A Collection of Secrets

Jericho Falls Cozy Mysteries, Volume 2

Brook Peterson

Published by GS Books, 2022.

A COLLECTION OF SECRETS
First Edition, January 2022
Copyright © 2022 Brook Peterson
G.S. Books
All Rights Reserved
Written By Brook Peterson
Cover Design By Beetiful Book Covers, www.beetifulbookcovers.com[1]
Edited By Melaney Taylor-Auxier

---

1. http://www.beetifulbookcovers.com

Also by Brook Peterson

Jericho Falls Cozy Mysteries
A History of Murder
A Collection of Secrets
The Present Predicament, A Jericho Falls Holiday Novella

Watch for more at https://www.brookpetersonauthor.com/.

With fond memories of our RV adventures, and in anticipation of all those yet to come.

Praise for the Jericho Falls Cozy Mysteries

A History of Murder

"FROM THE BEGINNING little 'roadside fiasco,' to the very real dread many of us feel when returning to our home towns, Peterson wrote a believable and compelling mystery."
-T.L. Brown,
Door to Door Mysteries
https://writertracybrown.com

"THE AUTHOR DID A GREAT job of weaving mysteries throughout the story as well as adding in some history and a touch of romance."
-Janna Rollins,
http://paulaniziolek.wordpress.com/

PROLOGUE

IT WAS ONE OF THOSE spring days that looked warm and inviting from the window. I left the house certain I could get by in short sleeves, but went right back inside for a jacket. And like the weather, the day's events didn't turn out as I expected either.

Grandma Lily and I worked in the front yard. It was springtime, and we needed to get everything back in shape. We'd raked leaves in the fall before the snow fell, but now was the time to trim wayward branches on the bushes and clean out the flower beds. Grandma's daffodils had recently popped out of the ground, and the tulips would be close behind. Soon, everything would be lush and colorful again at Jericho House.

I looked up at our impressive century-old mansion boasting three stories. A turret graced the left side, giving it an especially grand look. Every residence on our street was impressive. But none were as stunning as Jericho House. This part of Jericho Falls, situated high above the rest, had always been called Gold Mountain, because in the gold rush days, the townspeople referred to the women who married the richest miners, 'gold mountain wives'.

"Hand me that trowel, dear," said Grandma Lily with an outstretched, gloved hand. Her faithful feline, Elliot, who always dressed to impress in his 'tuxedo', lazed in the sun near my grandma. His eyes remained narrowed as if he were supervising our work. My fuzzy buddy, a young golden retriever named Jed, slept soundly beside Elliot—he was no taskmaster.

I gave Grandma Lily the trowel and continued to pull dry, crunchy leaves out from under a rosebush with my fingers held like claws. The ground's fresh, deep scent filled me with springtime gladness.

"Oh, look, a bird's nest," I said.

"Don't disturb it, dear."

I gave my Grandma a rueful smile. She told me this like I was still six years old and didn't know any better. Actually, I had turned twenty-nine in February. But I didn't mind her parental tone. I cherished every day as a new, full-time resident of Jericho Falls and co-hostess of this stately home. My grandma had done the job solo for many years and seemed thrilled to have me here.

I watched her, working hard to yank a stubborn weed from the ground. She was the youngest looking seventy-something I'd ever known. Her silvery hair was the only real give-away of her age. But even this she wore shoulder-length and usually swooped up in a high ponytail, giving her a girlish charm. After an unfortunate incident last summer, she had given up wearing signature ribbons in her hair each day and instead switched to trendy scrunchies. She now had a whole drawerful—one in every color. Today she'd chosen light pink.

I had just come back from dumping weeds from the wheelbarrow when my pocket vibrated. I pulled off one glove, then the other, before taking my cell phone out of my windbreaker pocket.

"Hello?" I answered. All I heard were sobs.

"Hello?" I said again, with more intensity.

Who could this be? I checked the screen of my phone. Bree Brandon, our local hair stylist and extra-bubbly friend, was calling.

"Bree, are you all right?"

These words and the worried tone in my voice attracted Grandma's attention. She froze, her gardening trowel shoved half-way down in the ground.

"It's Goldie," Bree managed, then wailed again. "she's...dead."

"Don't move, Bree. I'll be right there."

I hung up.

Grandma glanced at me, her eyes full of concern. "What's going on with Bree?" she asked.

"I'm not sure. But you wait here. If I need anything, I'll call." I didn't want to tell her that Bree had used the word 'dead'. My grandma had been through a lot. Last summer, the police suspected she killed a man who turned up dead in our flower bed. Sometimes she still seemed upset, sort of thin-skinned about these kinds of things.

I hustled to the back porch with Jed on my heels. Along the way, I stomped my feet and brushed my pant legs to shake off any dirt, weeds, or twigs that might be hanging on. I washed my hands in the deep farmhouse kitchen sink. Jed eyed me sadly.

"You know you can't come with me, don't ya, boy?" I gave his soft blond head a pat. "You stay here with Grandma and Elliot."

I nearly sprinted down Gold Mountain towards town. *What was I getting into? Has Bree called the police yet?* I half-hoped Jericho Falls Police Chief Lance Garner would be on the scene to save me from having to witness anything gruesome. I wondered, *Did this 'Goldie' lady keel over while Bree gave her a perm? Did she croak with her feet in the pedi-bath?* Whatever happened, this wasn't good.

At the intersection, I glanced at city hall just in time to see our newly elected Jericho Falls Mayor, Blake White, climbing the tall stairs to enter the building. Blake, my teen years' flame, chatted on his phone, so thankfully didn't notice me. I didn't have time to talk with anyone right now, let alone to *him*.

When I made it to Bree's Beauty Salon, there she sat on the shop's black and white checkerboard floor, her face in her hands.

With trepidation, I looked around the girly-themed salon for the deceased. Nothing seemed out of place. Aside from Bree, the place was completely empty.

"Bree?" I kneeled beside her and placed a hand on her shoulder.

She looked up at me with despair. Her bottom lip quivered, then she raised a shaky hand, pointing up at the counter where her cash register sat. I stood to find out what she meant. And that's when I saw Goldie. She was dead all right. She was floating, belly-up in a fishbowl.

"*This* is Goldie?" I asked, a little more exasperated than intended.

Bree rose and stood beside me, straightening her pink a-line skirt and lavender sweater-set.

"Yes," she nodded, "Goldie Prawn."

Internally, I rolled my eyes. Bree named her tiny white poodle Marilyn, as in Monroe. I should have guessed that she would name all her pets after blonde bombshells. I gave a relieved sigh and drew Bree into a hug.

"I'm going to miss her so much," she sniffed. "I only got her last summer at the Founder's Day Festival. What a horrible fish-mother I am... letting her die like this."

"Wait. Goldie is almost a year old?"

I felt Bree nod against my shoulder.

"Well, I'd say you're a wonderful fish mom." I pushed her away from me enough to see her face. "Carnival fish rarely last a week."

"Really?" A sad smile formed on Bree's innocent face.

I nodded reassuringly. "You gave Goldie Prawn a nice long life, Bree. Now, should we give her a funeral?" I suggested. "And a proper burial at Jericho House?"

Bree nodded quickly, making her chin-length flaxen hair bounce. She hugged me tightly once again.

I sent her into the shop's tiny bathroom to freshen up while I poured the lifeless Goldie Prawn into one of those plastic bags that ladies wore on their head underneath the dryer. I knotted the top for safe transport of the deceased. When Bree re-appeared, she seemed better. I brewed a pot of coffee and poured her a cup, stirring in a hefty amount of her favorite mocha creamer.

"After work today, come to Jericho House," I offered. "Grandma Lily and I will have everything ready."

Bree smiled, "Thanks, Chloe. That's why I called you. You always know exactly what to do."

1

I Never Imagined

GRANDMA HAD TIRED OF yard work and was back inside when I returned to Jericho House. She couldn't believe it when I told her this whole silly escapade was about a goldfish.

"Oh my goodness," she laughed. "Our Bree is such a hoot."

"That's one way to describe her." I shook my head. "And now I'm in charge of planning a fish funeral." I held the clear plastic bag up and inspected the lifeless Goldie Prawn.

"Today?" Grandma appeared genuinely shocked.

"Yeah, why?"

"Oh, Chloe, you should never hold a funeral on a Friday. Everyone knows it's bad luck," she replied.

I touched my forehead. "You and your superstitions, Grandma. It's only a *fish* funeral. I'm sure we'll all be fine."

After a brief deliberation, and some salt thrown over her shoulder, Grandma assured me she knew exactly how to handle the funeral and would take care of everything. She even suggested calling Anna Dunning, Anna's brother Dr. Leonard Dunning, and Karen Little from the Poison Pen Book Club. Maybe they would attend and lend support to Bree. I agreed, a few extra mourners in attendance would be nice. I wondered—would Grandma invite the group's final member, Chief Lance Garner? If so, would he come?

With our yard work done for the day, I told Grandma I'd be in my apartment if she needed me. Last summer, when I returned to Jericho Falls (reluctantly, by the way) Grandma Lily surprised me with my very own studio apartment. She had remodeled the back room of the garage, which had once been my grandfather's wood-working shop. It was now a small but cozy one-bedroom apartment. She knew, in order to convince me to move back to this turn-of-the-century gold mining town, I would need my own space. I was no longer a kid who spent every summer visiting Jericho House. I was an adult too, and we each needed our privacy.

Jed and I flopped onto the soft gray couch to cuddle.

"I'm sorry I didn't take you into town," I told him, giving his black nose a boop.

Jed yawned, turned a full circle, and curled up on the couch. Admittedly, he had grown much too large to be on the furniture anymore. But he was mine to spoil. I laid my head back and stroked Jed while I thought about Bree and the upcoming fish funeral. A pescatarian proceeding, you might say. *Something's always up with that girl.*

But like my Grandma, Bree had been through a lot. In solving the mystery of who killed Art MacMillan, I simultaneously uncovered damning information about Bree's fiancé. She was now single and incredibly sad. Bree took all her emotions to the extreme. Heartbreak was no exception. In the past few months, Bree had gone through a slew of strange hobbies and pastimes in an attempt to feel better. For a while she'd been into square-dancing, then came geocaching. Goldie Prawn was probably another one of her sidetracks. Bree, the fish mom.

Somewhere along this thought trail and in the comfort of stroking Jed's silky fur, I dozed off. The sound of knocking woke me. Jed, however, continued to snore. *Some guarddog you are*, I thought.

I took the mere three and a half steps necessary to reach the door and opened up to find Blake White. He still wore the same work-day attire I had spotted him in earlier, but he'd loosened his tie and undone the top button of his cream-colored dress shirt. His auburn hair was combed to the side, as always, perfectly.

"Hey, I saw you rushing through town earlier," he said, leaning on the door jamb. "Everything all right?"

"Yeah," I said, trying to ignore his macho stance. "I didn't think you noticed me."

Blake bit at his bottom lip. "It's like radar—I can always sense whenever you're around. I looked up just in time to see you."

I felt a jab of irritation. Blake just wouldn't let the idea of us being more than friends go, would he?

"Bree was in a panic. Her goldfish died."

Blake rolled his eyes and laughed. "Sounds like her."

"Well, she's been extra emotional about everything in her life after the break-up with *your* brother."

Blake made an "ouch" face. "Got it. I'll let her know I'm sorry for her loss when I see her next."

Somehow, I doubted it.

We stood there for a moment in silence. I wasn't going to invite him in. And he didn't seem to have any real reason for dropping by. I let the uncomfortable quiet sit between us for a few more seconds before making goodbye noises and pushing the door closed.

Blake said, "Wait," so I opened back up.

"Why didn't you tell me about Christy's diary?"

"What?" A tingly chill ran down my neck.

"For months now, I've been waiting for you to talk to me about it. I mean, what she wrote must bring back a lot of memories for you."

Blake was referring to the diary of our friend Christy, who tragically died when we were teenagers. When I arrived back in town,

Christy's mom sent me a shoebox of odds and ends, including the diary. I found it necessary to hide the box of stuff last summer when another of our mutual friends, Jeannie Smythe, tried to steal the diary out from under my nose. That's when it became clear the diary might contain important information about Christy's mysterious death. *But how did Blake know anything about it? Had Jeannie told him? Was he in on her thievery?*

"How did you find out about that?" I whispered, almost unable to make any noise at all.

"Don't be mad," Blake said, "but your Grandma Lily told me you got a box of stuff from Christy's mom in the mail, including her diary. I've tried to ignore it, but I just keep wondering, you know?"

So. My grandma had let the proverbial cat out of the bag. In her defense, Grandma Lily wasn't aware she should've kept her lips locked. In all the commotion around Art Macmillan's murder, I never told her that Jeannie tried taking the diary from me, or that it might hold important information. I simply hadn't found the right time, and I was reluctant to worry Grandma Lily about anything else unsavory.

I paused to decide how much to tell Blake.

"I haven't looked through Christy's things yet," I said.

Blake's eyes grew large. "But, why not?"

"Trying to get re-settled here in Jericho Falls has been hard enough without dredging up the past."

Blake nodded as if he was trying to seem understanding, but there was a definite look of concern in his eyes.

I went on, "One of these days, the time will be right. I mean, it's been almost fourteen years since she died. There's no harm in waiting a little longer."

Blake swallowed hard.

"I'm not sure we can wait until 'one of these days,' Chloe."

I frowned, confused.

"I found something in my new office at city hall," he said. "I think there may have been some kind of conspiracy."

I closed my eyes in exasperation. "Yeah, there was a conspiracy. Have you somehow forgotten that the cops tried to blame me for her death? No thanks to you, by the way."

Blake shook his head. "No, not about you. Well, that *might* have been a part of things, I suppose... "

I interrupted what I felt was his pointless theorizing. "Blake, listen. I'm finally fitting in here again. No one is pointing or whispering anymore. No one has asked me how I'm 'coping' with being back in Jericho Falls with all the 'memories' for weeks. The last thing I want to do is bring up the past all over again. Please, whatever you found, just let it go."

Blake held my gaze. His eyes looked disappointed, maybe even worried. "Sorry, Chloe, but I have to check on a few things. I'm going to ask the city records clerk to pull the case file for me."

"Do whatever you want." I threw my hands up. "Just leave me out of it."

My phone pinged. A text.

CHIEF GARNER: Fish funerals make me green around the gills.

"Who is it?" Blake asked me. He leaned towards me for a peek at my phone.

I put it face-down on the narrow table beside the door. "No one," I said, noncommittally.

"This 'no one' sure makes you smile."

I realized then that I was grinning from ear to ear at Garner's funny message. But this was none of Blake's business. I glanced at my wrist for effect (before remembering I wasn't wearing a watch) and told him I needed to get back to the house. Grandma Lily was expecting me.

He nodded, then waved goodbye as he rounded the corner of the garage. At that moment, I never imagined this brief visit from Blake would end up meaning so much.

2

A Public Gesture

JED AND I WENT INSIDE the house through the backdoor to find the lights turned low, curtains drawn, and unlit candles sitting on every available flat surface.

"Grandma?"

"I'm in the parlour, dear," she called.

"Are we holding a funeral or a seance?" I joked, watching her drape dark, lacy fabric over the few lamps she had left switched on for effect.

"You know, in the days before mortuaries, people held all funerals at home," Grandma Lily explained. "Families would lay their deceased loved one in the sitting room for friends and family to pay their respect. That's why we call it a visitation. People actually *visited* you."

I noticed the small card table in the center of the room. There lay Goldie Prawn in a narrow cardboard box lined with white satin.

Grandma ticked items off on her fingers. "Karen is bringing the flowers, her forsythia bush is in bloom. And Anna is going to play 'Wind Beneath My Wings' on her violin."

I giggled. "Don't you mean, 'The Wave Beneath My Fins'?"

Grandma laughed a little too, placing a hand in front of her mouth as if she felt guilty for it. "You know, I never thought I could have fun planning a funeral. When you don't give a hoot about the deceased, it's just like planning any other themed-party."

Our fishy-joke reminded me of Garner's text. I took my phone out and smiled again at his message. I replied,

ME: But will you attend?

In mere seconds, three little dots appeared, letting me know he was already responding.

GARNER: How could I miss it? Lily says I'm a pallbearer and the gravedigger.

I sent back a laughing emoji and pocketed my phone again. This freed up my hands to help Grandma cover the mirror over the fireplace with a tablecloth so the spirit of Goldie wouldn't get trapped inside. Grandma and her superstitions. *Geesh.*

Anna and Karen arrived a few minutes before five o'clock. They helped us set up by placing a flower arrangement near the deceased and lighting the many candles throughout the first floor.

"Isn't this a bit over the top?" Anna rolled her eyes in her usual cranky manner. "I mean, all this over a darned goldfish?"

"Yes, it is," admitted Grandma Lily, "and we wouldn't be doing it if it weren't for Bree. She may be pushing thirty, but in a lot of ways, she's still a kid. A kid who is heartbroken over Anthony and their ruined engagement."

"That's right," added Karen. "She's special to us, so why not make her feel that way?"

I had to admit, things did feel special. And so, at the last moment, I darted upstairs to Grandma Lily's closet to cover my plain white t-shirt with a black cardigan sweater.

I shook my wavy brown hair out of its ponytail and fluffed it out over my shoulders. I glanced at my reflection in the mirror of Grandma's antique dresser. Not too bad. I pinched my cheeks and rubbed my lips together. I told myself these last-minute preparations had nothing to do with Chief Garner coming over. But the butterflies in my stomach betrayed me.

I heard the home's original hand-turn doorbell and hurried out onto the landing to see if it was Bree. Sure enough, she came through the door, her hands over her mouth and an appreciative frown on her face. Her poodle, Marilyn, stuck her fuzzy white head out from the top of Bree's shoulder bag.

"Oh. My. Goodness," Bree said, as I went downstairs to meet them. "This is so nice of you all."

Karen, a large, soft woman, enveloped Bree in a tight hug. "Sweetheart, it's always hard to lose a pet," she said.

Anna, the Olive Oyl look-alike, was stoic as usual. However, she gave Bree's arm a pat and nodded along with Karen's comment. That was a lot coming from Anna.

Just then, there was a knock at the door. Dr. Dunning, Anna's brother, poked his head inside with a jolly, "Knock, knock." Officer Garner entered with him. Dr. Dunning sported his usual button-down shirt and knitted sweater vest. These, along with his round, gold-framed glasses, gave him the quintessential college professor look. Garner was still in his police uniform. I wondered if this was coincidental, or if Grandma Lily had asked him to show up this way—as the law enforcement official for the proceedings.

The men gave Bree a quick hug. Then, Grandma announced that since all the guests had arrived, we would convene in the parlour for the service in honor of Goldie Prawn.

The whole thing took about five minutes. Bree told the story of how she won the fish at the Founder's Day Festival last summer by successfully tossing a Ping-pong ball into an empty fish bowl. She seemed so proud. Grandma Lily read a short poem, and then Anna played the chorus to 'Wind Beneath My Wings' on her violin.

It was all I could do to not burst into laughter thinking of the alternate fishy lyrics. Thankfully though, it worked out, because in stifling my laughter, my eyes watered. Bree noticed me dabbing at them and assumed I was getting choked up over the dearly departed. She nodded sadly at me as if to say, 'It's okay to cry, Chloe.'

With the program finished, Grandma Lily ceremoniously went to the table, placed the lid on the box where Goldie lay, and asked for the pallbearers to step forward. Officer Garner and Dr. Dunning each took an end of the small box.

"Please follow me," said Grandma Lily reverently.

Single file, we went down the hall, through the kitchen and outside via the back porch. Once in the quiet, shady backyard, Grandma handed Officer Garner her gardening trowel. He gently dug a small hole between the base of the big maple tree and a cluster of daffodil leaves, just emerging from the dark, rich soil.

Dr. Dunning placed the box softly into the hole, pausing with his hand on top for just a second, as if saying a prayer. Garner then covered it over, smoothing the dirt flat. Grandma Lily presented Bree with a large flat rock from the Jericho River, suggesting she use it to mark Goldie Prawn's eternal resting place. Bree sniffed before accepting the stone and laying it on the grave.

"This concludes the service to honor the life of Goldie Prawn," announced Grandma Lily. "On behalf of Bree, I would like to thank you all for coming and invite you to convene for dinner at Joey's Steakhouse...my treat."

The group broke into various conversations as we all walked to the house.

Quiet enough so the others didn't hear, I said to Grandma, "Gosh, were you a funeral director in a past life?"

She chuckled, "When you get to be my age, you'll have attended enough of these to know how they go too, dear."

I put my arm around her as we went up the steps and into the house.

AN EXTENSIVE DEBATE over how to get ourselves downtown to Joey's Steakhouse ensued. Garner, Karen, and Dr. Dunning all had cars parked in the circle drive. Bree and her dog Marilyn had walked to Jericho House. Anna wasn't sure she wanted to come to dinner at all, considering all her dietary restrictions.

Discussion continued about whether to walk (since it would be dark and rather chilly by the time we finished eating) or maybe we should carpool so as not to take up too many parking spots on Main Street? I looked at Garner. He widened his eyes to express that he, too, was growing tired of this exhausting discussion.

"Tell you what," he said, breaking in, "I'd like to change out of my uniform before dinner, so I'll meet you there in about fifteen minutes."

I glared at him playfully. He had got himself out of this.

But then, he surprised me. "Chloe, want to ride with me?"

I felt a warm rush sweep through me. Never had Garner made such a public gesture, suggesting that we were good friends.

I simply nodded.

"See you in a few minutes, dear," Grandma Lily called, waving a hand at me and returning to the logistical debate still underway.

"Whew, thanks," I said to Garner, settling into the passenger seat of his police SUV. "I didn't think that was ever going to end."

"No problem, I'll just run inside and change real quick. We'll probably still end up beating them to Joey's."

I laughed. *Good chance of that,* I thought.

However, we had only made it down Gold Mountain, about to turn onto the side street that would take us to Garner's little brick house, when his police radio scratched to life. A female dispatcher barked a coded announcement I couldn't understand. Garner immediately lifted his radio handset and said, "This is the chief. I'm on it."

He flipped a switch and his cruiser lights flashed; the siren blared.

3

Her Eyes Were Wide

MY PALMS BECAME SWEATY with both excitement and a little fear. I had been inside a cop car before. First on that fateful day fourteen years ago when my best friend died at the waterfall. The police officers who arrived on the scene took us all home, recognizing that we were in too much shock to drive ourselves. Then, about a week later, another policeman arrived at Jericho House to take me to the station for further questioning. Because of the testimony of others (including my then boyfriend, Blake White) the police tried pinning Christy's death on me. Their theory was that she and I had continued a fight we'd started in the parking lot at the top of the falls. Then in anger, though probably not intentionally, I pushed her over the edge. Thankfully, my family hired an attorney whose investigators cleared me of any wrongdoing. In the end, officials called my best friend's death a mysterious and terrible accident. Still, it had been a harrowing experience. Garner's police vehicle was an eerie reminder of that terrible time.

"Where are we going?" I asked Chief Garner, noting that he had knit his dark brows together in a serious scowl.

"There's an issue at the RV Park," was all he said.

Garner maneuvered through the narrow, jig-jog streets of Jericho Falls with high-speed precision. This early American town didn't have the luxury of city development planners. Nor did the old-timers ever imagine automobiles traveling their streets in the 1850s when the town settled. But Garner seemed an expert at this. He simultaneously drove fast while on the lookout for other cars and pedestrians.

We headed to the outskirts of town, near the Jericho Falls Visitor's Center. This is where Pioneer RV Park had been built about twenty years before. It was a great boon to the tourist trade of Jericho Falls, accommodating travelers who intended to visit our town, as well as those just passing through, looking for a place to camp for the night.

Chief Garner turned off the paved road, crossed the bridge spanning a large man-made pond, and pulled into the park. He shut off the siren, but he kept the lights flashing. Up ahead, I saw a sign pointing towards the Office and Rec Center. Upon further study, it became clear that the park office was housed in a modest, well-kept home where the manager probably worked and lived. Through a breezeway at the back of the home office was a covered, fenced area that I knew included an in-ground pool and hot tub. A little farther was the laundromat building and a grassy yard which held a swing set, a small jungle gym and horseshoe pits. I knew all this because once, when Christy and I were kids, we'd snuck in and said our families were camping there in order to swim and play all afternoon. When Grandma Lily found out about our fib, I had to write a letter of apology and promise to never pull a "stunt" like that again.

I noticed several people gathered in front of the little house. They huddled together, almost in a group hug.

"Stay here," Garner told me. He put on his navy blue service cap that matched his uniform and went to talk with them.

There was a woman and two men in the small group. One man, who looked to be about sixty, wore Levis and a plain white tee. He also wore a sour expression. Were these the people having an "issue"?

I craned my neck around to read the name on the mailbox. It read, Duvall. I had heard the name around town before, but I couldn't say where. It wasn't the owner's name I'd addressed in my apology letter all those years ago.

There was a tan 1990s model sedan in the driveway and a potted geranium by the front walk. Everything looked neat and tidy. A homemade sign made of sticky plastic letters stated, "OFFICE HOURS 10-6." It was almost 6:45 now.

Garner dismissed one of the men and the woman. I watched them walk across the gravel pathway and return to separate RVs. He continued talking to the Levi-clad man, who kept running a hand over his thinning salt and pepper hair. Garner took notes and nodded as they spoke. I wished I could hear what they were saying. Realizing the vehicle was still running, I pressed the button on my door and lowered my window less than an inch. I hoped Garner wouldn't notice and that it would help me make out their conversation.

I had to concentrate to make out what they were saying, but I thought I heard, "She ain't answerin'."

Garner asked another question, to which the man replied sternly, "I told you already. The change machine stole my money."

I watched Garner nod understandingly, then clap a hand to the man's shoulder. He gestured toward the rows of campers, apparently suggesting the guy head home. I watched him storm away, still appearing frustrated. *Over some lost change?*

The chief came to my window. I rolled it down a bit more to speak with him. "Sorry, I should have taken you back to Jericho House, not brought you along to this rat race," he said.

"What's going on, anyway?" I asked.

"That guy's mad because the change machine in the laundry room ate his dollar bill for the second time this week. He's upset that Barbara Duvall, the owner of the park, won't answer her door. He's been beating on it, yelling and bothering everyone in the park."

"It couldn't wait until tomorrow, during her office hours?"

"Guess not. Wait here, I'll go talk to her," the chief said.

Garner didn't have any better luck than the angry camper.

With my head out the car window, I heard him rapping on her door. He hollered, "Barbara? This is Chief Garner. I'm here to check on you." It didn't seem like she was going to answer the door for the police chief, either. I wondered if there was a law against that.

That's when I heard the scream. It was shrill enough to make the hair on my arms stand straight up. It came from the direction of the pool and seemed to go on forever. Before I even knew what I was doing, I had opened the SUV door and ran in that direction.

The gate to the tall privacy fence that surrounded the swimming pool was unlatched, so I hurried inside. A teenage girl, wrapped in a beach towel as if she had intended to take an evening dip, stood at the side of the pool looking into the turquoise water. One of her hands was over her mouth, her eyes were wide.

I followed her gaze and knew right away why Barbara Duvall wasn't answering her door. She wasn't home. She was here, in the pool, looking a lot like Goldie Prawn had that morning.

My vision darkened around the edges, and I felt the familiar surge of adrenaline that often preceded a panic attack. Memories of seeing my best friend Christy floating in the Jericho River overlapped with the current reality. I sank to my hands and knees, afraid I might go in the pool too, if I tried to remain standing.

Chief Garner was right on my heels. In one fluid motion, he took off his hat, stripped off his police belt, and dove into the pool. He turned the middle-aged woman over, revealing her face. Her skin was a deathly shade of gray. With one arm expertly wrapped around her, Garner swam to the edge. By then, others were arriving, reacting to the teen's scream just as we had. In my foggy, anxious state, my mind snapped photograph-like images; campers watching in horror, the older man looking concerned, a pretty red-haired woman shrieking, then running away.

One man announced that he was a trained EMT. He helped Garner pull the RV park owner from the pool and stretch her out on the surrounding tile. They checked her pulse and attempted a few rounds of CPR. There didn't seem to be any hope of saving her, though.

"Chloe." Garner barked, running a hand over his wet hair, "Get my cell phone, I need to call for backup."

I stood shakily, went to his kit belt and with trembling fingers, fumbled his phone out of a velcro-latched pocket. I handed it to Garner and listened to him speak. He was the one to issue a coded message this time, but I didn't have to guess at its meaning. It meant someone was dead.

4

Simply a Stranger

OFFICER GARNER DIRECTED everyone away from the pool. "Thank you for your concern, but you must leave this area at once. Return to your RVs and wait for further instruction. You are not to leave the park."

Part of me just wanted to run as fast as I could from this horrible scene, which reminded me much too much of the way Christy died. But the other part of me needed to look at this woman—to reassure myself that this was simply a stranger, not my friend. I wanted to convince myself that this poor woman's death shouldn't cause such a powerful reaction in me. After taking a few deep breaths, I went over to get a closer look at her.

Barbara Duvall was fully clothed; definitely not planning on taking a dip. She wore slacks, a dressy blouse, and a sky blue cardigan sweater. Something about this hopeful spring color brought tears to my eyes. When she dressed that morning in this pretty shade, the RV park owner didn't know that she would be dead before dinnertime.

One item of clothing Barbara was not wearing was shoes. She only wore torn nylon stockings. My eyes moved up her body, to her hands. She had on light pink nail polish and a simple wedding band. I also noticed a hint of bruising around one wrist. I moved my focus to her face. Traces of mascara ran down her cheeks. Her short brown hair, sprinkled with gray strands, clung to her scalp to reveal a red, swollen area on her left temple. *What was Barbara Duvall doing out here? Had she been alone?*

I stood to inspect the pool. The skimmer tool used for cleaning it lay on the bottom. There were no signs of her shoes there, though. However, a sparkle in the deep end of the water caught my eye. I went to the edge, kneeling on hands and knees to get a better look. It might be a piece of jewelry, or a coin, but the shimmer and movement of the water distorted it enough that I couldn't be sure. *Maybe she went after this shiny object with the pool skimmer and fell in? But why then, a bruised wrist and a bump on the head?*

I turned around hoping to point out the shiny item to Chief Garner before any of his officers showed up. He was finishing a conversation with the man who'd assisted him earlier. Then he came my way.

"Chloe, you shouldn't be here. I'm so sorry you had to see this... considering."

My hands were still shaking, but the overwhelming shock waned as my interest in this curious situation grew. "Garner, I'm wondering about a few things."

"Oh, no, don't start, Chloe. This is a job for law enforcement."

"Just come here. There's something in the pool."

Garner took my elbow lightly and guided me toward the gate to leave. "We'll go over everything with a fine-tooth comb. Trust me," he said.

I nodded, but all the questions that bounced around in my head desperately wanted answers. "Why was she cleaning the pool in dress clothes?" I pressed. "That is, if she really *was* cleaning the pool. And she's barefooted. Is there any significance to that?" I asked.

"Chloe..." Garner took my shoulders, turning me towards the exit. "Don't worry about it. My officers and I are trained professionals. We'll handle everything."

I didn't think this was the right moment to remind him it was *me*, not his "trained professionals" who had cracked the last murder case in Jericho Falls.

But then, Chief Garner said something really concerning.

"Anyway, it looks like a simple slip and fall accident. I know this hits close to home, but don't read too much into it. Okay?"

I whirled around to look at him. "Did you see her wrist? And her head? I don't think this was an accident."

Garner didn't reply. He gave me a patronizing smile, then motioned with a lift of his chin, indicating I should look behind me. I turned around. Grandma Lily stood just outside the pool's fence, looking white as a ghost.

"I called you a ride," Garner explained.

"Why?"

"I saw how upset you were. And although I can't make it to dinner with our friends tonight, you can."

I glared at him before letting out a little huff. But I knew I couldn't win this argument. I went outside the fence to meet up with Grandma Lily.

"What in the world is going on?" she asked, fidgeting with her massive key chain—a collection of way too many souvenir bobbles and bling.

"Barbara Duvall sleeps with the fishes," I told her. I went in for a hug. Her warm embrace pushed me over the edge, so despite my attempt at humor, I began to cry.

"Oh, dear," Grandma whispered, against my ear, "that's terrible. Let's get you out of here."

Grandma Lily gave me a tight squeeze and handed me a tissue from her pocket. Before we could even make it to her little white Subaru, two police cruisers and an ambulance were crossing the bridge into the RV park. We sat in her car to wait for the parade of vehicles to maneuver past us down the narrow gravel drive. I laid my head back against the headrest and closed my eyes. *How could Garner decide so quickly this was an accident?* That's what the cops had decided about Christy's death, too. They simply gave up looking for answers and called it a tragic accident at the waterfall. That is, once they let *me* off the hook.

When I opened my eyes, it was with new resolve. I watched uniformed personnel erupt from their vehicles and make a bee-line to the open gate where Garner ushered them in. There was something I wanted to do before Grandma and I took off, so I hoped that their poolside duties would keep the first responders distracted.

"I'll be right back," I said, opening the car door. "Keep it running and be ready to make a break for it."

Grandma Lily raised her eyebrows, but gave me a thumbs-up.

I jogged to the front porch of the Duvall's house while bringing my cell phone out of my pocket and switching on the camera app. *How cute*, I thought, noticing the yard ornaments. *Mr. and Mrs. Duvall have the same ceramic gnomes as Garner. They must shop at Nick's Knacks, too.*

I climbed the stairs and walked across the small porch, which was carpeted with fake green grass, to peer into the door. This was a bust, considering the mini blinds covering the window. Checking first to make sure no one was around, I pulled the sleeve of my sweater down over my hand and tried the knob.

Locked. *Dang it.*

Jogging down the porch steps, I turned left to walk along the side of the house, conveniently hidden from the pool area. Sadly, the windows here were too tall for me to see into. I jumped repeatedly, but only caught glimpses of the room—the kitchen. As a last ditch effort, I stood on my tip-toes and raised my arm as high as it would go. I snapped a few photos of the room. Who knew if I got a shot of anything helpful, but it was worth a try. I didn't care what the chief said. Something about this whole thing seemed very fishy.

I hurried back around the little house and dashed to my get-away vehicle. Just before I sank into the passenger seat of Grandma Lily's running car, I looked up. Chief Garner was watching me, and he didn't look happy.

5

Adorned with Roses

I WASN'T UP TO EATING or socializing, but since Grandma had promised to treat our friends to dinner, we went back to town and stopped at Joey's Steakhouse.

"Let's not say anything about any of this," I suggested to her as we got out of the car.

Grandma nodded in agreement. "Good idea, it'll all come out soon enough."

We went inside to find Karen entertaining the group with a story about her grandchildren, who had recently come to visit. Apparently, the youngest wants to be an archeologist when he grows up and thought he had hit it big when he dug up a waterlogged 8-track tape near the river. "He asked me if it was from the Civil War," Karen said with humorous tears in her eyes. The table roared with laughter.

Dr. Leonard Dunning, our resident history professor, found the story especially funny. "I'd like to meet this young man next time he comes to town," he said. "Maybe, unlike Chloe, I can convince him to take one of my history classes." He looked down his nose at me playfully.

When I returned to town, I had fully intended to start a few college courses. But, more and more, I felt foolish about it. How would it be sitting in a classroom full of eighteen- and nineteen-year-olds when I was almost thirty?

I smiled at Dr. Dunning, but didn't reply.

"I'm only teasing you, Chloe," he said. "I hope you know that."

I nodded, "Yes, of course. I'm just a little tired."

Grandma looked at me with concern. She could tell I really wanted to get out of here, return to Jericho House for some cuddles with Jed and Elliot, and go over everything I saw at Pioneer RV Park with her.

When the waiter popped by to check in on us, Grandma Lily gracefully asked him for the check before he could offer the dessert menu. I caught her eye and gave a slight nod of thanks.

The group broke up. Apparently, their driving-versus-walking debate had all worked out because we were left on our own. I let out a sigh of relief as we eased into the gravel driveway of Jericho House. "I never tire of coming home to this place, but sometimes I'm happier than others," I admitted.

"I imagine so," said Grandma Lily. "What a terrible coincidence; you being with Chief Garner like that."

We went in through the back porch and instantly received love from the 'boys'. Elliot, our handsome tuxedo cat, stayed reserved. He never wanted us to know he actually missed us. But Jed hopped and panted and turned circles of joy at our return like a typical golden retriever.

Grandma filled their bowls and said she'd start a pot of tea. "I'll brew chamomile tonight, dear," she said. "After all you've been through today, you could use some help to sleep."

I kicked off my shoes and traipsed into the parlour. It was almost too warm these days for a fire, but I wanted the coziness of one, so I built a little house of kindling. I lit it with the long matches Grandma kept on the hearth. The fire crackled to life with pops and snaps.

I sank into the couch, drew my feet up under me, and thought.

Barbara Duvall. I didn't know her. Well, I remembered hearing the name over the years, but she wasn't someone I was friendly with. If I had to guess, I'd say she and her husband moved to Jericho Falls about the same time I stopped visiting as a teen.

Where was Mr. Duvall nowadays? I'd have to ask Grandma Lily. I replayed Garner's comment about Mrs. Duvall's demise being a "simple slip and fall"—an accident. It was possible, of course. But it bugged me that he suggested I was getting carried away simply because of my past.

Grandma came in with a tea tray and sat it on the table at my side. Steam rose from her yellow tea pot as she filled two dainty cups adorned with roses.

"Here, this will settle your nerves."

I breathed in the sweet, tart scent of chamomile—and was that lavender? The scent relaxed my shoulders even before I took a sip.

"Now, tell me what happened," said my grandma. She took a seat beside me.

I ran through the strange scenario I found myself in. I explained about the angry man and the others at the scene. Mostly, I talked about the shock of seeing the park owner floating in the pool face-down.

"Garner thinks she fell in accidentally. Like maybe she was using the pool skimmer, fell in and couldn't get out? It makes some sense, I suppose."

"Well, I'm not one to tell tales, but rumor has it Barbara Duvall had become somewhat of a drinker after Floyd died," Grandma Lily said. "I've heard that she's had to be driven home from the Saddles and Spurs Saloon more than once." She sipped her tea and raised her eyebrows at me over the rim of her cup.

"Maybe she had one too many this evening and lost her balance?" I suggested.

Grandma shrugged and gave a sad little smile.

I pulled my long hair back into a low ponytail and slid on the band I always kept around my wrist to hold it in place. I blew out a long breath.

"What is it, dear?" Grandma Lily set her teacup down.

"I just don't think this was an accident," I told her. "I can't say why, but something is just...off."

She patted my knee. "Chloe, I know it's been difficult for you to be back in town. Especially after helping me out of that fix last summer and having to face all the old questions about Christy. A woman drowning hits much too close to home for you. Is it possible that you expect problems in Jericho Falls, so you're simply looking for one?"

I looked at her and smiled weakly. "It's very possible, Grandma." Leaning my head on her shoulder, I suggested that I sleep in the house that night. I felt like staying close to her.

She didn't mind. In fact, she seemed thrilled. We made popcorn and took it upstairs. The round nook created by the turret on that side of the house gave Grandma the perfect spot for a TV in her room; the only one in Jericho House. We stayed up late watching old sitcom reruns.

I didn't mean to fall asleep in her bed, but I didn't mind either. Seeing Barbara Duvall's lifeless body and wondering if there was a killer in our midst had taken me back to places I'd rather not go.

THE NEXT MORNING I tiptoed out of Grandma Lily's room while she was still softly snoring. Jed jumped up from the rug where he'd been sleeping to follow me. We went quietly downstairs, and I let him out to do his business. Thankfully, last fall, Grandma and I completed the fencing around the home's backyard. Now Jed could go outside on his own without us worrying that he'd take off on another walk-about.

I started a pot of coffee in the large kitchen before going out to my apartment to get freshened up. But when I turned at the corner of the garage, it surprised me to find my flowerpot on its side, broken in half. This apartment space had once been my grandpa's woodworking shop, so I loved using his red, three-legged stool as a flower stand. I remembered sitting on it, swinging my legs and watching my grandpa work on furniture pieces or repair something for Grandma Lily. The red stool now laid on its side too. Dark potting soil littered the ground and my freshly planted petunias were toast.

Darn it. Probably a neighborhood cat on a midnight prowl, I thought. I set Grandpa's stool against the wall. Maybe I'd venture down to Nick's Knacks later in the day to buy a new pot and see if he still had flowers in stock to sit atop my beloved red stool.

I went inside the apartment, tossing my house keys on the tiny but functional kitchen counter and headed for the shower. As the hot water ran down my back, I relaxed and tried to let it wash away all the worry and suspicion yesterday's awful event brought me. I simply needed to let it all go. I lathered my hair and repeated soothing words to myself.

These mantras didn't last long before my mind went on another tangent... *What if someone is getting away with killing Barbara Duvall? We might go on living in a town with a killer who's never brought to justice!* I pressed my fingers to my temples and took a deep breath, trying my best to stop these thoughts. *Garner has it covered,* I told myself. He is a trained professional, after all. If he says her death was an accident? It was an accident. Right?

Stepping out of the shower, I remembered the cute look of frustration on the chief's face when I challenged him yesterday. It was kind of fun getting him wound up like that. I smiled into the mirror as I worked to detangle my damp, golden brown hair. The snarls that gathered at the ends made it hard for me to smooth it and reminded me I desperately needed a trim. Maybe I'd see if Bree had time to squeeze me in later.

In a clean pair of jeans and a white T-shirt with thin navy stripes, I was feeling as fresh as the spring morning and ready for a new start. I even swiped on some pink lip gloss. Yep, it was a new day for me. No more worrying about things that weren't my business. No more looking for problems in Jericho Falls.

Back in the house, Grandma was up and around. She'd sliced up an apple and made toast for us. "Thanks for starting the coffee," she said with a yawn. "It's been a long time since I've stayed up that late."

"Haven't slumber-partied in a while?"

"It's been decades," she laughed.

Grandma Lily wore her usual morning-walk attire, her hair in a high ponytail and a scrunchy decorated with tiny sunflowers. I knew that soon she'd be putting in her cordless earphones and heading out for her mile-long loop through town.

"Would you mind taking Jed along today? I'm going to do some errands and try to get a haircut at Bree's. He could really use the exercise."

"It would be my pleasure," she said, puckering her lips at Jed and ruffling his ears.

Soon Grandma Lily, Jed, and I gathered our various necessities and headed for the front door of Jericho House. I glanced back at Elliot and told him he was in charge. He meowed in agreement, then curled into a ball in his favorite morning sunning spot.

6

Old Worries

BREE HAD ONE LADY UNDER the dryer and another with her head in the sink when I pushed open the door to her salon.

"Hey girl," she called, raising her voice to be heard over the roar of the dryer.

I waved back.

Bree continued shampooing, but glanced over her shoulder at her client in the corner. The woman's attention was on an issue of Better Homes and Gardens. With the coast clear, Bree silently, but dramatically, mouthed something at me. It looked like, "Sit your ear amount miss too full?"

I frowned and shook my head. I had no clue what she meant.

Bree looked at the woman with her head covered in bubbles. She smiled at her sweetly, "Just a sec hon, I'll be right back."

Bree wiped her hands on her leopard-print apron, then grabbed my arm and dragged me to the front counter. She whispered in my ear, "Did you hear about Mrs. Duvall?"

"Oh. Mrs. Duvall," I said aloud.

Bree shushed me.

"Sorry," I whispered. "Yeah, I was *there*."

"What?"

"That's why I was late for dinner last night. Chief Garner got a call to respond before we even made it to Joey's Steakhouse."

Bree punched my shoulder softly and pushed her cute, blond eyebrows together. "And you didn't tell us?"

I explained I didn't want to take away from Goldy's funeral dinner. Plus, seeing another dead body had really shaken me up. Probably more than I liked to admit. Bree nodded apologetically.

"I get it," she said with a Bree-like pout. "Was it just awful?"

I nodded. "And strange. One of her wrists looked bruised, she had a bump on her head, and she was fully clothed—except for shoes." Before Bree could respond, I shook my head and swiped my hands in front of me. "Wait. You know what? Never mind. I'm trying to stay out of it. It's best to let Garner and the police department handle it."

Bree motioned to her two clients. "I wish we could talk more, but I'm swamped today." Then, as if to prove her point, the bell chimed and a teen boy who desperately needed his mop-top chopped came in the door.

"Darn," I said, screwing my mouth to one side. "And I was going to see if you could squeeze me in today."

Bree went to the spiral-bound appointment book she kept on the counter. Its pages were stained here and there with various shades of hair coloring. "It calms down after two o'clock," she said. "Want to come in then? I'll snip your ends while you fill me in."

I agreed. Bree jotted my name down in her book with a pink pen and I let her get back to work.

I DECIDED TO GO TO Nick's Knacks and get the supplies I needed. Then I could get my planting done before returning to Bree's later. I started walking in that direction. Main Street Jericho Falls was waking up for the day. Shop owners swept their doorways, placed sandwich boards on the boardwalk to advertise their daily specials, and greeted one another. Ragtime piano music swelled from the open doorway of the candy shop. I loved this little town. Once a booming gold mining settlement, now we operated on good old American tourism. Although things were slower this time of year, spring breaks and warmer weather were on their way, heralding the beginning of another busy tourist season.

On my way down the block toward Nick's, I stopped in at the Golden Grind Coffee Shop, where I was now working part time. I'd already had my cuppa for the day, but I hoped to find the owner, Kim Nagasaki, and check my work schedule. A veteran of coffee shop employment from my years living in Idaho, it seemed like an obvious job match for me. And one winter day, I helped save teen barista, Sandy Little (Karen's granddaughter) from a rush of caffeine-crazed Christmas shoppers.

After the holidays, Kim called to ask if I would be interested in working for her a few days a week. It was the perfect arrangement. I'd get to keep my coffee slinging skills polished up and still have time to help Grandma Lily with home tours and events at Jericho House. Grandma Lily told me she loved having my help around the mansion and didn't expect me to work otherwise, but it felt wrong not earning at least a little on my own. I suspected Grandma's real reason for condoning my unemployment was her wish for me to start college.

The Golden Grind was buzzing with people, folk music, and the scent of java. Several customers waited in line while Sandy Little handled them like the pro she had become over the past months. Other folks sipped their drinks at the rustic tables made from old wagon wheels topped with round-cut glass. Some of the people I recognized, others were strangers—typical in a town like ours.

I went behind the counter and into the backroom. Our boss, Kim, sat at her tiny writing desk filling out paperwork. She didn't look up but said, "I just posted the schedule. Hope it's all right to give you some time off. Dax and Jemma are home from college on their spring break and want extra hours."

I breathed a sigh of relief. With everything that had transpired over the last twenty-four hours, I could use some time to myself. "No problem at all. Business at Jericho House will be picking up, too. Believe it or not, Grandma Lily is actually letting me lead some of the home tours lately."

This made Kim look up from her work. "Whoa, that's a big step for Lily. What's she doing with all her free time?"

I laughed. "Mostly little renovation projects, but lately it's been directing pet funerals."

A smile grew across Kim's cheeks, and her eyes widened. "I don't know what that means, but nothing surprises me when it comes to Lily Martin."

"Kim..." we heard Sandy from the other side of the wall. "Can you print up a gift certificate for me?"

"Duty calls," Kim said. "Thanks for being flexible, Chloe. See you soon." She jumped up to lend a hand at the sales counter.

I followed Kim out of the backroom and wiggled my fingers in a little goodbye wave to Sandy. I wound my way around customers and tables toward the door. As I stepped out onto the boardwalk, the fresh air of the outdoors met the coffee infused interior, renewing the decadent scent for me. I breathed deeply and continued my walk.

Before rounding the corner to reach the side street, and Nick's shop, I spied Grandma Lily with Jed on the Riverwalk Greenbelt. My grandma pumped her arms at ninety-degree angles and was definitely working it. I chuckled. No one would ever believe she was in her 70s. I had a hard time keeping up with her, that's for sure.

Approaching Nick's Knacks, I was happy that he still had his vintage cart filled with plants on display outside. An old chalkboard announced *'Buy one Get One Free'* in a flourishing script. I found a pony-pack of white petunias and a bundle of lavender pansies. I went inside to peruse the choices for a new flower pot.

Nick's store was, in a word—eclectic. He carried everything from greeting cards to gardening supplies; antiques to cleaning products. It smelled of fertilizer and pot-pourri. Think hardware store crossed with a rummage sale. Thus, the quirky name.

Nick Newsom had moved to Jericho Falls *recently,* according to the long-time residents. But this simply meant he'd lived here less than twenty years. He had retired to Jericho Falls after a successful career as a radio announcer in some far-away big city. When he spoke, it always reminded me of his past life in semi-show biz—so suave, such impeccable enunciation.

"Top of the morning to you, Chloe," he boomed.

"Hi Nick, how are you today?"

"Fantastic. I couldn't be better. I see you're still planting more flowers at Jericho House?"

I told Nick about the feline prowler and my split flower pot. I asked him to point me towards a replacement. He directed me to a section of the store where I first found birdhouses, hummingbird feeders, and mops. Eventually, I discovered a variety of terracotta flower pots. I chose a medium-sized one and turned to make my way back to the sales counter. I found myself in the aisle with the brightly painted garden gnomes, pink flamingos, and those whirligigs that make the little man look like he's chopping wood whenever the wind blows. Seeing the gnomes made me think of Garner. And then, poor Barbara Duvall.

"Did you find everything you need?" asked Nick.

I nodded. Then quietly added, "Nick, did you hear about the RV Park owner?"

"I certainly did. Such a sad situation with her."

"What do you mean?"

"She was never herself again after Floyd passed."

I remembered what Grandma Lily told me. "Her drinking, you mean?"

Nick nodded sadly. "Rumor has it she was about to lose her job over it, too. They were forcing her to retire early."

"That's awful," I said. "But wait, Nick. I thought she ran the RV park."

"The park was Floyd's thing. Barbara's always worked an office job here in town. In fact, I think the stress of doing both after his death really weighed on her."

That certainly would be stressful, especially right after losing a spouse, I thought.

I smiled at Nick. "Hey, I noticed the Duvalls had a set of your garden gnomes. They're just like the girl gnome I bought for Chief Garner last Christmas, remember? To complete his pair?"

"That's right," Nick agreed with a grin. "The gnomes are my traditional housewarming gift whenever a new couple comes to town."

Couple?

I willed myself to maintain a cheerful expression even though my insides had suddenly constricted into a tight knot. *Garner came to Jericho Falls as part of a couple? Why didn't I know this?* The shock I felt at this news was rapidly turning into an emotion that might mean tears. I hurried to pay for my purchases and get out of there.

Once outside, I found it hard to swallow. Tears still threatened to spill out over my lids. I kept my head down and prayed I didn't run into Bree, or Sandy, or God forbid, Blake. I hustled all the way up Gold Mountain, huffing and puffing as I reached the top and crunched down Jericho House's gravel driveway.

I heard Grandma Lily before I saw her. "Hi dear, you bought more flowers? Those sure are pretty."

She was sitting in a white wicker chair on the deep, wrap-around porch of the mansion, sipping a glass of ice water and stroking Elliot in her lap. I stopped in my tracks and glared.

Right. At. Her.

7

Stunned Silence

GRANDMA LILY'S FACE went slack. She put Elliot down and stood slowly. "What's wrong, Chloe?"

The tears finally came. I grit my teeth while they ran down my face, making hot lines on my cheeks. "Why didn't you tell me about Chief Garner?"

"Tell you what?" Grandma came down the steps now, to meet me in the circle drive. She gently took the empty pot and the flowers from me, setting them carefully at our feet.

"Nick said that when Chief Garner moved to Jericho Falls, he was half of a couple."

Grandma closed her eyes and nodded. "Yes."

"How could you keep that from me? I've been assuming he was unattached—I've acted like a complete fool." It suddenly hit me how absurd it was for me to buy him that female gnome as a Christmas gift. *The gnomes are meant for couples in Jericho Falls.*

Grandma Lily tried to take my hands, but I pulled away. "Garner asked us not to talk about it," she explained. "I figured he'd tell you when he was ready."

"Us? Like he gave everyone a gag order about this?" Then it hit me. "Oh, my gosh. Is she someone I've already met? She's probably secretly laughing at me whenever we run into one another."

Grandma Lily spoke firmly, "Rachel is dead."

Her words quelled, at least for a moment, the wave of self-pity I was wallowing in. I stood in stunned silence.

She went on, "You need to talk to Chief Garner."

Without another word, I scooped up the gardening supplies and went past Grandma Lily, down the driveway at the side of the house and around to my apartment. I sat the flowers and pot beside my door—I didn't have the energy nor was I in the mood for planting happy flowers anymore. I went inside, flopped down on my bed with its soft chenille comforter, and covered my head with a pillow. *Ugh. Why had no one told me?*

Grandma was probably right. I wouldn't feel better about this bombshell until I talked it over with Garner. But what would I say? *"Oh hey, I realize we've never expressed feelings for each other besides friendship, but it really ticks me off that you didn't tell me you're a widower."*

Deep down, I knew I had no right to be mad, which just made me even more angry. I squeezed my eyes shut and cringed when I thought again about buying him that darned gnome. Did he think I was trying to say that I was his new girl?

Ugh.

True, Garner had offered to explain about the gnome statues at Christmas—in the thank-you note he left for me on Christmas night. *Where did I put that?* I lifted the pillow from my face and tossed it across the room. It landed in the kitchen a few steps away. I then began rifling through the drawer of my nightstand. When I didn't find Garner's note there, I went to the small bookcase on the far wall where I kept a vintage Hills Bros. Coffee can stuffed with various items I felt like keeping. There it was, at the bottom. I unfolded the note from Garner and read it with fresh, newly informed eyes.

For a long time, I haven't liked the holidays much. I wasn't sure I'd ever enjoy them again. Being with you and Lily at Jericho House helped change my mind.

I love the gnome. It's nice to have two of them in the yard again. Someday, if you want, I will tell you the whole story.

Merry Christmas to you all, and good night,

Garner

I never asked him to explain, and he never offered again. When I went to put Garner's note back in the coffee can, something else caught my attention. It was the "C" key chain from the stash of Christy's belongings her mother had given me. Because, although I'd told Blake otherwise, I most certainly had looked through my dead friend's things. I wasn't sure why I lied to him. Most likely, because these items of Christy's felt privately mine, and I felt territorial. But there was also a part of me suspicious of Blake's motives.

The truth was, I couldn't get back to Jericho Falls fast enough last summer to find out what was in Christy's diary. After taking it back from the thieving Jeannie Smythe, I hid it away for safekeeping in the one place I knew no one would find it—in Jericho House's broken dumbwaiter, which was forever stuck on the third floor.

Back in town less than twenty-four hours, I went upstairs and took the shoe box of stuff from its hiding spot and into my apartment with me. I tried on the red sunglasses, which I remembered Christy wearing nearly every day that last summer. I listened to The Killers, White Stripes and Green Day CDs, and I carried around this key chain in my pocket for a few days before deciding to put it in the coffee can. I read her diary too. Twice. And for the life of me, I couldn't find anything intriguing in it.

When Jeannie stole the diary, even breaking the lock to get inside, I hoped there was some explanation for Christy's death written on the pages. But all I found was typical teenage angst and her record of everyday life in Jericho Falls. There was one string of numbers

Christy had scrawled on the end paper that might have been a phone number or a date. Heck, it also could have been part of her math homework. But otherwise, the book was just a young girl's thoughts and wishes. And, really, that's all it had to be for me to cherish it forever. My best friend's *last* thoughts. Her *last* wishes. Now, I had her things hidden again. This time in my apartment where I could access them whenever I wanted to feel close to her.

I glanced at the digital clock on the microwave. It was almost one o'clock. In just an hour, I needed to have my emotions pulled together enough to chit-chat with Bree while she cut my hair. Maybe I'd take a run to clear my head. Jed certainly wouldn't mind another chance to get out of the yard today. I slipped into a pair of stretchy shorts and running shoes, then went to the house to find him.

Before I made it there, my cell phone pinged. A text.

GARNER: Hey, if I'm not mistaken, you snapped some photos yesterday. Mind if I come by and take a look?

The photos! In the aftermath since being at Pioneer RV Park, I'd completely forgotten about the photos I'd snapped of Barbara Duvall's kitchen. I was right about the chief noticing my snooping around, though. He'd busted me. Suddenly I felt very jittery. To be fair, feeling jittery at the thought of seeing the chief of police wasn't unusual. He often gave me butterflies. But I'd never felt nervous to see him because I had possibly tampered with a crime scene and because I wanted to know more about his late wife. Dread seeped over me. I took a deep breath and decided it was now or never.

ME: Sure. Headed to Bree's for a haircut at 2:00. Be home by 3:00-ish?

He sent me a "thumbs up". I was feeling more "thumbs down" at the moment, but whatever.

Outside, Grandma Lily was back at her yard work. This time, she was weeding around the back porch.

"Do you want some help?" I asked her, opening the gate to the yard. "I was going to invite Jed to take a run with me, but weed pulling would be just as cathartic, I bet."

She stopped what she was doing so she could look me in the eye. "I think getting your blood pumping would do you more good," she said. "I've been out here thinking about the uncomfortable spot we've all put you in and I find myself getting a little peeved, too. Secrets always take a toll, Chloe, even if they're kept for good reason."

I smiled at her, warmed by her understanding. "Thanks, Grandma."

Without another word, she went back to work while I fetched Jed's leash. He panted happily, hopping around a little when he realized he was going on yet another trek around Jericho Falls today.

8

That's an Order

A BRISK RUN DID THE trick. I was sweaty, and glad to be going in for a shampoo, but by the time I completed a loop down Gold Mountain, through Riverside Park and back up Main Street to Bree's, my mind felt clearer. At least, clear enough to sit through a haircut and not blast Bree with my anger the way I had done to Grandma Lily.

There was no doubt Bree also knew about Garner's past. And given Grandma Lily's use of the word "us" he'd probably asked her to keep quiet as well. It seemed like a miracle rivaling the Virgin Birth that Bree had done so... but as they say, the Lord works in mysterious ways. My best bet was to keep quiet too until I talked to Chief Garner later.

I tethered Jed in the shade under the awning of the shop, then went inside. Bree's Beauty Salon looked uncommonly messy. There were hot pink and leopard print styling capes draped on all three of her salon chairs. Fuzzy puffs of hair littered the floor, and permanent rollers filled a sink. She had had one crazy Saturday!

Bree popped out of the shop's tiny bathroom with a start. "Oh. Gosh, you scared me. I didn't hear you come in. Good grief, I had to tinkle so bad. Haven't had a break all day."

"Do you want me to reschedule?" I asked her, straightening the magazines and throwing a few empty styrofoam coffee cups in the trash can.

"Of course not," she said with her hands on her narrow hips, "after how sweet you were about Goldie?"

I smiled.

"Plus," Bree went on, "I want to hear everything about Barbara Duvall." There it was. Bree's real motivation.

Bree swept, and I helped straighten things up before she ushered me into a salon chair and swooped a pink polka dot cape around my shoulders.

"You get to talkin', I'll get to snippin'," she said.

I filled her in on what happened at Pioneer RV Park the day before, from the moment Chief Garner and I arrived to the end when Grandma Lily drove my getaway car. I told her how Garner suspected Barbara's demise was just an accident.

"Well, what did you find in those photos you took?" Bree asked, her eyes wide.

"Uh... I haven't looked at them," I said.

"Wait a minute." Bree stopped combing and cutting to whirl my chair around and stare at me. "You're trying to tell me that Chloe Martin, our resident sleuth who single-handedly solved a mystery last summer, hasn't looked at the photos she took of a potential crime scene yet?" Bree's eyes narrowed as she waggled the comb at me. "What's going on with you, Chloe?"

I didn't dare tell Bree what was truly bothering me. I knew that whatever melodramatic, sappy, hysterical things she might say about Garner and his late wife, Rachel, would inadvertently shape my conversation with him. Instead, I racked my brain for a different excuse for my preoccupation.

I said the first thing to pop into my head. "Um, Blake came by my apartment yesterday."

"And...?" Bree sang.

Where was I going with this? "And... he said he has a kind of radar for me. Like he can sense whenever I'm near. It just got me flustered, that's all."

Bree was back to work on my hair now. She wore a look of humorous satisfaction. "I knew it. I *knew* you two would end up back together," she said, batting her lashes.

"No, *no*..." I started.

"Chloe," she interrupted, "listen to me. If you've been holding back telling me because Anthony and I are splitsville just stop it. You don't have to keep your feelings a secret from me. I'm doing fine. And, it's not like this is a surprise. You and Blake have a long, romantic history together."

I managed a half-smile. I'd clear this up with her as soon as possible. But for now, I'd let Bree think she had me all figured out if that's what it took.

"Too bad he's out of town for a while, huh?" she asked.

"What?"

"Blake. He left for that mayor's convention in Albuquerque this afternoon. He was my first appointment of the day. Said he needed a fresh haircut before his trip."

I simply shrugged.

"Absence makes the heart grow fonder, right?" Bree chirped.

I seriously hope not.

ALTHOUGH BREE TRIMMED off less than an inch from my wavy tresses, my head felt about ten pounds lighter. The process put a little spring in my step too, because my hair smelled so darned good. On my part-time barista salary, I was too cheap to buy the expensive, yummy smelling shampoo that Bree used at the salon. My infrequent trips to get my hair done were always a treat.

My lightened mood didn't last long, though. As Jed and I climbed Gold Mountain, past the most stately old homes of Jericho Falls, I noticed Garner's SUV already sitting in our circle drive. *Gulp. Here goes nothing.*

"There he is!" Garner grinned and began patting his leg for Jed to come to him. I unclipped my feisty dog. He broke into a gallop to meet Chief Garner and his littermate, Mandy.

Mandy and Jed growled while they wrestled playfully. They were rescue dogs. Officer Garner had explained to me last summer that he found them at the local shelter and convinced Grandma Lily to adopt Jed when he adopted Mandy. Grandma didn't initially keep Jed. Rather, she gifted him to her then boyfriend, Art. But after Art's death, Jed became my very own good boy. Whenever these two canine sibs got the chance to play together, they had a ball. They were now dashing around the front yard, wearing the same happy expressions on their nearly identical faces.

"They'll sleep well tonight," remarked the chief.

I nodded. "You have no idea. Jed has already taken two long walks today."

He laughed. "Uh oh, you might find it challenging to sleep through his snoring, then."

When I didn't respond, Garner turned to look at me. "Everything all right?"

I gave him a tiny shake of my head, frowning.

His smile faded away.

"Let's put these two in the backyard," I suggested, my insides filled with a fluttery nausea. "We need to talk."

With the dogs playing safely in the fenced backyard, I asked Garner if he'd like to come to my apartment for a glass of lemonade and a chat. He agreed by nodding. We went around the garage silently to enter my humble abode.

Grandma had furnished the apartment with a small 1950s yellow kitchen table and two chairs with coordinating yellow and gray fabric. I invited Garner to have a seat while I poured each of us a glass of lemonade. I thanked my lucky stars that Lilian Martin was my grandmother and had trained me to always have a beverage on hand for drop-in visitors.

When I turned to face him, drinks in hand, Garner had placed his hat on the table. He looked worried. "Is this about the thing at the RV park yesterday? I'm sorry you got wrapped up in that."

I shook my head and sat down across from him at the table.

The chief took a sip of lemonade, then frowned. "Is it because I haven't told you how nice your hair looks yet?" He smiled coyly.

I shook my head again. I didn't even attempt to smile. Breaking the stoney expression on my face might cause another round of tears. *I will not cry.*

"What is it then?"

I guessed that this must be the feeling a skydiver has before leaving the plane, because there would be no turning back—no getting back to the safety of the aircraft. What I was about to say would change things between us... forever.

I began. "When I came back to Jericho Falls, I didn't expect to stay. There were too many terrible memories for me here. I told you *everything* about what happened the summer Christy died. Having your support played a big part in my decision to stay."

Garner nodded. "Good," he said, "I'm glad I could help."

I went on, "I started to believe you and I had a connection—or that we could. But today I learned something that let me know, you don't care about me at all. Not really."

Garner blew out a breath and shook his head in confusion.

"If you cared about me, you would have told me about Rachel," I said.

I had never seen the expression the chief now wore on his face. It bore a close resemblance to the sad look he gave when he unwrapped the gnome I gave him at Christmas. Now it made sense why. Garner ran both hands over the top of his head slowly and looked at the ceiling. Then he dropped his face towards his lap.

"It's not that I don't care, Chloe."

"Then how could you keep this a secret and embarrass me like this?"

"*Embarrass* you? That's what you're concerned about here? Being embarrassed?"

I swallowed. "You should have told me."

"I offered to, remember? At Christmas. It's not my fault that you never brought it up again."

"You mean in the note you left?" I asked.

Garner nodded.

I felt a surge of anger at him. Was he saying that it was *my* fault I had stayed in the dark about this? That was ridiculous! I had no way of knowing how important the information was that he vaguely hinted at in that short note.

"Oh, forgive me if I wasn't fascinated by your offer to tell me the history of your ceramic yard decorations," I snapped. My cheeks suddenly felt hot.

Garner chuckled, but it was without humor. "You know what, Chloe? Not everything is about you and you don't have a monopoly on pain. You lost your best friend? Well, guess what? So did I. And just yesterday, a woman I've known for years tragically died. Try putting yourself in someone else's shoes for a change. Maybe you'll realize you're not the only one who's ever been hurt."

Garner stood up, putting his hat on roughly, and headed for the door. "Thanks for the lemonade. When you get a minute, text me the photos. That's an order."

"Garner, wait."

He didn't respond, only slammed the door behind him.

What had I done?

I picked up the pillow from my kitchen floor where it'd landed earlier, flopped onto my bed, and once again buried my head.

9

What's Done is Done

GRANDMA LILY AND I had fallen into a predictable daily routine since I'd returned to Jericho House. We had coffee and breakfast together each day to report our daily plans and then, if nothing else, met up again at dinnertime. The point is, when I didn't show up inside the main house for dinner, Grandma came looking for me.

I was still pouting on my bed when I heard her tap on the door. I knew it was her because she always knocked the same little rhythm.

"Come in," I groaned, muffled by the pillow still covering my face.

I heard the door open slowly. "Chloe, dear? Are you feeling all right?"

I moaned.

Grandma hurried to my beside, uncovered my face, and touched my forehead with the back of her hand.

"I'm not sick. I'm stupid."

I scooted over. My grandma took a seat on the bed and I told her the whole sordid story about my visit with Chief Garner.

She sighed, "Gosh, I thought you might play the 'I'm so sorry for your loss' card and wriggle your way right into his handsome little heart."

I flopped over onto my stomach. "Waah, why didn't I do that?"

She patted my back. "There, there now. Stop wallowing. What's done is done. The good news is that this whole thing is out in the open now. You two can move on."

I wasn't sure Garner wanted anything to do with me. Let alone to "move on."

"Jump up, now," she told me. "Bree called and invited us to the Opera House. The new manager has arranged a variety show with all local talent."

I shook my head. "No. Please, Grandma. Make an excuse with Bree for me? I have a pity party to plan and attend."

Grandma Lily pursed her lips and frowned at me. "Okay, I'll give you tonight. But by tomorrow morning, I want you to shake this off and start fresh. He's a man, dear. Just apologize and let him get a whiff of that shampoo. He'll see reason."

With that, Grandma Lily pulled a blanket over me and went to leave.

She was almost out the door when she mumbled something.

"What's that, Grandma?"

"Oh, I was just talking to myself. I need to remember to have someone come look at the back gate. Today when I came home, it was open. I'm sure I shut it tight. I'm afraid there might be something wrong with the latch."

"We better get it checked or Jed will go on one of his famous walk-abouts."

Grandma winked. "Speaking of that cutie, he's in the backyard. I've fed him his dinner." She shut the door behind her.

I laid there, staring at the ceiling for another few minutes. This wasn't helping. Maybe I'd clean my apartment. Sometimes that did the trick to get me out of a funk. Under the kitchen sink, I took out my cleaning supplies; I swished the toilet, polished the mirror and sink, scrubbed the claw-footed tub, and even the bottom of the shower curtain that tended to turn orange. I swept the kitchen and living area, then ran my cordless vacuum over all the rugs. I washed the lemonade glasses, then wiped down the countertop and took a moment to toss a few questionable looking items from the fridge. I even wiped the shelves in there. In exactly 23 and a half minutes, I had cleaned my entire apartment. It was the blessing of living in a tiny space. But this evening, I could've used a longer distraction.

Jed was always good for distraction.

I changed into a pair of sweats and a pullover hoody. I grabbed my phone, locked up, and headed for Jericho House. It was almost dusk now and Jed let out one big bark when he saw me approaching the fence.

"Just me, boy," I told him.

We went inside, where I treated myself to a cup of tea. Jed laid by my feet while I waited for the teapot to sing. This quiet moment got me thinking. *Should I call Chief Garner?* I could apologize—admit that I let my surprise turn into anger and I shouldn't have reacted that way. But something told me he wasn't ready to have that conversation. The only thing he wanted from me at this point was the photos I took of Barbara Duvall's kitchen.

The photos.

I reached into my hoody's front pocket for my cell phone. I swiped open the photo album and began thumbing through pics I snapped yesterday. The poor quality and weird angles reminded me of the equally poor and weird stance I had to get into in order to take them. I could make out the Duvall's circa 1970 avocado green dinette set. Sitting on it was a plate with a half-eaten sandwich, a bottle of wine and a wine glass with about one swig left inside. I flipped to the next frame that was almost identical except for one difference. I had managed a slightly wider angle, which showed me that one of the dining chairs laid on its side. Also visible from this angle was a pair of Barbara's slippers stashed in the corner.

I grabbed the magnetized pad of note paper Grandma Lily kept on the refrigerator and jotted down a few things:

-Wine

-Sandwich. Old or fresh?

-Chair knocked over

-Barb needed to update her kitchen

I scrolled through the shots one more time to make sure I wasn't missing anything. I wondered, why didn't Garner have his own photos of the house? Weren't his "trained professionals" on the scene with their big fancy cameras? I wished I could ask him. But for now, I thought it best to simply follow his instructions and text him the images before he subpoenaed them. Or worse yet, sent my least favorite officer, Ellie Porter, over to get them from me. *Blech.*

I tapped on each photo, even the ones that seemed too blurry to matter, and attached them to a text for Chief Garner. *Should I add a message?* I couldn't think of anything to say right now, so I pressed 'send' and heard the chime sound as the photos floated through cyberspace. I waited. Soon, the word 'delivered' appeared. I waited some more, staring at the screen to see if the chief would reply. He didn't.

The teapot whistled. I poured scalding water over a peppermint tea bag I had placed in my favorite red mug with the words, 'I'm a history buff, my jokes are historical' on the side. Grandma Lily told me it was a coffee mug, not meant for tea. I didn't care.

While I sipped from the steaming cup, I thought about Barbara Duvall. I remembered her bruised wrist, the bump on her head, and how she was fully clothed right down to her torn stockings. I thought about what Nick had told me—that she had been depressed since her husband died and possibly drinking too much. If her job was on the line too, she might have been feeling desperate. Maybe Garner and I were both wrong. Maybe Barbara wasn't the victim of an accident or an assailant. Maybe she was a victim of... herself.

10

Cloud of Dust

BY THE TIME I DOWNED that gigantic cup of tea, I'd decided to return to Pioneer RV Park. Looking back, I'm not sure why I cared so much at that moment whether Barbara had an accident, did herself in, or had been murdered. But it likely had something to do with taking my mind off the terrible ache that sat underneath my rib cage ever since my talk with Chief Garner. I liked the idea of getting out of the house and putting my brain to work instead of my emotions.

I stuffed the list into my pocket before leaving. Elliot was in the parlour giving himself a bath. I told him Jed and I would be back soon. He gave us a "as if I care what you two do" yowl and continued licking his nether regions.

I loaded up Jed in the bed of my little red Toyota truck and we were off. It was officially dusk now. Twinkle lights decorated many of the shops' windows, giving Main Street a festive feel. It was fun to think of the busyness we'd soon be experiencing when the warm weather and tourist season officially hit. Families from far and near would come to spend a few days in the wild west. They'd pan for gold at the booth in the park, eat ice cream at Sarsaparilla Sally's and watch the live shoot-out reenactment that took place every day at noon in front of the Jericho Falls Opera House. Seeing the visitors' enjoyment of the place helped keep the magic alive for those of us who lived in this old-time town year round.

When I crossed the bridge into the RV park, the first thing I noticed were the campfires sprinkled here and there. There weren't many RVers here yet, but the few people who were camping were taking advantage of the opportunity to roast a marshmallow or a hot dog on this peaceful spring evening. I stopped near the Duvall's home office. I gave Jed a pat on the head as I got out and told him to stay put.

The growing darkness afforded me suitable cover to meander around outside the little house. *Darn it.* Yellow crime scene tape was wrapped around the front porch and pool fence. There was no way I could get inside to look around. Well, no way, that is without committing a crime. And face it, I was already in enough trouble with Garner. I looked out into the rows of campers and recognized the thin, balding man from yesterday—the one upset over the broken change machine. He sat alone in a lawn chair near his campfire, strumming a guitar. I wondered if he would talk to me.

I swished through the ankle deep grass in his direction, feeling a little vulnerable out here. But just one row over was a family with three rambunctious kids playing and singing, so I figured I'd be safe. I was only twenty or thirty feet away from the man when he finally noticed me.

He jumped a little and gasped, "You scared the bejeezus out of me."

"I'm sorry, I didn't mean to."

He squinted, then motioned for me to come closer to his fire. "Aren't you the girl from yesterday?" he asked.

I nodded.

"I don't talk to cops," he said. The man turned his back as if to go inside his camp trailer.

"I'm not with the police, I promise."

He looked back at me with a glare. "You sure? You're not trickin' me?"

"I'm not a cop. It was only a coincidence that I was with the Chief of Police yesterday. He was giving me a ride when the 911 call came through."

"So whatcha doin' here again?"

I shrugged. What *was* I doing? "I guess I'm just interested in knowing what happened to Barbara Duvall."

The man stayed quiet. He seemed to be stuck in deep thought. This gave me a moment to look around his campsite. He'd tucked straw bales around his small trailer, had several potted plants growing, and a wooden free-standing clothes line to one side.

"Looks like you've lived here awhile. You must have known Barbara pretty well."

He grumbled and swatted at an imaginary fly. "Barbara and I had our ups and downs."

"Over the change machine?" I smiled.

He smiled too. I had effectively softened him up. "That. And other things."

A vehicle pulled in and parked behind my pickup. Light from a single lamppost cast only enough of a glow for me to see it was a dark-colored minivan. A man got out of the driver's seat and went towards the porch of the Duvall home. He didn't heed the warning of the yellow tape, but simply lifted it up and slipped underneath.

"Hey," I yelled. Come on, if I was going to obey the CAUTION and resist snooping, this guy was, too.

I wasn't the only one watching this rebellious person. A pudgy woman in pink sweatpants and foam curlers called out toward him and rushed in that direction.

"Uh, oh," said the man at my side, "there goes Lottie. That guy better watch out."

"Looks like she means business," I added.

He pushed his chin out in her direction. "That's Lottie Sloan. She works here. Barbara hired her after Floyd died to watch the park office while she went to work. Lottie gets free rent in exchange."

I nodded. *Good to know.*

The woman I now knew as Lottie reached the home office and convinced the visitor to come down off of the front porch. Judging by the amount of her arm waving, she was also berating him for ignoring the police tape. I had to applaud her on that point. I wanted to hear what they were saying, so I began wandering closer, through the increasing darkness. I heard Lottie say, "You best get outta here right now."

The man, who was probably in his early thirties, spit on the ground before obeying Lottie's request. He walked around the dark green minivan and went to open the driver's door. But as he reached for the handle, Jed, who was still in the back of my pickup a few feet away, did the strangest thing. He lunged, barking. His front feet came to rest on the top of the tailgate. The man jumped back.

I took off in a run toward the commotion. *What had gotten into Jed?* He didn't have a mean dog bone in his body. By the time I reached them, Jed was no longer barking, but he gave a low, continuous growl.

"I'm so sorry," I told the man and Lottie. "You must have startled him." I placed a hand on Jed's neck to pet him. He didn't stop growling.

Now, standing this close, I could see that the stranger was quite thin and rather greasy. His jeans looked dirty and his sweatshirt bore paint stains. He wasn't from around here. Still, I felt like I'd seen him before. He glared at me without saying a word. Then, he got into the dark green minivan and left. Lottie and I were left in a cloud of dust.

"Who are *you?*" Lottie asked, waving a hand in front of her to clear the air before pushing up her thick and terribly out of style eyeglasses. I hadn't seen Lottie here yesterday during the commotion. She was a memorable enough character I would have remembered.

I put my hand out. "My name's Chloe Martin. I was here yesterday when they found Mrs. Duvall."

"Oh. Just another thrill seeker, then. Like that last yahoo." She motioned in the direction the minivan had taken.

"Not exactly. I'm a local. I live with my grandma, Lily Martin, at Jericho House," I explained.

"So?" Lottie said, thoroughly unimpressed.

"So... I'd like to know what happened here, wouldn't you?"

"I doubt they'll ever find out what really happened to Barbara," she whispered. I couldn't tell whether this possibility made Lottie sad or relieved.

I took a deep breath and let it out slowly. "Well, a long time ago, I had a friend drown too. We never found out what caused her accident and believe me, it's terrible. Maybe this time, things can be different."

She narrowed her eyes once again and tilted her head to one side cynically. One of her hair curlers bounced against her cheek, threatening to come undone from her graying hair.

"Lottie, I hate to pry, but do you think Barbara Duvall might have hurt herself?"

Lottie's eyes grew large. "Why would you say that?"

"Well, the talk around town is she hasn't been well since Floyd died and was being pushed into early retirement."

At first, Lottie shook her head, making her curlers bob and twirl in every direction. But suddenly she stopped short. A thoughtful look crossed her face. "I don't think so, but who could say for sure? She has been through a lot."

I could tell Lottie wouldn't talk with me much longer. She'd already taken a few steps towards her camp trailer. I switched gears while I still had the chance. "Was Barbara especially close to anyone? A new boyfriend, maybe?"

She frowned. "No. Oh, old Jim over there tried, but Barbara wasn't interested." Lottie pointed at the man's trailer where I had been before.

"You mean the guy who was mad at her? About the broken change machine?"

She rolled her eyes and nodded. "That's Jim Holt. He was over there harping at Barbara about something nearly every evening. Just an excuse to see her, if you ask me."

"But Barbara wasn't interested?" I asked.

"Not in the least."

A small dog's incessant barking could be heard inside a nearby trailer. A definite no-no in the RV park rulebook.

"I better go rap on that door and tell them to keep their yappy dog still. Quiet hours start at 8:00."

"Thanks for chatting with me," I told her. "If you want to talk more, you can call me at Jericho House."

Lottie murmured something noncommittal, then shuffled off toward the shrill barking.

I thought about going back to visit with Jim some more, but he had doused his campfire and there weren't any lights on inside his small trailer. Just before I opened my truck door to leave, I noticed a piece of wadded paper in the gravel. It was right where the minivan had been parked. That grimy guy might have kicked it out of his car accidentally. I bent down to pick it up and found it was a receipt from The Golden Grind. *At least he appreciates good coffee.*

I tossed it into the trash bag in the cab of my truck.

11

Tough Guy

IT WAS ALMOST TEN O'CLOCK before Grandma Lily arrived home that night. I was waiting up for her in the parlour.

"Bree and I had such a delightful time," she said. "I wish you felt up to joining us."

Grandma told me all about the community variety show. Nick Newsom acted as the emcee and there were acts of every kind.

"I had no idea Mr. Cooper could juggle like that," said my grandma with amazement, "or that Claire Harland plays the spoons. Imagine, we've been neighbors all these years."

It seemed to bode well that the new Jericho Falls Opera House Manager would organize such a fun event as one of his first orders of business. He seemed community-minded, wanting to get acquainted with the townspeople in such a way.

"What have you been up to, dear?" Grandma asked me.

I told her I went back to the RV park to look around—just to raise my spirits.

"Oh no, Chloe," Grandma shook her index finger at me. "I do not want you getting tangled up in another ugly situation. I know this is upsetting, but please, leave this whole thing to Chief Garner and his officers."

"I'm just afraid that he is missing something. He thinks it was an accident."

"Maybe it was."

"Maybe it wasn't," I argued.

"Speaking of Lance Garner," Grandma threw me a scolding look, "I sure hope this thing about Blake isn't some conniving ploy you're using to get his attention. Believe me, it won't work with him."

"*Thing* about Blake?" I asked.

She looked at me pointedly. "Bree told me you are having feelings for Blake again, but have been too scared to tell us. I knew that was hogwash right away. But, young lady, you better have a good reason for making up such a thing."

I dropped my head into my hands. "Oh, no. It's nothing but a huge misunderstanding. And I didn't make it up, Bree *assumed* it." I exhaled loudly. "I'll clear it up with her right away."

"Good. Now listen. I'm cooking up a little something. Maybe you could help me. It would be a good way to take your mind off the RV park situation."

I raised my eyebrows, signaling her to go on.

Grandma grinned and rubbed her hands together. "I think we should play matchmaker for Bree and the new opera house manager. His name is Stan Duncan. He's around her age, very handsome, talented, and clearly wants to put roots down in Jericho Falls."

"Do you think Bree's ready to move on yet?" I asked. "It hasn't been long since her engagement to Anthony fell apart."

Grandma shrugged. "I guess we'll find out." She scooped up Elliot and rubbed him underneath the chin. As she left the room, I heard her tell the cat sweetly, "Oh, that young man might be nice-looking, but no one is as handsome as my Elliot."

Grandma Lily soon announced she was ready to hit the hay, so I went out to my apartment with Jed. I wished I felt tired, but between the heartache I still felt over Garner and the nagging questions about Barbara Duvall, not to mention the mix-up with Bree—my mind would not let me rest. I sat down at my kitchen table with the list I started earlier.

I read over my notes, then added:

-Lottie doesn't think Barbara would have killed herself.

-Jim had the hots for Barbara.

If Lottie was right, I was back to considering the possibility that Barbara Duvall was murdered. I simply couldn't reconcile the bruising, torn stockings, and bump to the head with accidentally falling into the pool. Unless... she was very drunk? Could that also explain her injuries?

I dug my phone out and opened up the photos again to investigate the kitchen scene. As I remembered, the wine bottle was mostly empty—meaning Barbara could have been quite tipsy. I scanned the image closely, looking for any other minor details to help me. That's when I noticed it. A second wine glass. It was almost hidden from view behind the napkin holder, but I could definitely make out the rim of another stemmed glass. Barbara hadn't been drinking alone.

I paced the room. 'Pacing' within my studio apartment meant taking a mere five or six small steps in one direction before turning back again. It wasn't as helpful as walking the long hallway inside Jericho House, but it worked in a pinch.

What if Barbara rebuffed this Jim fellow one too many times? Could he have become angry enough to do her in? Was Jim Holt more than just the pest that Lottie seemed to consider him?

And then there was the man in the green minivan. Lottie guessed he was a thrill seeker, just out to glimpse a real-life crime scene. And it would be unwise for him to come back if he was the killer. Unless he needed to clean up a loose end or two, like a wine glass with his fingerprints on it.

Even though Chief Garner probably already knew all this and would only tell me to stay out of his official investigation, I really wished I could talk with him. I liked the way his eyes narrowed when he went into cop mode—so serious, so handsome. And I needed to convince him to look deeper, not just assume Barbara Duvall's drowning was an accident. But going over things with Garner wasn't likely right now, considering how miffed he was with me. I was on my own. Tomorrow, after what was probably going to be a restless night's sleep, I'd go back to Pioneer RV Park to get answers to more of my questions.

I wasn't wrong. I slept terribly. And surprisingly, after such an active day, so did Jed. For whatever reason, he found it necessary to pee at the top of every hour. Then, when I took him outside, he'd growl and puff up like some tough guy, which he most definitely is not. *What has gotten into him lately?*

Finally, when Jed woke me again around six a.m. I gave up trying to sleep and simply got out of bed. I showered before going inside the house to start some coffee and breakfast for Grandma Lily and me. It shocked me when she was already up, too. She typically slept until seven a.m. on the dot.

"The handyman said he'd swing by to look at the fence before heading to a project he's working on in Lakeview," she explained when I questioned her early morning start.

I nodded while getting out the bacon and eggs. Grandma was already grinding coffee beans.

As our breakfast sizzled in the cast iron pan, I considered how to broach the subject I wanted to discuss with her. Unfortunately, tact before bacon isn't my specialty, so I ended up blurting, "Did you know her?"

"Hmmm?"

"Garner's wife. Rachel. Did you know her?"

Grandma smiled sweetly, took the spatula from my hand, and motioned for me to have a seat at the kitchen island.

"Not well," she said, cracking another egg into the skillet. "They hadn't lived here long when she had the accident. I didn't get to know Lance until after she was gone. Karen Little invited him to join our book club to help him get out and about again."

"It was an accident, then?" Over the past hours, since learning that Chief Garner had once been married, I played a dozen scenarios out in my head. Tuberculosis, gunshot wound, death during child-birth. *Jeez, I seriously needed to get out of this old-timey town once in a while.*

"It was a car accident." Grandma plated the food, slid one to me, and sat down beside me. "I'm going to say it again. You need to talk to Chief Garner about this, not me."

I let out a long, slow breath. I certainly did. But how, now that I'd made things so uncomfortable between us?

A knock on the back door interrupted our conversation and our breakfast. Grandma stuffed a sizable piece of bacon into her mouth and went out to meet the handyman. I fed the furry family members and left through the front door. I didn't want Grandma Lily to know I was going back to the RV park to snoop around.

12

A Grieving Child

THAT MORNING WHEN I arrived, there was a sign posted at the entry to the park, "CLOSED UNTIL FURTHER NOTICE." Most of the trailers were now gone, except for those which had clearly been there for some time, like Jim's and Lottie's. I drove down the narrow gravel lane and parked in front of Lottie's trailer space. When I knocked on her door, I could hear country music and the sound of a vacuum cleaner inside. I knocked again, a little harder.

Lottie popped her head out of the door, holding a cordless vac in one hand. "Oh, hi," she said, pushing up her glasses. "Just doing some cleaning. I'll be right out."

I used the few moments before Lottie came outside to look around the park. Jim's trailer was two rows over, almost directly across from hers. A little farther down on this same row was a large, brand new behemoth of a 5th wheel trailer. It had professional skirting installed, blooming flower pots, a patio set, and a wire dog kennel. Also set for long-term, I guessed.

When Lottie came down the steps of her RV, she was wearing the same pink sweats I had seen her in the night before with a purple bathrobe over the top. Her fuzzy slippers might have once been blue, but were now a dingy gray.

"You're back," she said with a grin.

Her lighter mood pleasantly surprised me.

"Yeah, I wanted to pick your brain some more. I had a long, sleepless night of too much thinking."

"Well, you'll never guess what happened after you left last night."

"What?"

Lottie told me that the man in the minivan came back to the RV park accompanied by a police officer. The man, who she learned was none other than Daniel Duvall, Barbara's son, informed them that since he would inherit the place, he expected to be treated with respect whenever he showed up. He went door-to-door, kicking out campers, and closed the place down.

"What about you and Jim? And whoever that is?" I pointed toward the fancy trailer at the end of the row.

She went on, "Officer Porter told Barbara's son that because we have been full-time residents, he has to give us thirty days' notice. But in a month? We're all out of a place to live."

I resisted the urge to roll my eyes. Officer Ellie Porter and I had a contentious relationship. As Christy's kid sister, she never gave up the idea that I had something to do with her sister's tragic death. This became especially clear when I returned to town last year and she quickly jumped to the conclusion that my grandma was a murderer. In the months since, we'd done our best to avoid one another.

"What if one of the campers knew something to help solve the case? Were they at least questioned?"

Lottie said yes. They were all interviewed by officers on Friday night and instructed to leave contact information.

"What's the point in Daniel Duvall closing the park?" I asked. "Surely it turns a profit and the tourist season is about to start."

"He said he doesn't want the hassle. I bet he's just going to sell it and get a fat stack of cash." Lottie rolled her eyes to emphasize this sleazy sounding plan.

"Lottie, you know how to run this place. You should buy it."

She laughed out loud. "I live in an old camp trailer and barely scrape by one month at a time. Where am I going to get the money to buy a whole RV park?"

Every time I turned around lately, I found another problem brewing; Barbara Duvall's suspicious death, Bree thinking I was falling for Blake all over again, Garner giving me the silent treatment, and now impending homelessness for the settlers at Pioneer RV Park. While only two of these issues were actually any of my business, somehow I felt compelled to solve them all.

"Don't give up on the idea, Lottie. Maybe you can come up with some financing."

"Whatever you say, kiddo." She sounded unconvinced. "Now, what are these ideas that kept you up last night?"

I told Lottie that, unlike the police, I didn't believe Barbara's death was an accident. "How long had she been home from work when Jim started knocking and carrying on about the broken change machine?"

Lottie narrowed her eyes in thought. "I'd say a half-hour, forty-five minutes tops. I finished up at the office and left a few minutes after five. I had to hurry home because I always video chat with my daughter and her new baby on Fridays at 5:30."

"Did you see anyone coming or going from Barbara's place in that span of time?"

"Sorry," she said sadly, "I was too busy watching my grandson coo and slobber. I wasn't paying attention to anything else."

I smiled. "You and Barbara must have been pretty close, huh?"

Lottie's expression became unreadable. She shrugged. "Barb could be hard to deal with. I only started working for her once Floyd died. Like you heard, she didn't handle his death well."

"Anything particularly difficult?"

She hesitated. "I hate to speak ill of the dead, but she paid me next to nothing—aside from the free trailer space, I mean. Recently,

I told her I was going to have to take a second job if she didn't raise my hourly rate."

"This upset her?"

"Yeah," Lottie said, "she wanted me at her constant beck and call."

"Why constant?"

Lottie pantomimed drinking. "Even though I was supposed to have weekends off, she usually called me in."

I took a deep breath and asked, "Lottie, was Barbara ever violent with you?"

"Barbara? Violent? No. Weepy and pitiful, maybe, but not violent." We were quiet for a moment, then Lottie made a comment that I considered rhetorical. "Someone might have gotten violent with her, though, huh? I wonder who."

I had two suspects high on my list. First was Barbara Duvall's son. He seemed to be in a big hurry to evict the campers and liked the power he held as the heir to this place. He wasn't exactly acting like a typical grieving child—more like someone who saw a big paycheck on the horizon. Then there was the camper named Jim with his unrequited love for the RV park owner. His anger last night might have been about more than a broken change machine. But I didn't want to show my cards to Lottie just yet. Because if her issues with Barbara ran deeper than she was letting on, she too might be to blame for the woman's death. Instead, I changed the subject.

"Who lives back there?" I pointed again at the shiny, brand new trailer.

"That's the Browns. They won the lottery a few years back, and ever since, they've been summering here and wintering in Arizona. They pulled in again last week."

Interesting timing.

"Were they friendly with Barbara?"

"Yeah. When Floyd was alive, the four of them hung out all the time."

It looked like I had another visit to make.

"Thanks, Lottie. I appreciate your help."

I went toward my truck.

"Hey, where's your dog?" Lottie asked, noticing the empty bed of my Toyota pickup.

"I left him home today, after his rude behavior here last night."

"I wouldn't call him rude," Lottie remarked. "Maybe just a good judge of Daniel Duvall's character."

I chuckled and waved goodbye. I started my truck to drive the short distance to the Brown's trailer. The couple had a rectangular bamboo rug underneath their patio set and a small electric fountain bubbling for ambience. The scent of breakfast food wafted out of an open window.

I knocked lightly and at once a man, presumably Mr. Brown, answered the door.

"Can I help you?" he asked. He wore a light blue polo shirt that was at least one size too small. He'd slicked his graying hair back over the top of his head a la 1950s gangster, and donned a gold chain with a small medallion around his neck.

"Hi, Mr. Brown, I'm a friend of Lottie's," I fibbed. "I wanted to come by to express my condolences about Mrs. Duvall."

His expression changed in a flash from mildly bothered to extremely sad.

"Oh, thank you," he sang in bass. "The missus and I are terribly broken up over the whole thing."

I clicked my tongue and drew my eyebrows together in mock understanding, but stayed quiet in order to let him talk.

"I was just telling the missus we should have Barb over for dinner. She must be so lonesome with Floyd gone. But we didn't make good on that invitation in time."

"Did you see her at all since you've been back?"

He shook his head firmly. "No, sadly. Lottie was manning the office when we arrived. Then, we've been so busy getting everything set up." He waved around the little yard with its heavy dose of decor.

I found it interesting. Lottie said the Browns had been friends with the Duvalls. Yet, they didn't make a point of saying hello since they arrived. *Was that simply a coincidence or were they on the outs?*

"How is it you know Lottie?" Mr. Brown asked me. "Do you have an RV here?" He craned his neck around, looking throughout the park for a space that might be mine.

"No, I live in town. My name's Chloe Martin. My grandmother owns Jericho House."

"Ahh, yes. Me and the missus toured that place a year or two ago. Magnificent."

"Thank you, it is."

Suddenly I heard 'the missus' from inside the trailer say something about getting rid of me. Mr. Brown's face flushed, but he obediently said he needed to go. His breakfast was ready.

I took the not-so-subtle hint and excused myself from their doorstep.

So far, the day hadn't netted me enough information. Should I try talking with Jim again? He'd been pretty tight-lipped the night before. Still, my new worries about him played on my mind. In the end, I decided it couldn't hurt. It would have been another ridiculously short drive, so I simply hoofed it over to his meager camp trailer.

Unlike the other two, Jim's campsite didn't show any signs of life. I checked my phone. It was only 9 a.m. I hated to wake the guy if he was sleeping. But I risked it anyway, rapping out what I hoped was a friendly rhythm on the door. Several moments passed before I heard anything. What I heard was grumbling. Soon, Jim poked his head out, eyes puffy and hair ruffled. Uh oh, I woke him.

13

Nothing to See

"YOU'RE BACK." HIS WORDS were the same as Lottie's had been, but his annoyed tone gave them a completely different meaning.

"Hi, sorry to wake you. I was next door," I motioned towards Lottie's RV, "and wanted a chance to visit with you, too. I didn't properly introduce myself yesterday. Chloe Martin." I offered a handshake.

He accepted, and I shook his limp and somewhat sweaty hand through the narrow sliver of his open door. I realized then he was only wearing boxer shorts. And while fit for an older guy, his bare chest and legs were so white I could see every vein like a roadmap. I quickly looked away so as not to embarrass him, or myself, any further.

"I'm Jim Holt. And, as long as I'm up, want a cup of joe? I'll put on my clothes and the coffee pot if you'll gimme a minute."

Jim didn't wait for my answer before shutting the door behind him. I noticed the trailer rock from side to side as he moved around in there. I heard rustling and clanking, some water running, and more grumbles. Eventually, he unlatched the door once again, and I climbed the three steps to go inside.

Surprisingly, the interior of this little house-on-wheels was chock full, yet nicely organized. The tiny trailer seemed to contain everything you might have in a full-sized house, all squished into a 25 foot space. There were several green plants, a collection of vinyl records and a small fish aquarium gurgling near the one upholstered chair.

Jim moved a stack of books from the booth-like dining area and asked me to have a seat. He sat a steaming mug of brew in front of me. It smelled divine. It tasted even better. I turned to look at his miniature stove. "How did you make this? It's probably the best cup of coffee I've had outside of a gourmet coffee house."

He was pouring a cup for himself, and lifted a blue enamelware coffee pot so I could see it. "I use a good, old-fashioned percolator. Sometimes it's a waste of time trying to improve upon the way our ancestors did things."

This sounded like something Grandma Lily might say. Looking around this neatly organized space, sipping great coffee and hearing Jim's words, I was warming up to the old crank. And he must not think I was too bad either, inviting me inside and all.

"So what were you doing talking to Lottie?" he asked.

He took a seat across from me at the little table. Our knees briefly touched underneath.

"I'm curious about how Barbara died. Just gathering information."

Jim sipped and nodded. "Well, don't put too much stock in anything she tells ya."

"What's that supposed to mean?"

"Lottie Sloan's not the most trustworthy gal in my book."

In my head, I went through the details Lottie shared with me. I'd focus on the most pressing details to verify with Jim. "All right then, did you really get a thirty-day eviction notice from Barbara's son last night?"

"Yup." Slurp.

"Were The Browns and Duvalls friendly with one another?"

"Eh," Jim shrugged, made a so-so gesture with his hand and took another sip.

"Was Barbara Duvall taking advantage of Lottie?"

"Negative."

"Care to explain?" I asked.

"Lottie likes to complain about her hourly wage. But Barbara gives her the trailer space and electricity for free. Plus, she always stocked Lottie's fridge. The woman doesn't own a car, so she doesn't need gas money. As far as I can tell, aside from her cell phone, Lottie can't have many bills."

"How'd she end up here without a vehicle?"

"Her *fiance*," Jim seemed to use this word lightly. "He up and left her in the middle of the night. That was four years ago."

"Whoa."

"Yeah, I'd say she's pretty lucky things have turned out this well."

I raised my eyebrows at him. "I guess. But this arrangement might make a person feel a little... I don't know, trapped."

"Only has herself to blame. Lottie's the one who suggested it to Barbara."

That was interesting. Lottie would have me believe she was being victimized by Barbara. Had she really made the deal herself?

"What about you, Jim? Looks like you've been here awhile, too."

Jim took a gulp of coffee and stretched his neck before answering. "I went through a divorce. This trailer's about all I ended up with. Never meant to stay this long, but I like Jericho Falls. I do odd jobs around town and get by. One of these days, it'll be time to move on. Probably sooner than later now that Barb's gone."

I felt tension coming from Jim's side of the table, like he was about to tell me my time was up. I had to go for it.

"Jim, what do you think happened to Barbara?"

"According to the police, she fell in accidentally and drowned."

He took another drink, watching me over the rim of his mug.

"That's not what I asked. What do *you* think happened to her?"

He put his coffee down, then stared into the jet black liquid for several seconds. When he looked up, he had tears in his eyes. "It didn't seem like an accident."

I simply nodded, unsure what to say to soothe his sadness. *He was feeling sadness, right? Not guilt?* Oh gosh, here I was inside this little tin can with a man who was pining away for a woman found dead mere hours before. I glanced at the door and tried to estimate how many steps it would take for me to get out of here. Could I beat Jim to the door if I needed to? Could I operate the weird RV door handle thingy? Thankfully, what he admitted next calmed my concerns.

"To be honest, I only complained so much about things around here 'cause I liked the playful banterin' with Barbara. Heck, I knew she wasn't sweet on me, but I think she at least enjoyed my company. Kinda loved to hate me, ya know? I worried about her and I know what it's like to have a broken heart." His chin quivered, and a tear spilled down his cheek. He cleared his throat and stood, wiping his eyes.

I hated to do this to the guy, but I needed to know, "Could Barbara have done this to herself?"

Jim leaned against his tiny kitchen countertop and shook his head thoughtfully. "Doesn't make sense. If she was gonna knock herself off, it would've been that first year after Floyd died. Gosh almighty, she was a wreck. Nah, slowly but surely she's been gettin' better."

"Need a refill?" he asked with a shaky, tearful voice while turning toward the stove.

"No thanks, Jim. I better be going." I stood now too, gulped down the last bit of the divine brew, and handed him the empty mug. He promptly put it in his tiny sink.

"Listen," I told him, "I'm going to find out what really happened to her, I promise."

"Why do you care so much, Chloe Martin?"

"Let's just say I've been there, too. With a broken heart and a friend gone with no explanation why."

Jim smiled sadly.

As I stepped to the door, something caught my eye on a narrow table against the wall. Next to the aquarium sat a tiny T.V. set with tin foil around the antenna for better reception. That's not what interested me, though. One shelf down I saw a book titled, *Wildflowers of Nevada*.

The idea of flowers tickled something in the back of my brain. *Why? When have I been thinking of flowers recently?* We had flowers at Goldie's funeral, of course, but those had been forsythia. And I bought flowers from Nick's Knacks, but those were typical garden varieties. Then it came to me. I was almost certain I had seen a small bundle of wildflowers lying on Barbara Duvall's kitchen table in the photographs I took. They didn't seem important at first glance. But were they?

"I need your help, Jim. Come on."

I rushed out of the trailer, leaped down the steps, and went toward Barbara's house. When I glanced behind me, Jim was hopping into a pair of shoes. I stopped to let him catch up.

"Where are we going?" he asked.

"I need a boost to look into Barbara's kitchen window, police tape or no police tape."

Jim didn't seem the slightest bit concerned with the crime I was asking him to commit. I was glad, because while I wanted to know what variety of flowers were in the victim's kitchen, I didn't want this armchair florist and potential suspect to know what I was interested in.

When we reached the house, we ducked under the yellow ribbon and I motioned for Jim to follow me around the far side of the house where I had taken the photos on the day Barbara died.

"I need to see in there." I pointed to the window above my head. Jim made a cradle with his hands where I could put my left foot. Then he hoisted me up with a grunt.

I got my first clear view of the room. It wasn't exactly what my photos had shown me, of course. Now gray fingerprint dust littered most surfaces and yellow plastic markers sat nearby anything the officers considered important. They did not, however, mark the little bundle of white flowers that lay on the table beside the bottle of wine. There were about ten of the blooms, tied together with a rubber band. Some of their petals had fallen off, or perhaps someone had pulled them off on purpose. Because at the bottom of the wine glass there was a confetti sprinkling of tiny flower petals.

"You about done?" Jim lamented. "You're killin' me."

I hopped down. "Sorry, and thanks."

"Well?" he asked, still in the dark about the hunch I was following.

"I was wrong," I lied. "There's nothing to see."

14

Circling Back

I DROVE HOME WITH MY heart pumping like crazy. Had I cracked another case? If the flowers in Barbara Duvall's wine glass were poisonous, wouldn't that prove that someone drugged her and caused her death? Sure, she may have drowned, but only because she was under the influence of something—something stronger than wine.

Although my suspicions about Jim Holt had diminished some, the book he had on his shelf bothered me. Did he learn about poisonous plants in order to harm Barbara? Or was this simply a coincidence?

The speed limit changed to 20 mph, and I eased down Main Street. That's when I spotted the dark green mini van parked on the curb in front of The Golden Grind. I quickly found a parking spot of my own and dug through the trash bag that hung around my gearshift. There it was. The Golden Grind receipt I'd picked up from the ground at the RV park. I opened and smoothed it to read.

The receipt was from yesterday at 10:47 a.m. Heck, that's about the time I'd been here checking my work schedule. I scanned to the bottom of the slip to see if barista Sandy Little had entered the customer's name. The shop's system was set up for it, but we only used the feature when we were extra busy. But there it was. The name

'Dan' appeared on the receipt. *Had he been one of the unfamiliar faces I saw here yesterday morning?*

Unfortunately, I didn't move quickly enough. Daniel Duvall suddenly appeared outside the coffee shop with a muffin and coffee in hand. He immediately got in and took off in his van. *Dang it.* Well, if he was becoming a regular at The Golden Grind while in town, maybe I would catch him here tomorrow morning and have a little chat.

Back on the move, I turned down a side street to reach Nick's Knacks. Nick was outside, sweeping the boardwalk, when I pulled up.

"Hello there, Chloe," he said with a smile.

"Hi, Nick. By any chance, do you stock books on wildflowers?"

He leaned against the broom handle and looked upward in thought. "I'm fairly certain I have a guidebook intended for hikers. Let's go look."

We zig-zagged through the amply and oddly stocked aisles until we came to a wire display rack. Nick spun it first one way and then the other. The books for sale ranged from romance novels to car magazines and daily devotionals. Like everything in Nick's shop, the keyword here was eclectic.

"Shucks, I don't see it." Nick sighed. "It must have sold."

Maybe to Jim Holt, I thought.

"That's all right," I told Nick. "I'll ask around."

I started for the door, but Nick stopped me.

"Many thanks for sending Chief Garner in."

"What?"

Nick shrugged. "He said something you two talked about the other day inspired him to do some shopping. I appreciate the referral."

I was about to ask Nick what Garner purchased, but the shop's phone rang. Nick hurried away to answer. As I turned to go, I heard his elegant vocal skills greet whomever was on the other end.

I went back to my pickup in a bit of a fog. What could our conversation (which was better described as an argument) have inspired the chief to buy? I started my little truck, hung a right, and continued toward Gold Mountain. I could have flipped a u-turn and gone down Main Street, of course, but my current route put me in the best position to view city hall's employee parking lot. It gave me the chance to see if Garner's SUV was there. It was, meaning the chief was likely inside the building.

I wanted so badly to go inside and patch things up with him. I wanted things to be back to normal so I could tell him about the flowers—and what I thought they might mean. But there'd be no privacy in the PD office. Officer Ellie Porter might even be there to listen in. *Ugh.* The realization suddenly hit me that even *Ellie Porter* had known about Garner's past relationship this whole time. There was no way I could show my face in there, where everyone knew the secret he'd withheld from me.

A professionally dressed brunette woman in a skirt and blouse went through the employee entrance. She gave my truck a look, probably wondering who I was, stalking the employee parking lot. I sped up and drove away.

"WHAT'S GOTTEN INTO you now?" Grandma Lily asked as I entered the front door to Jericho House.

"Huh?"

"I can see that you're out of sorts. Tell me what's going on. But make it quick. I have a group tour starting in fifteen minutes."

Leaning against the foyer wall, I sighed. "I'm more sure than ever that Barbara Duvall was the victim of something sinister. I just don't have enough evidence to put it together."

"Oh, for goodness' sake, Chloe. Didn't I ask you to leave that whole thing alone?"

"Yes. You did. But I can't, okay? So, can I talk it out with you? To see if any of my theories hold?"

Grandma glanced at her watch, then audibly exhaled. "Only if I can sip some tea while you're at it. I better make it peppermint or maybe lavender. You're fraying my nerves."

She shooed me towards the kitchen. I started talking on the way. "All right, here's what I know so far."

I explained to Grandma Lily that there were four full-time residents at the RV park, aside from Barbara Duvall. Jim Holt, who had an unrequited crush on her; Lottie Sloan, her part-time office assistant who seemed a little disgruntled, and the Browns who had only recently returned from their wintertime RVing in sunny Arizona.

"Lottie and Jim knew her best. They said that Barbara was depressed before, but lately had taken a turn for the better. Both say it's doubtful that she would have offed herself."

Grandma cringed. "I don't like it when you talk like that Chloe. Don't be so crass."

"I'm sorry," I said. "How about—they don't believe she'd *harm* herself?"

"That's better, thank you. But it might have been a terrible accident, just like Chief Garner thinks."

I winced at this. "Grandma, the Duvall's son showed up last night and kicked all the campers out. They think he intends to sell the place right away to make a quick buck. Doesn't exactly sound like a grieving son, huh?"

With a thoughtful look, Grandma dunked a tea bag into the cup of hot water she'd poured. "I remember something about that boy ending up in juvenile hall," she mused. "Always was a bit of a trouble-maker, I'm afraid. In fact, there was a whole rash of teenage troubles for several years in a row... pregnancies, shoplifting," Grandma shook her head and clicked her tongue. "I'm glad you didn't get caught up in any such falderal, Chloe."

I murmured an agreeable noise before circling back to the subject at hand. "Wait until you hear this. As I was leaving Jim's trailer..."

Grandma interrupted me, "Goodness!" she cried. "You went inside a strange man's camp trailer?" She sat her teacup down on the counter a little too abruptly, sloshing the hot drink onto the back of her hand. She let out a short yipe.

I hurried to the sink to grab a towel and wet cloth.

"I had to find out what he knows, Grandma. His unreturned affection may have driven him to murder." I mopped up the tea and gave her the cool cloth to soothe her hand.

Grandma Lily sighed, while closing her eyes. "I think I need something stronger than peppermint tea to handle you and your antics, Chloe. Go on, though. What did you find out?"

"At first, our visit reassured me he wasn't a suspect."

"At *first*?"

"Yeah, he seems like a sweet guy and makes a mean cup of coffee."

Grandma Lily threw her hands up. "Oh, of course he's innocent, then. A murderer couldn't *possibly* know how to use a coffeemaker."

"Percolator, actually." I smiled.

"Whatever, dear. Just explain."

"As I was leaving, I noticed he had a book about wildflowers. It reminded me of something. Look at this."

I pulled out my cell phone and opened the photo gallery. I swiped to the images of Barbara Duvall's kitchen table. "It's pretty hard to tell, but if you look closely, you'll see a small bundle of..."

"Cut-leaf Nightshade," Grandma whispered.

I looked at her in astonishment. "You recognize it?"

"Yes." She wore an intent look on her face. "My father taught us to stay away from the plant with white, star-shaped flowers and berries that resemble green tomatoes. They're pretty, but can be extremely poisonous."

I swallowed hard, thinking about how someone had gifted Barbara Duvall with a toxic bouquet. "What happens if you ingest it?"

"A little would only make someone dizzy or sleepy. Too much though, and they'll become disoriented and eventually go unconscious."

"They'd certainly be in danger of drowning if they found themselves in a swimming pool."

"Most definitely. But who would do such a terrible thing to Barbara?" Grandma Lily asked.

"Daniel Duvall has the most to gain here," I said. "Even though Jim had the wildflower book, he, Lottie, and the others won't benefit from Barbara's passing. In fact, they'll lose their homes if Daniel sells the RV park. Barbara's son is the most likely suspect to me at this point. Now, I just need to prove it."

The doorbell sounded. Grandma jumped up to smooth the front of her crisp white cotton blouse. She adjusted the red scrunchy holding her ponytail. "Sorry, dear. Tour duty calls. We'll chat more later."

I told her I'd tidy up the kitchen and began gathering our cups and saucers.

She was almost out of the room when she paused. "I just thought of something, dear. Why don't you talk to Barbara's co-workers? They might have an opinion on her mood and know if that delinquent son of hers has been coming around."

"Good idea," I said, "especially with the rumor she's being forced to retire because of her drinking problem. I'll check into it. Where did she work?"

"City Hall. The Records and Evidence Department," Grandma said off-handedly.

She dashed down the hall to the sound of the doorbell ringing once again. This sound matched the chimes going off in my head. *City Hall? Records and Evidence Department? Was Barbara Duvall the one helping Blake look into Christy's death?*

In the blink of an eye, this case just got a lot more personal.

15

Keep it a Secret

WAS IT POSSIBLE THAT Barbara's death was connected somehow to what Blake White was trying to warn me about on Friday afternoon? I grabbed Jed's leash and went to find him in the backyard. He was digging near Goldie Prawn's tombstone.

"Jed, no," I scolded him while repacking the dirt around the flat river rock. "Come on, let's go for a walk."

I clipped my mischievous yet loveable dog to his lead and opened the back gate to go into the open field behind Jericho House. It was just sage and scrub brush back here, where we'd dug for buried treasure and played hide and seek as kids. If I went far enough, I'd reach the edge of the Jericho River and that's precisely where I wanted to go. Jed and I walked through the rugged terrain until we finally made it to the riverbank. Jed traipsed through the water, chomping at it to get a drink. I picked up a handful of pebbles and tossed them, one by one, into the current—thinking.

The theories about Barbara's death I had pieced together so far now seemed paper thin. Could she actually have died because of something she found out about Christy? It seemed unlikely after all these years. *I really need to talk to Blake.* Too bad he was out of town at that conference.

Maybe there was a way for me to reach him. As his hair stylist, Bree probably had Blake's phone number. But oh, jeez. She was practically planning our wedding after the mix-up on Saturday. The last thing I needed to do was add fuel to her ridiculous fire. Who else would have Blake's information? Chief Garner, I guessed. The chief of police would have the mayor on speed dial, right? But let's face it, I would only make my precarious situation with Garner worse by asking him for my ex's phone number.

As I plunked pebbles into the water watching rippling circles form, overlap, and then dissipate, I contemplated my next move. For now, I would put the investigation at the RV park on hold. I needed to look into this new angle. Just to put my mind at rest, if nothing else.

Jed brought me a stick. I threw it into the water for him a few times, admiring his fluid, athletic swimming skills. Then I clipped him back on his leash and began the walk home. That's when I remembered the carving I found in the grove of trees last year. I'd only come out here to cool down after a particularly irritating conversation with Chief Garner, but I ended up discovering an interesting artifact.

I went into the trees, the grass swishing around my legs. I looked for the carved initials once again. It took me a few minutes, but eventually I located them. There, on a cottonwood just a bit higher than my head, a heart had been crudely etched in the tree. Inside the shape was the message, *B+C4ever.*

After I originally found it, I ended up asking Blake whether he had been the one to carve it. After all, they were our initials, and we were two teenagers who thought they would be in love forever. But he denied it. If it wasn't him, who else had been in love and wanted to record it on this tree?

I pulled out my phone and snapped a quick pic. I'd show it to Blake later. He may have forgotten carving it and a photo would remind him. I turned to go, but noticed Jed was busy digging again. His river-wet paws were now covered in mud. "Good grief," I sighed. "Please don't tell me you're attempting another grave robbery." It was meant as a joke. But when I looked into the hole, I saw that Jed had uncovered bones.

I screamed before I realized I was going to. It was nothing more than the skeleton of some little woodland creature. The miniature ribcage and skull with tiny teeth proved it. Still, with everything that had happened recently, it made me shiver.

"Come on, boy," I said, encouraging Jed to leave the remains alone. "Let's get out of here."

THE BACK GATE WAS ONCE again unlatched when I returned to Jericho House. Whoever Grandma had hired, he wasn't very skilled. I hoped she hadn't paid him yet, because he obviously hadn't completed the job. I went inside to tell her, but she wasn't there. Surprisingly, her home tour must have already finished. Usually, large groups wanted to linger and ask questions forever. But the house was quiet. I found a note on the kitchen island which read,

Gone to see Stan Duncan at the Opera House, Grandma added a little smiley face.

I rolled my eyes. Let the matchmaking begin. I took up the pen lying there and added my own line at the bottom,

I've gone to see Bree. To clear up the misunderstanding about Blake.

I fed Jed and Elliot, gave them each a squeeze, locked up, and left through the back porch. I parked on Main Street in front of Bree's Beauty Salon. Through the large plate-glass window, I saw her sweeping. She waved, smiling brightly when she noticed me.

"I'm so glad you came in," she said. "I know you've probably been worried sick about why your lover-boy isn't calling. But never fear, he only lost his phone."

Lover-boy?

Bree reached into the front pocket of her hot pink stylist's apron and pulled out a black cell phone. "It must have fallen out of Blake's pocket when I cut his hair. Then, with that whirlwind of a day on Saturday, it got squished into the gap between the back and the seat of the chair. Cranky Miss Violet found it this afternoon when it poked her in the tush."

Bree handed me the phone as if it belonged to me.

"I don't want it," I told her.

"Well, you're the best person to keep it safe for Blake until he gets back on Wednesday."

Blake was going to be out of town until Wednesday?

"No, Bree. I'm not. There's nothing going on between Blake and me."

Bree smiled coyly and batted her eyelashes. "I told you, silly. You don't have to hide the truth from me anymore."

I slipped the cell phone back into Bree's apron pocket and took her by the shoulders. "Listen to me. It was all a misunderstanding. What had me flustered was nothing to do with Blake." I took a deep breath before saying, "On Friday, I found out that Garner used to be married."

Bree sat down hard in a salon chair. "Oh."

I eased into the one beside her. "More like, oh, no."

She gave me an understanding look. "I wanted to tell you before, but he forbade us to talk about her. Ever."

"Ever?"

Bree nodded, her eyebrows were knit tightly together. "After Rachel died, if anyone around town so much as mentioned her name or asked the chief how he was doing, he would blow up and tell them to 'never talk about her again'. So, we didn't."

I remembered feeling that way after Christy died, too. It was easiest to avoid the topic altogether. "So, maybe Garner wasn't specifically keeping this a secret from me?"

Bree frowned, "Gosh, no. This might sound weird, but it's almost like he wanted to keep it a secret... from himself."

"Like he wanted to pretend it never happened," I said.

"Yeah."

A silence hung between us as I took this information in and mentally replayed the conversation I had with Garner in my apartment. "Well then, I really blew it," I told Bree.

"What do you mean?"

I told her all about our talk and how Chief Garner had stormed out, accusing me of being self-absorbed. "He said I don't have a monopoly on pain."

Bree made an "ouch" face and bit her bottom lip.

She reached out and placed her hand on mine. "Don't worry, Chloe. It'll all work out, I just know it. In the meantime, what should we do with this thing?" Bree reached back into her apron pocket and withdrew Blake's phone.

I felt the prickles of goosebumps on my arms when I realized it might hold the answer to my question of whether Barbara Duvall was the person Blake was working with at city hall.

"Can I check something?" I asked Bree. She handed the phone to me. But when I pressed the front button, nothing happened. Either the phone was powered down or its battery was dead.

I said a little prayer and pressed the power button. A melody played, giving me hope the phone was about to come on. I looked at Bree with anticipation. She widened her big blue eyes. The phone's screen lit up. For a split second, a notification was visible.

INCOMING MESSAGE FROM B. DUVALL

The phone beeped and went dead. My heart was pounding—my thoughts raced. Blake lost his phone on Friday afternoon. Barbara died on Friday night. Her message to him may have quite literally been her last words. I shoved the phone back towards Bree. "Put this in your cash register drawer and keep it locked up, okay?"

"All right," she said with a pout, "but what's going on?"

"I'll explain later," I called, running for the door.

16

A Million Pieces

I HOOFED IT TO CITY Hall and took the cement steps two at a time to enter the grand, historic building. I found myself in the large foyer where a pretty thirty-something woman sat behind a dark mahogany desk. Long hallways ran down each side of her where various city departments maintained their offices.

"Does Mayor White have a secretary?" I asked the woman, discovering I was out of breath when I spoke. Her name plate read, Missy Bray. I realized that this was the woman I'd seen in the employee parking lot the day before.

She smiled and said, "Yes, that's me."

"Thank goodness." I leaned against the massive desk and took a deep breath in preparation to speak. "I need to get in touch with him right away."

Ultra-professional Missy gave me a concerned look. "I'm sorry, but he called yesterday to report that unfortunately he's lost his cell phone. He's directed me to take all messages for him. He'll be returning calls on Wednesday." She took up a small pad of lined paper and poised a pen, ready to take my message.

"That won't work," I told her. "This can't wait. I need to talk to him today. Can I call the hotel where he's staying?"

The secretary put her pen down sharply and crossed her arms. "I'm not at liberty to share private information about the mayor with you, ma'am."

"Come on, it's an emergency."

Her eyes widened. "Well, why didn't you say so?" She hopped up and started down the hall to her right, her kitten heels clicking on the shiny vintage tiled floor. "I'll get a police officer right away," she called over her shoulder.

Gulp. Police officer? There was no way I was going to stick around for whoever was about to come to my aid. Odds were it would be Chief Garner or Ellie Porter, neither of which I wanted to see today.

Hurriedly, I scanned the desktop where Blake's secretary had been sitting. Her workspace was excruciatingly tidy. But there, slid half-way underneath her computer keyboard, was a glossy brochure. I carefully slid it out to get a look. It was for The Radisson of Albuquerque. Missy had written "Reservation complete for Room 709" in pretty cursive across the top.

With the sound of footsteps approaching, I returned the brochure to its original spot and ran for the door. I was half-way down the steps of city hall when I heard my name.

"Chloe Martin? Is that you?"

I turned back. It wasn't Chief Garner or Officer Porter, thank goodness. It was the rookie, Billy Meyers. Billy was the newest member of the force. He'd been at Jericho House last summer when it was the scene of a crime. I still remembered how sweet and caring he'd been with Grandma Lily.

Officer Meyers motioned with his thumb over his shoulder. "Missy said you have an emergency?"

I rolled my eyes and did my best impression of Bree's eyelash fluttering. "Oh, it's silly. I just had a quick question for Blake, nothing *urgent*. Sorry if his secretary got the wrong impression."

The young officer looked confused. He tried to speak, but I interrupted him.

"Anyway, sorry I bothered you. Have a good afternoon." I jogged down the last few steps and back to the salon.

When I got there, I went straight in and grabbed a marker from the jar beside Bree's cash register. I wrote RAD ALB 709 on my arm so I wouldn't forget. Now I just needed to look up the number and call the hotel.

"I found him!" I said to Bree, suddenly regretting not taking a moment to find a piece of paper to write on. Now I had vibrant, 2-inch-high purple permanent marker scrawled on me. *Ugh.* The regret I felt about the marker, though, paled in comparison to the remorse I was about to experience. Because when I looked up, I learned Bree was no longer alone in the salon. Standing right beside her was Chief Garner.

"Uh, hi," I said.

Garner frowned, "You found who? And what's that?" He pointed at the scribbles on my arm, which closely resembled a preschooler's art project.

"Um. Jed. I found Jed, he ran off again. And this? Oh, it's just something I need to remember."

The chief raised his eyebrows and seemed genuinely concerned about my sanity. Bree tried to giggle, but even she was feeling the heavy awkwardness of the moment.

Finally, Chief Garner cleared his throat and said, "I saw your truck out front. I need to talk to you."

"Here?" I squeaked.

"Outside."

He led the way, which gave me a quick minute to make urgent eye contact with Bree, meant to say, *"What the heck?"* and *"Oh my gosh, I have so much to tell you!"* all at the same time.

She met my gaze with a worried expression and crossed her fingers at me for good luck.

Garner stood outside on the boardwalk. He kept a wide stance, his arms folded across his broad chest. Today, he wasn't in full uniform. Instead, he wore a nice pair of jeans, a blazer, and a dress shirt. His badge was on his belt. "Can we take a walk together?" he asked.

"Sure," I shrugged. "Is this about Barbara Duvall?"

He looked down at me puzzled. "No, why would I want to talk about her?"

"No reason." *Gulp.*

We proceeded to the crosswalk to enter Riverside Park. We didn't speak a word as we went through the grass to reach the greenbelt that ran alongside the Jericho River—a wide asphalt path intended for morning joggers, biking families, and the occasional rollerblader. Garner's pace slowed while my heartbeat picked up. I felt so nervous I worried a butterfly might fly out if I opened my mouth.

"I owe you an apology," Garner said.

I looked at him, surprised. "What?"

He put his hand up in concession. "I do. I should have told you about Rachel a long time ago. The truth is, I never talk about her. Not with anyone. So, if you got the idea that I was trying to keep something from you..." his voice trailed off and his gaze moved from my face to the rushing Jericho River.

He went on, "Rachel and I had been married a year when I got a patrolman position in Jericho Falls. It was a dream come true for both of us since we both grew up in small towns. Before long, the chief started talking about retiring and I was pegged for the position. I couldn't believe my good luck. The girl and the job of my dreams were mine. Rachel was a veterinarian. She was going to open her own practice here in Jericho Falls, but was still commuting to Lakeview every day until we saved enough money."

Garner paused, preparing himself to go on. "Our second winter here was severe. Several times she had to stay over because the roads were too icy to drive home through the pass. On the night of our anniversary, there was another snowstorm, but Rachel drove home anyway to surprise me. After work, she and our golden retriever, Jiffy, headed home. A few miles out of town, a semi-truck lost control on the ice and hit them. She died instantly."

"I'm so sorry," I whispered.

Garner looked at me and cleared his throat before continuing. "When I heard the call on my radio and recognized the description of our car, I couldn't go. I stayed behind. In fact, I couldn't leave my house for several days. The guys came by and told me and I just lost it, you know?"

I reached out and touched his arm. Tears filled his eyes.

"I don't even remember her funeral, Chloe. I was in such a fog."

I nodded, but couldn't find any words to comfort him.

Garner pinched the bridge of his nose to gain composure. "That day, though, when I got home from her service and went up the side-walk—those stupid garden gnomes were standing there, looking so happy together. They were smiling, but I was completely ruined. I grabbed the female statue and threw it into the street. She shattered into a million pieces."

"She broke," I said quietly, recalling the words Garner used last Christmas. Now I wondered if he had been referring to the ceramic gnome or Rachel herself.

Garner looked away again.

A few quiet moments passed. We walked, watching the water and listening to the birds sing.

"What happened to your dog, Jiffy? Did she make it?" I asked.

Garner shook his head. "Just long enough to give birth to her puppies. Only two survived."

He stopped, turning to face me with a smile; the knowing smile I was getting used to seeing on his handsome face.

I frowned, "You don't mean... Jed and Mandy?"

Garner nodded.

"You told me they were from the shelter."

"It's true, they were. I wasn't in any shape to keep them, since they needed lots of special care without their mother. But after a few weeks, I went to see them. I wanted one of Jiffy's puppies—*needed* one, I think. And, thankfully, your Grandma Lily adopted the other one. With just a little coaxing."

"And now, he's mine." I said.

Garner reached out and took my hand. "Yes, he's yours."

Suddenly, Garner's pocket buzzed. He frowned, making his 'cop face', and answered. "This is the chief," he said.

As the caller spoke, though, Garner's expression changed. His eyes searched my face. He dropped my hand. "I don't need to *go find* Chloe. She's right here. With me."

His eyes narrowed as he listened again to the caller speak. All at once, he pushed the phone out to me. "It's Blake White. For you."

17

Not Without Invitation

TENTATIVELY, I TOOK the phone from Garner's hand. "Hello?" I answered.

"My secretary said you're looking for me because of an emergency. Is everything all right, Chloe?"

"I'm not sure," I said. How I wished I wasn't having this conversation in front of Garner, let alone on his phone (which smelled just like his woodsy cologne, by the way).

"What do you mean, you're not sure?" Blake asked.

Garner glared at me in concentration, as if he were trying to decipher what this phone call from my ex was all about. Once again, he had his arms folded across his chest.

"We need to talk," I said to Blake.

"Go on."

I turned my back on Garner. "Can I call you back? Later?" I whispered.

"I'm staying at the Radisson in Albuquerque," Blake said, "room 709."

"I'll call you in about an hour," I told him. My face felt hot as I looked at the scribbles on my arm, reiterating his words.

I pushed the button to end the call and simultaneously turned around to hand the phone back to Garner. He held my gaze as he forcefully shoved it into this shirt pocket. Then he turned on his heel and walked away.

"Garner, please. Wait," I called.

"Just forget it, Chloe," he said, still moving in long, determined strides.

"It's not what you think."

He came to a stop, but didn't bother to turn around. "That's what you always say about Blake White."

The chief took off again. I didn't even try to keep up.

HOW HAD I LET ANOTHER important moment with Garner turn out so badly? His words had been so touching, so honest. And then our sweet moment of connection was obliterated in an instant by none other than Blake White.

Of course, I couldn't let on to the chief, but the business I had with Blake was vitally important. His questions about our old case might have led to Barbara Duvall's death—information Blake held might track a killer. Whether I wanted to or not, I needed to have a conversation with him.

I took my time going back to my truck. My moping mood had returned. *Why couldn't I get things right when it came to Lance Garner? And why was ever-annoying Blake always complicating things between us?*

Though parked right outside, I didn't go inside the salon. I couldn't possibly relay to Bree the rollercoaster ride of emotions I had just been on. Plus, I needed to get home and talk with Grandma Lily. It was time for me to come clean with her about how Jeannie had stolen Christy's diary last summer and how issues from the past might be responsible for Barbara's death. I wanted her guidance and wisdom before I returned that call to Blake.

With a familiar ache in my chest, I slipped behind the driver's seat of my little pickup and did a quick mirror check before flipping a u-turn to head home. As I drove up Gold Mountain, passing the many large homes flanking the street, I spotted Grandma Lily up ahead. She stood in front of Claire Harland's beautiful two-story house with Jed on his leash at her side. This was 'Harland's Haven Bed and Breakfast'. Claire held a broom and wore a straw hat to shield her face from the afternoon sun. Both women waved as I approached. I pulled up against the curb and pressed the button to roll down the passenger window. "Hello, ladies, and gentleman," I said. That's when I noticed that Grandma seemed flushed. Claire was patting her back sympathetically. "What's wrong?" I asked.

"Claire just told me she saw a man in our yard earlier today. When she called out to him, he took off through the back gate."

I gasped. Maybe there wasn't anything wrong with our gate after all—except a trespasser coming in and out without us knowing. Suddenly, the broken flower pot at my apartment door came to me. Neighborhood cats probably weren't to blame for that, either.

"I think we'd better call Chief Garner," Grandma said. "I don't like the idea of someone snooping around."

I felt a wrenching in my gut. I was pretty sure the chief didn't want to be anywhere near me right now. But, Grandma was right. Something was amiss at Jericho House, and we needed to report it. "Hop in," I told her. "Let's go home and call."

Claire gave my grandma one last hug while I dropped the tailgate for Jed. Claire blew me a kiss goodbye and went back to sweeping the walk.

"I'm in a dither over this," Grandma said with a sigh. "I mean, Jericho House is open to the public, but not without invitation."

"You're right to be concerned. I'm sure this explains the gate being left open lately and my broken flower pot a few nights ago."

"Looks like we have a peeping tom." Grandma rolled her eyes. "Who could imagine?" She looked my way, frowning. "What's that on your arm, dear?"

I brushed off her question while parking in the wide circle drive in front of our mansion. "I'll explain later."

Grandma Lily seemed reluctant to go inside, so I told her I'd go first—to check it out.

"Take Jed with you," she said before handing me her ridiculously large key chain holding the house keys. I went up the steps and crossed the deep covered porch. When I turned the key and opened the door, the familiar spicy floral scent of the house filled my nose. I called a "hello," not expecting an answer, but still felt relief when there was no reply...no noise at all. Jed and I looked through all the rooms on the first and second floors. Nothing seemed out of place. I went back to the porch and motioned for Grandma to join me inside. "The coast is clear," I said.

Grandma Lily reached for the receiver of the home's landline as soon as she arrived in the foyer. I watched her place the phone up to her ear and listened as she asked to speak with Chief Lance Garner. This was my cue. Maybe I was being a big chicken, but I didn't want to hang around to see him. I called Jed, we left through the back porch for the safety of my studio apartment. Grandma could deal with reporting the trespasser to the chief without my input. I would simply disappear and stay completely invisible.

Unfortunately, as I rounded the corner to reach the back of the garage, things weren't as I'd left them. Papers, which turned out to be a few of my bills and an old grocery list, were fluttering around in the breeze. The doorknob of my pretty little sanctuary had been broken off. Through the open doorway, I could see that the apartment was a wreck. Jed barked. The hair between his shoulder blades stood as he peered into the open doorway. *Was the intruder still inside?* I grabbed his collar and pulled him with me back to Jericho House.

It stunned Grandma when I told her what I'd found. She sank onto a barstool at the kitchen island, putting a hand to her forehead. "Thank goodness the police are already on their way."

I went to her for a hug. "It's going to be okay, Grandma. I promise."

Just then, the hand-turn doorbell rang. I hurried down the long hall to answer. It wasn't Garner. Apparently, I was right about him not wanting to see me. Because in his stead, he sent Officer Ellie Porter to check on us.

18

Reliving the Agony

"GOOD AFTERNOON, CHLOE," Ellie Porter said without sounding like she meant it.

"Hi. Thanks for coming. Unfortunately, it's worse than we originally thought."

Grandma Lily and I relayed to the spunky female officer how we had been experiencing strange happenings for a few days, but thought little of them. Claire's sighting of the man in our backyard put us on alert. I explained that after we called the police, I found my ransacked apartment. Officer Porter asked us to wait inside the house while she went around back to check the apartment. Eventually, she showed up again on the front porch. She had her clipboard out and made notes with a concerned look on her face. "I'll have you come with me now, Chloe. To tell me if you notice anything missing."

I agreed, and we went to the apartment together.

With everything strewn around the room in such a mess, it was hard to tell if anything was gone. Thankfully, I kept very little in the apartment, so I began an inventory of items.

"It looks like he was searching for something specific," Officer Porter said. "Make sure you aren't missing any cash or jewelry. You know, valuable things."

A trickle of worry ran down my spine. Suddenly, I suspected it wasn't money or precious gems the intruder was after. I dashed to my bookcase where the vintage coffee can filled with my mementos should be. It was gone. My breathing was shallow now as I frantically scanned the room for the items that had been in it. I hoped the dummy had just dumped them out somewhere. Sadly, I didn't see Christy's key chain or the Christmas note from Garner anywhere.

"What is it?" Officer Porter asked, noticing my concern.

Should I tell her? In her lingering anger at me over her sister's death, I couldn't let her in on any of this—not yet. "I... had a few hundred dollars in a coffee can," I fibbed.

She shook her head and made a tsk-tsk noise. "That's what the bank is for, Chloe. It'll be impossible for us to get that back, you know."

I fought the urge to roll my eyes at her condescending tone and shrugged. "It's just money, right?"

Officer Porter went around the room, looking at the mess left by the burglar and snapping photos. "I'll send over the team to do fingerprinting, but I don't have much hope. If Claire Harland can give us a solid description of the guy she saw, it may help."

I nodded in understanding. And impatience. I couldn't wait for her to just *leave* so I could check the hiding spot where I had stashed Christy's diary and the rest of her things. *If they are gone too, what will I do?* Not only could they possibly hold the key to solving a murder, they were the last pieces of connection I had with Christy. I felt tears fill my eyes as I willed Ellie Porter to get a move on.

"Okay," she said with finality, "I'll go back to the house now and get a statement from your grandma, then go next door to Claire's. I would advise you against spending time out here until you get a new door knob. And how about a deadbolt this time, Chloe?"

Another jab.

"Is there anything else you need?" she asked me.

"No. But is it okay for me to clean up?"

Officer Porter said it was, but to contact her if I found anything that might indicate who had done this. She gave me a firm nod goodbye and left.

I waited a moment or two to make sure she was really gone. The last thing I needed was Ellie Porter coming back with a Columbo-esque last question and finding me holding her dead sister's diary. I wasn't even sure if she knew I had it. Gossip around town was that Ellie and her mom were on the outs. So, if her mom sent those things to me without Ellie knowing... or wait. *What if Ellie found out I had Christy's diary and she was the person trying to get it back?* Oh jeez, now that was just plain crazy. My racing mind wasn't making any sense.

Anyway, when I was sure she'd gone, I went into the tiny bathroom, stood on the toilet and turned to face the oak highboy dresser Grandma had put there for bathroom storage. On the top was a tall carved decorative piece, perfect for hiding something behind. I stood on my tiptoes and felt around. A flood of relief hit me so hard I almost fell into the bathtub. The shoe box of my friend's belongings was there, safe and sound. I pulled it down, hugging the box to my chest.

One thing was certain. The lightbulb moment I experienced last summer, that Christy's diary might be important, now felt like a floodlight. Whatever happened, I needed to keep these things safe and do my best to decipher what information they held. But who could I trust? Jeannie, Blake, and Ellie each made me suspicious in their own way. Jeannie because she tried taking the diary from me; Blake because he'd originally lied and said I played a part in Christy's death; and Ellie, Christy's younger sister, who still wasn't completely convinced of my innocence. I needed to talk this out with the person I *knew* I could trust. Grandma Lily.

I spent a few minutes picking up my apartment. I arranged the kitchen chairs, picked up the garbage can, including its contents (yuck), and swept up the pieces of a broken coffee mug. In all this, I didn't find the keepsake items from the coffee can. Instead, I found a lump in my throat when I realized I had probably lost Christy's "C" key chain for good.

"I'm so sorry, Christy," I whispered.

When I'd straightened things enough so it no longer looked like a bombing zone, I took up the shoe box, pulled the broken door as tightly shut as possible, and started for the house. As I turned the corner, I remembered the packs of petunias and pansies I never got around to planting. I went back in for a glass of water and gave them a big drink. When this was all over, I'd get things spruced up again around here.

Once inside Jericho House, I placed the shoe box on the kitchen island. When I knew Ellie was gone and I wouldn't get caught, I'd take Christy's things back to the third floor. There, in the safety of the defunct dumbwaiter, no burglar would ever find them.

Grandma Lily's voice filtered into the kitchen. I assumed she was still with Officer Porter, or maybe on the phone, rehashing the day's excitement with Claire Harland. I went toward the sound of her speaking. There, sipping tea with Grandma in the parlour, was Chief Garner. He looked up at me and gave a half-hearted smile.

"Lance came over as soon as he heard we had an actual break-in," Grandma explained.

"Thanks," I told him, forcing my lips into a tight grin.

Chief Garner sat his cup down on the side table. "Lily, I'd like you to show me around now. To make sure Officer Porter didn't miss anything important."

The police chief and my grandma stood, going out of the room chatting about where to begin. His shoulder brushed mine, but he didn't say a word to me. My heart clenched. Elliot, with his feline tendency to enjoy human suffering, let out a long and mournful meow. His yellow eyes narrowed.

I told the cat, "I know. I can't seem to do anything right with him lately, but you don't have to rub it in." I sank into the chair where Garner had been sitting. The spot was still warm, and I caught a whiff of his cologne, causing me to feel equally wonderful and awful at the same time.

Elliot meowed again while jumping up onto my lap. I stroked the back of his head and listened to him purr. "At least I know how to make you and Jed happy. Cuddles and kibble, right?" Elliot's eyes closed in pleasure.

I took out my phone to check the time. Over an hour had passed since my brief conversation with Blake. He would have expected a return call from me by now. But not only did I cower at the idea of having Chief Garner catch me talking with Blake again, I wasn't sure how to approach things.

I supposed I needed to tell Blake that Barbara Duvall had left him a message before she died. And I needed to know whether she was the person looking through the old case files for him. *But should I trust him, or was he in cahoots with Jeannie?* If I could ever get the chance to talk with Grandma Lily, I'd decide. If she thought it was safe, I'd discuss things with Blake.

To pass the time until Chief Garner left, I scooped up Elliot and took him to the front porch. I was straightening the cushions on the wicker chairs when I heard my name. Bree came up the walk with her dog, Marilyn, on a bright purple leash.

"Oh. My. Gosh. I heard about the break-in. You must be terrified," Bree squealed.

I was still getting reacquainted with the speed at which town gossip whizzed through Jericho Falls.

I shrugged, "It's strange, that's for sure."

"Do they know who it was?"

"Not yet. Chief Garner is with my grandma, looking around."

She was in front of me now. She threw her dainty arms around my neck and squeezed. "If you both want to stay at my apartment for a few days, I don't mind." Bree had an upstairs apartment above her salon on Main Street.

I chuckled. "I think we'll be fine," I said. "But maybe Grandma Lily will finally get that alarm system I've been trying to talk her into."

Bree frowned and nodded. In a flash, her expression switched to intrigue. "So what in the world happened earlier today? Where'd you go? And what about Garner? I mean, tell me. Like pronto."

I rolled my eyes as a wave of heartache passed through me. "Well, I blew it again. We were finally talking things over when darned *Blake* called Garner. He immediately asked to speak with me, completely giving Garner the wrong idea."

"How'd Blake call? I have his phone." Bree withdrew the now familiar 'lost' phone from her little yellow fanny pack.

I explained to her my escapade with Missy, Blake's secretary, and the follow-up call he made to me via the chief. I left out the personal details Garner shared with me and the new angle about Barbara's death I was considering. Still, I felt my face flush, reliving the agony of it all.

Bree squeezed her eyes shut, then clutched her chest. "Oh, no," she cried, "exactly what you *didn't* need."

"I know."

She patted my arm in sympathy, then handed Blake's phone to me while she dug around inside her fanny pack. "I found an old charging cord that fits it."

"What are you talking about?"

"So you can charge Blake's phone and get that message from Barbara Duvall."

I swallowed hard. "That wouldn't be right. Not without Blake's permission," I said, shaking my head.

Bree pushed the charger at me. "Suit yourself. Marilyn and I need to scoot. But hey, if you change your mind and want to crash at my place later, just let me know." She gave me a parade-worthy wave and lilted away.

Before I made it to the porch, I heard footsteps crunching towards me on the gravel. Grandma and Chief Garner were approaching. I ran up the porch steps and into Jericho House before either of them could spot me.

19

Hasty and Rude

AT THE KITCHEN'S DEEP farmhouse sink I ran warm water and lathered a handful of lemon scented soap. I squirted a little extra onto the vegetable brush and went to work on the unsightly marker I'd scribbled on my arm. The rhythmic movements, rushing water, and lovely scent were rather hypnotic. I felt myself slipping into reminiscence.

My life had truly never been the same since the day Christy died. And not just because I'd been considered responsible for her death for a time. Since she died, I had never stopped feeling guilty for having a life to live. That's why I didn't go to my senior prom or pursue the history degree I had always dreamed of. It's why I put a damper on everything. How did I deserve to have milestone life experiences if Christy didn't?

Even worse, it was nearly impossible for me to form lasting or meaningful relationships. I knew that just like my best friend, anyone I loved could be taken away from me. I wasn't sure I could survive losing someone close to me like that ever again. So, I simply didn't get close.

Is this what I was doing with Chief Garner? Keeping him at arm's length so we would never get close and I'd never risk losing him? I shook my head. That seemed like psycho-babble. *Time to lay off the self-help books, Chloe.*

I was churning this over in my mind as I dried my hands and arm. Then, still in a bit of a trance, I went to the back porch and unloaded the clothes dryer. I folded the warm items of clothing—some Grandma's, some mine. With this batch finished, I'd go out and strip my bed and gather all the towels from my little apartment. I wanted to disinfect everything in that place. It gave me the heebie-jeebies knowing that a stranger had been inside. I wondered what all he had touched. It made my skin crawl.

I heard Grandma enter the kitchen and go to the sink. Probably washing up the cups from her spot of tea with the chief. When I went in, carrying the laundry basket in my arms, Grandma had taken the lid off the shoe box. She lifted out the diary.

"Why are these things out?" she asked.

I put down the laundry basket. "I think it's what the burglar was after."

Grandma Lily looked at me, confused. "Why do you say that?"

I sighed. "It started last summer."

At last, I told Grandma how Jeannie Smythe had come to Jericho House under the ruse of bringing us baked goods for our daily home tours, when what she really wanted was an excuse to look through the house. "I was at her restaurant a couple of days later and found Christy's diary sitting beside the cash register."

"She stole it from your bedroom?"

I nodded. "Then *I* stole it back and hid everything in the old dumbwaiter."

Grandma pointed at me. "Good thinking. But what could be special enough about a teenager's diary to steal it?"

I took the book from her hands and flipped through the pages. "That's the problem, I don't know. I've read through it twice and for the life of me, I can't find anything compelling. But Blake dropped by last week asking me about the diary. He said he was interested because he found something troubling in his new office—about Christy's accident. Grandma, Blake planned to ask the city records clerk to pull the old case files for him."

Grandma Lily's eyes grew wide and her hand went to her throat. "Barbara Duvall is... I mean, she *was* the city records clerk."

I nodded slowly, watching realization seep over her.

"Oh, dear," she whispered.

I told her that Blake would be out of town until Wednesday and he didn't have his cell phone, but I'd found a roundabout way to get in touch with him. (I left out the part about making Garner mad at me again in that process.)

"My question is, should I tell Blake all of this, Grandma? I've come a long way in forgiving him for betraying me. But I'm still not sure I completely trust him."

Grandma Lily narrowed her eyes and patted an index finger against her bottom lip. "The way I see it, Blake wouldn't go stirring up questions at city hall if he was up to no good. And, better for him to keep quiet and go about his own business if he was trying to get the diary from you."

She made good points. Blake was too smart to call attention to himself at work or with me if he had ill intentions. "Hey, did Claire get a good look at the guy in our backyard?" I asked her.

"Only that he was a slight man, wearing a gray sweatshirt and jeans. He had a red baseball hat pulled down tight, so she wasn't able to see his face or hair color."

I rubbed circles into my temples. "That doesn't give me much to go on."

"Hmm," Grandma raised her eyebrows and gave me a suspicious grin. "Do you think Jeannie would send her cowboy husband over here to do her dirty work?"

Eric Smyth was a slim guy and crazy enough about his wife, Jeannie, to do something nefarious at her bidding. If nothing else, Jeannie's past bad behavior earned them a visit from me about this possibility.

"Grandma, do me a favor. If Blake calls Jericho House, stall him. Play dumb like you don't know anything about this. And, whatever you do, don't tell him about the break-in yet. I'm going to have a talk with our friends at The Vintage Grill." I swiped up the diary to take with me and slipped on my jacket.

Grandma hollered a 'be careful' at me as I went to the front door. I hurried down the mansion's steps and jumped in my pickup to head into town. On my way, I thought about all the things I'd wanted to say to Jeannie Smythe these past months. I wondered if she knew, that I knew, she stole Christy's diary.

I pulled into the small parking lot next to The Vintage Grill, a barbeque restaurant owned and operated by ebony beauty, Jeannie, and her blond, hunky cowboy husband, Eric. Cars filled the small parking lot. The place was hopping.

Inside, there was standing room only. A woman with an alluring, smokey voice sang a country number, accompanying herself on an acoustic guitar. Apparently, this live entertainment had drawn in the crowd. I scanned the space, which was originally a blacksmith's shop, to see if I could spot Jeannie. She wasn't at the register or waitressing. I wound my way to the front through the pine tables decorated with red and white checked tablecloths. A teenaged boy at the register swayed to the beat.

"Hi," I said, straining to be heard over the music. "Is Jeannie here?"

He smiled. "No, but she'll be right back. She's delivering a call-in order."

I pointed to a table against the wall, indicating that I would wait for her return. He gave me a thumbs-up. Nerves threatened to take over now that I was here. What would Jeannie do or say when she saw me? I drew in a long breath and blew it out slowly. I tried to simply focus on the music and relax until she returned.

I pulled the diary out of my jacket pocket and laid it on the table. With my fingertip, I flicked at the ripped cardboard strip that once kept it locked. It was torn open like this when I took the diary back from Jeannie—a hasty and rude action for her to take, in my opinion. Everyone knows that cheesy diary locks are worthless except to stall nosy younger siblings or inquisitive parents. All Jeannie had to do was poke a bobby pin inside the clasp and turn it. The lock would have popped right open. Instead, she vandalized it.

Absent-mindedly, I flipped through the book. I turned it over, cussed at it for being both useless and somehow valuable at the same time. I flopped it onto the table and pushed it away from me. That's when I noticed it. From this angle, looking at the diary from its end, I could tell there was a void about three quarters of the way through. Pages were missing! No wonder I didn't find anything of interest when I read the diary—the important part had been removed.

Now, more than ever, Jeannie had some serious explaining to do.

20

A Vague Memory

A GUST OF COOL EVENING air let me know the restaurant door opened. I turned quickly to see who it was. Jeannie was back. In a flash, I swiped the diary off the table and put it back in my pocket. Jeannie exchanged smiles with the crowd of customers, but her face changed when she noticed me. She went to the front and opened the cash register, where she deposited the money from her recent delivery. She seemed to be ignoring me.

Once again, I finagled my way through the crowd to reach the front counter.

"Hi," I said, "do you have a minute to chat?"

"About what?"

I cleared my throat. "Christy."

Jeannie's dark eyes darted up at me, then back down to the money she was counting and bundling. She formed a tight, fake smile and said, "This isn't a good time, we're busy."

Just then, Eric popped his head out of the kitchen door. "Oh hi darlin', you're back," he said to Jeannie with a smile. "Howdy, Chloe."

I wiggled my fingers in a wave at him. He winked before returning to the kitchen.

"I can wait... or come back at closing time," I suggested.

She stared at me, her eyes displaying resignation. "No. I'll come to you. I don't want to involve Eric in any of this."

I nodded, "Okay, I'll be at Jericho House."

I turned to go, with the sound of the raspy-voiced singers' rendition of Folsom Prison Blues filling the restaurant. She was good, and if the circumstances were different, I might grab a seat and listen for a while. But it wasn't wise for me to lurk. Because I knew I had just thrown a curve into Jeannie Smythe's world, and I wondered exactly what she was thinking right now. Not wanting her husband privy to our conversation said a lot to me.

I went outside the building, along the exterior wall, to stand by the window where I could see Jeannie behind the register. I watched. She cashed out a customer with her usual kind demeanor. Once free, she withdrew her handbag out from under the counter and rummaged through it. She looked frantic when she couldn't find whatever it was she was searching for. She placed both hands to her ribcage before reaching into her pocket for her cellphone. Jeannie dialed, waited for an answer, then placed a hand in front of her mouth before speaking. Her eyes looked worried. She listened for a moment, blinking. She made one more brief remark and ended the call. Jeannie rubbed the back of her neck. Then, with resolve, she pulled her shoulders back and turned on a smile for her customers. I was dying to know who Jeannie called. I would do my darndest later to find out.

On my way back to my truck, I decided that although this hadn't gone as planned, it actually worked out perfectly. Now, I would get to talk with Jeannie on my own turf. Also, a stroke of luck, was noticing the missing pages before showing the diary to her. She'd already cut the binding of the lock to get inside. Was Jeannie also brazen enough to rip out the pages?

BLAKE DIDN'T CALL WHILE I was out. This was a relief to me since I wasn't sure Grandma Lily could have stopped herself from spilling the tea and telling him everything. I sat at the kitchen island, did an online search for the number to the Radisson in Albuquerque, and dialed. As I waited for an answer, I took the diary and laid it in front of me, just as I had at the Vintage Grill. I needed to assure myself I hadn't imagined things. It was true, though. A thin but definite void existed in the book's binding, proving that there were missing pages.

"The Radisson, may I help you?" a deep, male voice said.

"Room 709, please."

"Just one moment."

The extension rang about seventeen times. Darn it, I'd probably waited too long and Blake was at some stuffy evening reception schmoozing with the other small-town mayors. I wondered if they all thought as highly of themselves as he did. I strummed my fingers on the granite countertop while Elliot wound through the legs of a bar stool, meowing.

"What is it, buddy?" I asked him. He looked up at me and gave another mournful cry.

"Don't try convincing me that Grandma didn't feed you dinner. I know better."

"I most certainly did," Grandma said as she came into the room. "It's those new treats I bought him. He's been begging for them all day." She scooped up the cat and pet him while cooing baby talk in his ear about getting him a treat. He gave me a side-eye glance as if to say, "And that's the way it's done."

Once the kitty treat package crinkled, Jed came running. Grandma Lily made him woof "please" before she tossed him a Tuna Num-Num too. "All right," Grandma said, "what did Jeannie have to say for herself?"

I explained that Jeannie would come to Jericho House after closing to talk because she didn't want her cowboy hubs involved.
Grandma raised her eyebrows. "Interesting. And a clue that he's not
our burglar."

"True. But get this. After I left, I watched Jeannie through the
window. She called someone right away. She looked pretty upset."

Grandma squinted. "Who do you think she called?"

I shrugged. "Don't know. But I'm going to ask her. Hey, what did
Chief Garner have to say about our break in. Any theories?"

I could have sworn I saw a flicker of the suspicious expression
Grandma makes whenever she's trying to keep a secret. She said,
"Only that you can't stay in the apartment until we get a more secure
door. He also wants me to get a security system. With a property this
large and it being open to the public during the day, he's probably
right."

I rolled my eyes. "And it's something I've been asking you to do
for years, Grandma."

She didn't seem to hear me. "I'll call the security company tomorrow."

In the end, I knew it wasn't important whether she took the advice from me or the chief. It would keep us both safer. *But really.*

"Do you think we need to tell my mom and dad about the break
in?" I asked Grandma Lily. My folks were currently on their retirement world-tour which had been in the works for years. Grandma
Lily and I only talked with them sporadically, but I figured they'd
want to know about something as important as a break in at Jericho
House.

My grandma shook her head and screwed her mouth to one side.
"There's no use trying right now. They're on that mountain climbing
expedition in the Alps. They won't have cell service for another ten
days." She sighed. "Your father has always had such a wanderlust. I
never understood why he was so anxious to get away from here."

I put an arm around her and looked her in the eye. "I guess the love for living in a tiny town that celebrates the past must skip a generation." This got a warm smile from her and she touched her forehead to mine.

"I've been wondering," Grandma Lily said, changing the subject back, "would it help to call a meeting with the Poison Pen Book Club? Once you hear from Blake and talk to Jeannie, of course."

I hadn't thought of it, but the group had been quite helpful to me in clearing Grandma's name last year. They read and discussed mystery fiction every week and tended to have a knack for crime solutions.

"Yeah, I think so," I said. "But wait. No Chief Garner. I can't have him knowing I'm looking into Barbara Duvall's death." *And anyway, he pretty much hates my guts at the moment.*

Grandma winked. "Leave that to me."

I tried Blake's hotel room three more times over the next hour while waiting for Jeannie's arrival. On my last try, the front desk clerk gave me a cranky huff before connecting me to the room. But my attempts were in vain. At 10:30, when I heard a knock at the front door, I still hadn't reached him.

"I heard a knock," Grandma whispered. She shuffled in her slippered feet to the kitchen, Elliot padding after her. I kept Jed at my side. Even though I doubted our talk would turn threatening, it made me feel safer having him with me when meeting with Jeannie.

Grandma Lily and I had made a plan. I'd talk with Jeannie in the library. Grandma would wait in the kitchen until we were settled and then creep down the hallway to listen from the foyer. I knew that my judgment was clouded, given the emotions I still felt towards Christy's death. So, I wanted Grandma's opinion on anything I was about to learn.

I went to the front door and peered through the edge of the stained glass window. It was Jeannie. I unlocked the door to let her in. With one glance at her face, I could tell she'd been crying.

"COME IN," I SAID STOICALLY, not wanting to fall for false remorse. I held my right arm out, inviting her into the library.

Jeannie sniffed and wiped at her eyes with the back of her hand. I sat in one green velvet chair and she took another. It was hard, but I held myself back from consoling her or telling her not to worry.

Instead, I waited.

"Is this about the diary?" she finally asked. She bit at her bottom lip.

I nodded.

Her pretty face crumpled, and she hid it behind her hands, sobbing.

"Why did you steal it from me?"

Jeannie shrugged. "I wanted to read it."

I glared at her. "Then why not just ask me?"

She shrugged again.

I was tiring of her playing dumb. "You *know* why. So tell me."

"I was afraid Christy said bad things about me in it. I thought you'd read about what I did to her and hate me."

"What did you do?"

Jeannie cast her eyes to the floor. "Christy and I weren't getting along that year. I started hanging around some girls at school that liked to pick on her and I'd join in."

"Pick on her about what?" A vague memory of Christy mentioning the 'mean girls' at school swirled around in my mind like a fine mist. *What had she told me about them?*

"You know, Christy was a goody-two-shoes, and those girls were sort of wild. They enjoyed making fun of her for being prim and proper."

I frowned. "I don't get it. You were worried enough about me finding out you'd bullied Christy to steal from Jericho House? That seems extreme."

Jeannie tried to smile, but tears took over. "With you back in town, I hoped we'd be friends again. But I knew it would be impossible if you found out I had been so mean to your best friend."

Jeannie seemed sincere. In fact, I thought she was probably telling me the truth. Just not the whole truth.

"So you tore the clasp in order to get inside?"

"I was going to fix it."

"And cut out the incriminating pages?"

Her eyes met mine with a look of confusion. "What? No."

"Stop lying and tell me what you did with the pages."

Jeannie's cheeks had lost their flush. She shook her head and frowned. "I promise, I didn't do that. I barely read any of it. When it turned up missing from the restaurant, I didn't know what to do or where it went."

I crossed my arms. "I took the diary back from you. And there are pages missing, Jeannie. If you didn't remove them, who did?"

"I promise, I don't know."

I glared at her, then looked away pointedly.

Jeannie used this as an opportunity to leave. She gathered her purse from the floor and stood to go. She rushed past me, heading for the front door. But I stopped her with one more question.

"Who did you call after I left the restaurant tonight?"

She turned back to me with a jerk, her eyes filled with stark surprise. "I don't know what you mean."

"I watched you, Jeannie. You made a call. To whom?"

She waited a beat too long before saying, "My mom. She knows all about this. I wanted to talk to her."

All at once, a loud clanging, almost like a gong, erupted from the foyer. I turned toward the sound in time to see my grandmother breeze into the library as if nothing was amiss.

"Well, hello, girls," she smiled, her cheeks extra pink. "I didn't know you had company, Chloe. I was just, uh... dusting and knocked over the old spittoon in the hall. It's only decorative, of course."

Grandma's interruption was just the distraction Jeannie needed. She announced politely that she must go and hurried to the door. I locked up behind her and gave my grandma *The Look*.

"I'm sorry, I was having trouble hearing," she explained, "so I tried creeping closer. That's when I quite literally kicked the bucket."

I laughed, shaking my head. How could I possibly get upset with her when this was something I could see myself doing?

"Did you learn anything?" Grandma Lily asked.

"Only that Jeannie's not telling me the whole truth. And clumsiness runs in the family."

21

An Ultimatum

I TRIED BLAKE'S HOTEL room one more time. There was no answer. I hated to admit it, as I crawled into bed in my room upstairs, but I was worried. For all I knew, whoever killed Barbara Duvall went after Blake, too. If they'd checked her cell phone and found the outgoing message to him...a chill ran down my back.

I snuggled down deeper into the frilly covers but only tossed and turned, worrying that Blake might have also met his end. To soothe my worries, I played devil's advocate with myself. *I don't actually know what the message from Barbara Duvall to Blake says. I only know that she sent one.* Yeah, maybe I had it all wrong. Maybe her message is something completely innocent, like wishing him a safe trip to Albuquerque.

I tried convincing myself.

It didn't work.

I flopped around some more, clearly annoying Jed. He whined from his spot on the nearby rug.

"Sorry, boy," I whispered into the dark room.

Finally, I decided I wouldn't sleep until I found out what her message said. Like I told Bree, I didn't like the idea of snooping around in Blake's phone without his knowledge. However, if he was in danger, we needed to know, right? I slipped a baggy sweatshirt over my t-shirt and pajama pants and crept downstairs by the light of my cell phone screen. Jed's nails clicked along behind me on the cherry staircase.

I went to the side table in the foyer where I'd put the phone and charger earlier. There I gently, and hopefully quietly, jiggled the antique drawer open just enough to slip my hand inside and grab the items. Jed and I went to the kitchen, where I switched on the under-cabinet lights and plugged in the charging cord.

"Here goes nothing,'" I told my cute doggo, readying myself to see if the charger really fit this phone. It did. Impatiently, I stared at the screen. At first, nothing happened.

"Great," I told Jed. "It's not going to work." But the device must have simply been extra drained, because eventually a red blinking battery icon flashed in the corner.

I bit at my bottom lip and twirled a long strand of hair. *Was I really going to invade Blake's privacy like this?* He'd hopefully understand when I had the chance to tell him why I'd gone to such lengths. Suddenly, the phone's screen lit up. It was charged enough to operate.

"What are you doing up?"

I did a spinning jump move that ended in a karate chop motion to find Grandma Lily standing in the kitchen doorway, bleary-eyed.

I steadied myself against the counter and panted to catch my breath. "Good grief, Grandma. You scared me half to death."

She scratched her head and went to the fridge, tying her baby blue bathrobe a little tighter. "Sorry, I couldn't sleep either, thought I'd get a snack. What do you have there?"

"Blake's phone."

She looked at me with sleepy eyes and squinted. "Am I sleep-walking? Still dreaming? I thought that thing was lost."

I laughed, then explained how Bree found Blake's phone in her salon and handed it off to me. "I'm worried about him. So, I'm struggling with the moral dilemma of whether or not to snoop through his phone."

Grandma Lily ate a spoonful of strawberry yogurt. "Would Blake go through *your* phone if given the chance?"

I looked at her out of the corner of my eye. "Even without the excuse of an ongoing murder investigation."

She swirled her spoon in the air above the phone. "Fire that baby up."

Grandma watched over my shoulder, eating, while I thumbed through Blake's phone. I wondered...had Barbara sent Blake a text message or voicemail? I opted to check for voice messages first, given that Barbara was a mature woman and less likely to be an avid text messenger. I had just touched the icon shaped like a little green phone receiver when insistent knocking rang out from the back porch.

I let out a yipe. Grandma's spoon clanged onto the tile floor, and Jed jumped to his feet, growling. I went to place a hand on his neck, realizing that Jed's recent spurt of protectiveness wasn't unfounded. He'd been the only one of us aware that someone was lurking around Jericho House. "Good dog," I whispered, patting his head.

The knocking stopped.

I looked over my shoulder at Grandma Lily while moving toward the back porch.

"Chloe, be careful."

I tiptoed across the wooden floor of the porch in the darkness, careful to avoid the squeaky boards. The eyelet cafe curtains furnishing the windows of the porch prevented me from seeing who was out there. Another quick series of knocks rang out and although I flinched, I held in the scream that wanted to escape this time.

Carefully, I lifted the corner of the curtain hanging across the door. Blake White, looking exhausted and worried, was about to knock again. I opened the door before his knuckles made contact.

"What in the world are you doing here?" I asked, ushering him inside.

"Oh, Blake, it's only you," Grandma Lily said with relief.

He looked out into the dark backyard while closing the door behind him. He seemed jumpy. His usually perfectly coiffed auburn hair was sticking up on top, and he could use a shave.

"I've been trying to reach you all evening," I told him. "I must have called your hotel room two dozen times."

He rubbed his upper arms as if chilled. "Sorry, after we talked this afternoon, I went back to my room to wait for your call. I think someone was in there while I was out."

"Like a maid?" I asked sarcastically.

"No. Like my briefcase may have been gone through. Anyway, I threw everything into my suitcase, called a cab, and headed straight for the airport. It was a nightmare changing my flight, but I managed to get home. I thought I should come right over and check on you."

"I'll put the kettle on," Grandma said after picking up her spoon and wiping up pink yogurt splatters from the floor.

Blake was usually ultra cool. He never wanted anyone to know he could feel nervous or worried. So I didn't take his nerves tonight lightly. I pulled out a barstool and asked him to take a seat.

"I assume as the mayor, you already know about Barbara Duvall's death," I said to him.

He rolled his eyes in exasperation while removing his suit jacket and cuffing his sleeves. "Yes, but not easily. Without my cell phone, Missy could only leave messages for me at the hotel desk. I didn't find out about the accident until this morning. First that sad news, then your urgent message, and finally my room being gone through. What the heck is going on around here?"

I stepped over to get his phone, which now showed a twelve percent charge. I unplugged it and handed it across the kitchen island to him. "Check your messages, would you?"

Blake frowned. "How'd you get my phone?"

"You lost it in a salon chair, but that's not important right now. Listen. On Friday afternoon, you told me you planned to ask the city records clerk about Christy's case. Hours later, the city records clerk wound up dead and I think she left you some information before..." my voice faded away.

Blake still wore a look of disbelief. "Wait. From what I've heard, Barbara had a slip and fall accident. You think she died because of me? That she was *murdered*?"

Grandma set a cup of tea in front of Blake and placed her hand on his shoulder. "No one is blaming you, dear. We're just trying to figure out what really happened."

I sat down beside him and waited a moment for the news to sink in. Blake drank some tea, then rubbed the top of his head. He loosened his tie and undid the top two buttons of his shirt.

"Let's start at the beginning," I suggested. "What did you find in your new office that made you think there's more to Christy's case than we were ever told?"

Blake looked up. "A letter. It was wedged behind a desk drawer. When I took out the drawer to clean it, the letter dropped right out."

"Who was the letter for?"

"Mayor Luna. Remember him? He was in office when we were young?"

I nodded. "He and his wife had kids around our age."

"Yeah, he even hired a couple of high school students each year for summer jobs. I applied but never got hired. I can't believe it, either. I mean, *I* was the one with straight A's and political aspirations."

"Blake," I said with a groan, "stop wallowing. You couldn't win everything."

"Just most things," Grandma Lily mumbled before taking a healthy sip of tea.

He went on. "Anyway, it's a handwritten-letter giving Mayor Luna an ultimatum. The sender tells the mayor to get rid of 'the b.s. interview about the drowning girl' or his secret would get out."

I shot a quick look at Grandma Lily. "Secret? Was Mayor Luna the type of guy to have secrets?"

"Everyone has secrets, Chloe," Grandma said dryly.

Even Garner, I thought.

"Was the letter signed?" I asked Blake.

He shook his head, no.

"So apparently," I said, "the sender of the letter believed some interviews taken after Christy's death were false? Trumped up?"

"That's what it seems like to me," said Blake. "And they wanted the false information taken out of evidence."

"I remember some false information given to the authorities," Grandma remarked before taking yet another meaningful sip of tea.

Blake cast his eyes down.

I swallowed hard to fight the anger that still filled me whenever I remembered what Blake, my boyfriend at the time, had done. At the urging of his parents, he told the cops that a fight Christy and I had started in the parking lot continued at the top of the waterfall. His testimony led authorities to assume that in anger, I'd pushed her. Blake and his younger brother were in the clear, while I suffered weeks of interrogations and accusations.

I cleared my throat for effect. "That's true. We know there was false testimony given. Still, this doesn't make any sense. If the letter refers to Blake's 'bs' testimony, then it was sent by someone in my circle to get me out of the hot seat. *My* family wouldn't blackmail the mayor."

I turned to face Grandma Lily. "Would you?"

She put her hands up, surrendering. "No way. Your parents and I went the legal route. We hired that attorney and thank goodness his investigators proved that the allegation against you was a lie."

A silence fell between us. I looked around the room, unable to focus on anything in particular. I wanted desperately to understand what the threatening letter meant, but I was missing too much information.

"That isn't all I found," Blake said, undoubtedly relieved to change the subject. "Folded inside the letter was this."

He reached into his shirt pocket and withdrew a photograph. It was a picture of Mayor Luna, with two women and another man. They were all smiles, wearing golf attire and holding a massive trophy. Across the bottom, someone had scripted I KNOW in red ink.

Grandma Lily took the photo from me. "Just a minute," she said. Blake and I waited while she explored the kitchen junk drawer to find a magnifying glass. She held it over the image, her eyes growing wide. "That's the governor. I mean, she was at the time. Governor Kate Finney."

"Do you recognize the others?" I asked her.

"No, I can't say that I do. But they all must be important if they're golfing with the governor."

A stillness came over the room.

"That blackmail letter isn't referring to Blake's bogus testimony, is it?" I whispered.

"I don't think so," Grandma said.

"If anything," I added, "the blackmailer's instructions might have pressured the mayor into finding an alternate suspect—as in me."

"A scapegoat," Grandma whispered.

Blake nodded. "Plan 'B.'"

The three of us each took this news differently. I paced and twirled a piece of my hair around my index finger. Blake sat pensively, studying the grain in the marble countertop while chewing a fingernail. Grandma Lily rinsed and polished the kitchen sink.

"Blake, we need to know what Barbara Duvall had to tell you," I said finally.

Blake nodded, but I wasn't sure he'd heard me. He looked like a kid too enthralled with their TV show to hear what their parent was trying to tell them.

"Blake," I said, waving my hand in front of him.

He blinked hard. "Oh, yeah."

He fumbled when he went to pick up his phone, but managed to swipe it open and look through his notifications. "It's a voice message," he looked up at us.

I met his gaze. "Play it."

22

Way Too Long

BLAKE TURNED UP THE volume and pressed play.

Hello Mayor White, You're probably in the air by now but I wanted to let you know I found a necklace in evidence that sheds light on what the letter means. You see, it's not what we thought at all. I know I've crossed a line here, but I brought it home with me to show you—no one's going to miss it for a few days after all these years. And I'm a short-timer, now anyway. Right? (a sad attempt at laughter). Call me when you land. Bye-bye now.

"That's it?" I barked.

"That's it."

I sank onto a bar stool and put my head in my hands. It wasn't nearly enough. And now that she was dead, how would we ever find out what Barbara Duvall discovered?

GRANDMA LILY SUGGESTED Blake stay at Jericho House for the rest of the night. He still seemed shaken by everything we discussed and exhausted from his impromptu return trip from Albuquerque. She offered him the bedroom next door to hers, but he declined, saying he'd be fine on the couch in the parlour. Before I went upstairs to bed, he pulled me into a hug. My arms remained at my sides while he squeezed me tightly. "Trust me, Chloe. We're going to figure this whole thing out, I promise," he said. *As if I needed his reassurance.*

The next morning, though, Blake was already gone when I arrived downstairs. This concerned me. Had he gone to the police? I wasn't ready to let Chief Garner in on our suspicions just yet. While making a pot of coffee and pouring kibble into the pets' dishes, I dialed Blake. I felt surprisingly thankful that we had exchanged numbers the night before. Sadly, my call went straight to his voicemail.

"Hi," I said after the beep, "just checking to make sure you're okay. Give me a call."

I waited for his response, busying myself by toasting bagels and slicing fresh strawberries. When Grandma came downstairs, she looked drained.

"I'm sorry we kept you up last night," I told her with a peace offering of coffee in hand.

"No apology necessary," she smiled. "I'm just as concerned as you are, dear. Which reminds me, I think we should have the Poison Pen Book Club over tonight. Like we discussed."

I had forgotten about her suggestion to solicit the group's opinion. We could use their input now more than ever. "All right, tonight." I told her. "But how do you plan to keep Chief Garner occupied? He is a regular member of the book club, after all."

"*I'm* not going to keep him busy. You are."

I nearly spit out the coffee I had just slurped up. "Oh, no," I choked, "he doesn't want to see me."

"You might be surprised," Grandma Lily sang.

I took a seat and screwed my mouth to one side. "Grandma, I haven't told you about my latest mess up with him. Blake called at the most inopportune time and now things between Garner and I are a disaster again."

Grandma Lily put a thick layer of cream cheese on a bagel and added some sliced berries to the top before saying, "I heard all about it. In fact, I took it upon myself to clear things up for you."

"What?"

Grandma licked her fingers. "When Garner and I were looking around after the break in, I took the opportunity to pry a little. Of course, at that point, I only knew about your first falling out. The chief told me about the call from Blake and how you were being secretive, you didn't want to talk in front of him."

I groaned.

"Lucky for you, Chloe, I'm quick at coming up with a fib. I told the chief that *I'm* the reason Blake called you—that the two of you are helping me in my sneaky matchmaking venture. Anyway, my point is, I think Garner would happily accept an invitation from you to get a cup of coffee or something to talk things out. Shoot for around seven o'clock and I'll meet with the others here at the house."

I grinned. "How do you do it, Grandma?"

She shrugged. "It's a gift. Now I need to put on my walking shoes and get a move on. I thought I'd make my way to the opera house this morning and check on Stan." Grandma Lily looked thoughtfully at the ceiling. "If he should happen to drop by Jericho House about the same time the book club finishes up..."

I left her to her matchmaking daydreams and went to the backyard with Jed. I sipped my morning brew while watching him sniff all his favorite spots in the backyard. Thankfully, the back gate was secured, and nothing looked amiss this morning.

I couldn't decide what my next step should be. Aside from inviting Garner for coffee, that is. My insides fluttered. Maybe something stronger than coffee was in order—but only to get the nerve up to ask him out. Once with him, I'd be a teetotaler. Who knew what kind of trouble my mouth would get me in if I lubricated it with liquor.

Watching Jed gave me the perfect idea. No beverages required. I patted my leg and called him to me to stroke his handsome, silky face. "Hey buddy, wanna make a deal?" I asked. "You be my wingman with Garner, and I'll get you one of those fancy dog treats from Blue Bonnet Bakery."

Jed panted, then lifted his front paw to shake. "OK, deal," I said with a smile.

I took my phone out and thumbed a text message to the chief. I knew it was a wimpy move even as I did it, but I wasn't brave enough to call him. This way, if he declined, I would only have to read the words—not hear him say them.

ME: Hi. Jed asked me to see if Mandy is free this evening for a trip to the dog park.

I was already pushing my phone back into the pocket of my jeans, not expecting a prompt reply from him, when it dinged.

GARNER: Her social calendar looks open. 6:00?

I smiled and felt a thick wave of relief. But six o'clock was too early, according to Grandma's plan.

ME: How about 7:00? It's staying light later.

He sent back a thumbs up with no questions asked. *Whew.* I let a few minutes go by before sending,

ME: See you then.

I drew in a long breath. Finally, I could relax. At least a little. If Garner and I met, we'd surely be able to have a mature conversation about these things. Well, not *all* the things. I wasn't ready to discuss the possibility that Barbara's death was connected with Christy's somehow. Or that I had been poking around at Pioneer RV Park. But I certainly wouldn't mind hearing about the progress on *his* end of the investigation. Maybe I'd get some inside info on the case while throwing tennis balls for the pups at the dog park. Two birds, one stone. Win-win.

With the opportunity to talk with Garner later, I wanted to have a strong theory in place. I needed to think this whole thing through—to find out where the missing pieces were and see whether I could make any more fit before day's end. Then, tonight I'd know what careful questions to ask the chief.

Jed brought me a ball. I tossed it from one hand to the other, thinking. "Okay boy," I said, throwing it for him, "let's say this whole thing has nothing to do with Christy or what happened all those years ago."

Jed had already retrieved the ball, sprinted back, and dropped it at my feet. I threw it again. "That would mean I was right all along and someone connected with the RV park did her in." Jed sped out to retrieve the ball and jauntily loped back. "In that bunch, Daniel Duvall is still my primary suspect."

Ugh! Daniel Duvall! I was going to look for him at the coffee shop today. I checked my phone; it was 8:30. If I hurried, I still had time to haunt the place and try to catch him.

Without a minute to spare, I ran up to my room. I swooped my hair into a messy bun and dressed in my typical jeans and T-shirt ensemble. I tied a sweatshirt around my waist to account for the unpredictable spring weather and hustled downstairs. Just as I reached the bottom step, my phone dinged. Blake was finally responding to my voice message.

BLAKE: How do we know it wasn't an accident like Chief Garner says?

ME: I don't think so—she had bruises, ripped stockings.

BLAKE: Maybe we should meet with Garner and hand over everything.

Oh no, he didn't. I wouldn't let Blake wimp out now.

ME: Not yet. We need more proof or he'll never believe us.

BLAKE: Chloe, I'm the mayor. I can't hide evidence from a police investigation. I'll lose all credibility.

He had a point. While I didn't have any lovey-dovey feelings left for the guy, and it might be kinda fun to watch his reputation implode after what he'd done to mine, I didn't have it in me to stoop to that level. I didn't want Blake to lose his position as mayor.

ME: 48 hours.

BLAKE: Huh?

ME: Give me 48 hours. If I haven't figured this out by then, we'll go to the police.

BLAKE: 2 days is way too long.

ME: Remember, this is personal. We need to follow it through.

And then,

ME: I'll take all the blame if it blows up on us.

Several seconds ticked by before I saw the sign that Blake was texting back.

BLAKE: OK.

That's Blake for ya, I thought.

I slipped my phone into my pocket, then hugged the animals. "I'm going to see what I can find out from Daniel Duvall," I told Jed.

He whined. Probably just because he wanted to go with me, but the sound made him seem concerned.

I slung my backpack over one shoulder, then kneeled down to look him in the eye. "I promise to be careful. You hang out with Elliot. I'll be back before either of you wake up from the naps I know you're about to take."

I patted his head one last time and took off to find the man in the dark green minivan.

23

Like a Magician

I SPOTTED DANIEL'S van parked outside the Golden Grind once again. I whispered a little prayer of thanks for the addictive qualities of caffeine, then hustled to get inside before he left again.

Like most mornings, the line for java was long and winding. Daniel was about half-way to the counter. I considered joining him in line for our little chat, but instead, waited at the table right by the door. Once he'd purchased his coffee, he'd have to come past me to leave. And this way, I had time to study him. Today, he looked cleaner, less greasy than before. His clothes might have been the same, but at least they looked like they'd been washed. His hair was combed, too.

At last, with coffee in hand, he approached me.

"Daniel?" I said, just as he reached for the door.

"Yeah?"

"Can I have a minute? It's about your mom."

Recognition came across his face. "You were at the park Saturday night. With that pushy Lottie."

"Yes. My name is Chloe Martin. But I wasn't *with* Lottie, I'd only just met her."

"Martin? Like the Jericho House Martins?"

"One and the same," I smiled. "It was a strange coincidence, but I was at the RV park the night your mom died, too." Daniel frowned, showing concerned interest in this. I opened my palm to the chair beside me. "Have a seat?"

He considered the offer for a moment, lifted one shoulder to show resignation, then sat. He put his coffee and the muffin he'd bought on the table.

"How are you doing?" I asked him. "It must be tough losing your mom like this."

He raised and lowered that shoulder again.

"Have you spoken to her recently?"

He nodded. "Yeah, thankfully I did."

Today, Daniel Duvall seemed like a normal, grieving son. *Time to turn up the pressure*, I thought.

"Lottie says you're planning on making a quick buck by selling the RV park."

Daniel gave a tired, sarcastic laugh. "Of course she does. What I'm *doing* is putting a stop to that woman's thievery. Listen, I've already gone over all this with the cops..."

"Thievery? What do you mean?"

Daniel huffed. "The sooner the cash stops rolling in at Pioneer RV Park, the sooner Lottie Sloan will go find another business to steal from."

"Lottie was stealing from your mom?"

"She arranged a pretty slick deal for herself, didn't she? My mom left for work at city hall every day and Lottie had the run of the place. You know what I think? I think my mom finally caught her with her fingers in the cookie jar on Friday. And look what happened."

My mouth felt dry. *Was Lottie the killer?*

"Forgive me for asking, Daniel. But where were *you* on Friday?" After all, he could be throwing shade on Lottie to divert attention away from himself.

Daniel reached into his back pocket. He unfolded a piece of paper and handed it to me. It was a flier for an art show in Portland, Oregon. The exhibit's closing reception had been Friday night, six to nine p.m. The most interesting part was the featured artist's photo in the corner. It was none other than 'Renowned Metal Sculpurist, Daniel Duvall'.

"You're an artist?"

He tipped his head. "I had a hard time in my early years. Thankfully, I finally found meaning in my life through making art. But as you can see, I was nowhere near Jericho Falls on Friday night. As soon as I got word of my mom's death from law enforcement, I threw some things in my van and drove straight through." Daniel scrubbed at his chin, distracting himself from the tears that wanted to come.

Suddenly, my judgment of his griminess made me feel terrible. I, too, had made a similar frantic drive last year when I thought Grandma Lily was ill. I, too, looked worn out and bedraggled when I arrived. And no wonder he'd been gruff with us; he had just lost his mom, and the woman who he suspected was responsible told him to go away.

"Anyway," he went on, "I'm putting business at Pioneer RV Park on hold until I find out what happened to my mom."

"I see."

He stood to go, taking up his coffee and muffin. I folded the flier and handed it back to him.

"Anything else you're curious about, Miss Martin?"

"No, that does it. Thank you for talking with me, Daniel."

He nodded curtly, then lifted his to-go cup in a 'cheers' goodbye before leaving the shop. Daniel Duvall had given me a lot to think about. He'd effectively cleared himself from my list of suspects, but he'd added Lottie Sloan.

It was time for me to get back to the RV park and ask more questions.

MY PLAN OF ATTACK WAS woefully underdeveloped. What I needed to do was rule out Jim and Lottie. If neither of them was guilty, Barbara must have been killed because of what she knew about the blackmail letter. With the RV park residents in the clear, plus the things Blake found, I just might convince Chief Garner that Barbara's death was connected with Christy's.

As I drove past the Jericho Falls Opera House with its grand brick facade, I noticed Grandma Lily standing outside with a man who must be Stan Duncan, the new manager. She hadn't lied. He was cute. His black hair was cut in a short, almost old-fashioned style that suited him. He wore a white oxford shirt rolled up to his elbows with neatly pressed khakis. He nodded intently as Grandma spoke. *Oh, boy.* I thought, *I wonder what she's talking him into.* No time to worry about the consequences of her matchmaking mission right now. I focused back on the road and drove on toward Pioneer RV Park.

I turned past the town visitor center, slowing to let two kids on bikes go past me on the narrow, gravel road. They waved their thanks, making me smile. This was such a friendly town we lived in, it seemed impossible to imagine that a murder might have taken place here just a few days before. And worse still, the murderer might get away with it.

Crossing the bridge over the pond to enter the park, I wondered... What excuse should I use with Lottie, Jim and the others as my reason for returning? Perhaps I lost something? I needed to cover my tracks? I wanted to see if the security tape was down so I could finally peek inside the Duvall's house? None of these sounded good enough. Out of time, I opted for the least of my bad ideas—I wanted to make sure none of them let on to Chief Garner that I had been snooping around.

I saw Jim right away. He was at the side of his little trailer watering a wimpy-looking tomato plant. Its brown leaves were a dead giveaway that he'd left it outside on a night that got too cold. I surveyed Barbara Duvall's place. Unfortunately, police tape still surrounded it. *Darn. No getting in there yet without breaking the law.* Lottie's trailer was quiet. So was the Brown's. I'd start with Jim.

I left my red truck near the office again and took my time meandering towards him. We'd come a long way since my first visit, yet I didn't feel like startling him again and risk making him cranky. He glanced up and waved with one hand while the other one held a hose trickling water into the tomato plant's soil. "Not sure I can save this one," he smiled.

"Yeah, the nights are still pretty chilly," I added. I put my hands in the front pocket of my jeans.

He nodded.

An awkward silence followed. Finally, I said, "Hey, so have the police still been coming around here?"

He shrugged. "Not much in the past day or so. I heard they're done collectin' evidence."

I stifled a huff. *Of course they've stopped collecting evidence. The chief immediately jumped to the conclusion that Barbara's death was an accident.*

I said, "Well, can you do me a favor and not mention to the chief or any of the officers that I've been poking around? I don't want to get in trouble."

This got a grin out of Jim. "You're a bit of a rebel, ain't ya?"

I returned a sly smile. "Like I told you, I just want to know what really happened to Barbara."

"You might be the only one," Jim said. His happiness faded, and he focused on winding up his garden hose.

"What's that supposed to mean?" I asked him.

He tilted his head. "Doesn't seem like anyone around here really cares that she's gone. Life's just goin' on as usual."

I remembered feeling something like that when Christy died. Whenever I'd see a smiling family or a cheerful group of kids, I'd wonder how they could be going on normally when I was such a wreck. It didn't seem fair. "It's terrible losing someone we care about," I admitted.

"Okay, I won't tell the cops you've been comin' around. Anything else?" Jim said. He looked like he wanted to get back inside, away from this sad topic.

"Yeah, actually. Jim, have you heard rumors about Lottie stealing from Barbara?"

Jim's cheeks reddened. "Ain't rumors. Lottie and Barbara had it out a few months ago 'bout that."

"Why didn't you tell me this before?"

"None of my business. I told Barbara I'd have fired Lottie over it, but they seemed to make up."

I bit at my bottom lip. "Do you think Lottie could have...," I let my words fade away. I knew Jim would get my meaning.

24

Specifically the Mermaid

"WOULD LOTTIE KILL BARBARA?" Jim's face scrunched into a scowl of disbelief. "Heck no. Look where this leaves her; without a place to stay, without a job, and without a cash cow—if she was still stealin', that is."

I considered this. Jim was right. Lottie wouldn't want Barbara Duvall out of the picture. It ruined a great setup for her.

"But ya know, I do find it odd," Jim went on, "that she weren't nowhere around when we found Barbara in the pool."

I hadn't seen Lottie on Friday evening either. The first time I laid eyes on her was Saturday evening. Then it came to me.

"Lottie told me that she always video chats with her daughter and grandbaby at 5:30 on Fridays," I said. "She was probably busy with that."

"Maybe so." Jim lifted his hands in a 'let bygones be bygones' manner. "I'm just sayin' it's strange that the assistant manager didn't come out to see what was goin' on. I told your cop friend that, too."

I looked across the way to Lottie's trailer. "When Lottie's at home, can you tell from here? Did you notice if she was inside her trailer that night?"

Jim shook away my question. "Nah, too far for me to tell. Anyway, I wasn't here. I was doing my wash. Me and old Brownie were watchin' the game together in the laundry room. He's got himself a washin' machine in his fancy trailer, but he keeps me company sometimes."

"Brownie? As in Mr. Brown?" I pointed to the extravagant trailer Jim must be referring to.

He nodded, but scrunched his nose. "Not my favorite person, kinda hoity-toity for my taste, but he likes baseball and so do I."

"Was Mrs. Brown with you?"

This got a braying laugh out of Jim. "Heck no, that woman never leaves her heated and cooled mobile palace. I'm not sure how Brownie ever convinced such a princess to go RV'ing. Or how he affords all the electricity she burns."

Good old Jim. Despite his rough exterior, I liked him. I wondered if deep down, Barbara Duvall did, too. "Was Mr. Brown still with you when the change machine started acting up?"

"Nope, his wife texted him around the sixth inning to whine about being hungry. Said she needed him to come home and bar-b-que dinner for her." Jim rolled his eyes.

So, if Lottie was occupied with her weekly grandbaby video chat and the Browns were in their trailer having dinner when Barbara took her fatal dive into the pool, what about Jim? I still wasn't sure if he was off the hook or not. On the one hand, why would he create havoc around the office area if he knew she was floating face down a few feet away. Unless it was intentional... like a magician waving his wand in one direction so the audience looks away from what's really going on.

"Who called the police, Jim?"

"Hmm?"

"On Friday. When you were upset about the broken change machine and Barbara's refusal to answer her door, who called the police?"

"I did."

I frowned. "*You* did? I got the impression that your outburst caused one of the other campers to call for help."

He shook his head. "I was yellin', but only trying to rouse her. I was worried."

"You weren't threatening her?"

"Heck, no," he said. His eyes softened along with his voice. "I figured she wasn't answerin' because she drank too much again. I thought she might have fallen down or passed out. It's happened before." He let out a long breath. "And it looks like she *did* fall. Into the pool this time."

I wasn't sure who to believe. Chief Garner's explanation on the night Barbara died led me to believe Jim was upsetting the campers with his anger. But whether Jim was angry with Barbara or simply concerned for her safety, he'd have been nuts to kill her and then call 911. For now, at least, it seemed to me that Jim Holt was in the clear too.

Jim also seemed to be worn out. He swatted at a bug. The gesture turned into a wave goodbye. "I'll be seein' ya, Chloe. And don't worry, I won't say a word about you to the fuzz."

I waved too. "Take care of yourself, Jim."

I headed for the Brown's trailer.

Just as before, the place looked pristine. Since my last visit, they'd added a string of lights across their trailer's awning and several solar luminaries to light a pathway to their chic color-coordinated picnic set.

When I approached the trailer steps, I could hear raised voices. Were the Browns having an argument? Their words were too muffled behind the metal of the RV and the whirring of the HVAC unit on the roof for me to make anything out. But it definitely sounded like these two were at odds.

I waited a beat before I knocked. This time, it was Mrs. Brown who opened up. I was utterly shocked. She was not at all what I expected. While Mr. Brown was easily sixty, a little paunchy and white-haired, this woman looked close to my age. She was tall, curvy in all the right ways and had flowing red hair the color of a brand new penny. Jim wasn't kidding. She looked like a princess—specifically the mermaid one. Not as cheerful, though.

"Who are you?" she scowled.

"Uh, hi," I stammered, trying to regain my footing after such a big surprise.

Mrs. Brown stood frowning with her hand on her hip, displaying a diamond the size of a peach pit.

"My name is Chloe. I dropped by a couple days ago."

"And?"

I swallowed. "I spoke to your husband about Barbara's death. Is he here, by any chance?"

The glamorous redhead let out an irritated sigh and turned her back on me without saying another word. With the door standing open, I heard what sounded like someone flopping onto a couch, then an exasperated, "It's for you."

Mr. Brown appeared in the doorway, looking identical to the first time I'd seen him. The only detail that had changed was the color of his shirt. Light yellow today.

"Chloe, isn't it?" he didn't seem thrilled, but at least he wasn't glaring at me.

"That's right. Could I have another moment of your time?"

He motioned to the picnic table and shut the door behind him, no doubt required to preserve as much temperature controlled air for his wife as possible. He came down the steps to join me and we sat on opposite sides of the picnic table.

"What's the reason for the visit today?" he asked.

I tried a different tactic with him, since Mr. Brown seemed like someone who would enjoy having his ego stroked. "I was hoping I could pick your brain. You're obviously a successful guy who is much more worldly wise than most of these...," I paused for effect and flipped my hand around as if looking for the right word, "trailer park people."

He gave me a tight-lipped smile, edged in satisfaction.

"What's your opinion about Barbara Duvall's death? Do you think it's possible someone *here* could have harmed her? I mean, wouldn't it be terrible if one of them gets away with it?"

Mr. Brown leaned back a bit, puffing out his chest. "I understand your concerns," he began. "In fact, I nearly packed up and drove away that night for fear there was a maniac on the loose or something. But then I realized that running away would only make me and the missus look guilty ourselves. With nothing to hide, we needed to stay put. And anyway, the police seem sure that it was nothing but a terrible accident. I have no reason to think otherwise. I'm siding with the experts."

I gave him a look of appreciation. "That's good advice. You're probably right." I turned my palms up and hoped my next fib rang true. "Well, that makes me feel better. If the accidental death explanation satisfies a guy like you, who am I to argue?" I stood to go and Mr. Brown rose as well.

"There's one more thing that's bothering me," I said after taking a few steps.

"What's that, hon?" he addressed me as if I were a child.

"I don't remember seeing Lottie at the scene that day. As Barbara's assistant and friend, I would have expected her to come running like everyone else."

"Come to think of it, I didn't see her either." Mr. Brown seemed puzzled. "But she was bragging to me about her new grandbaby and video chatting with her daughter that evening. Too enthralled with her progeny to be distracted, I'd say. And she showed up, eventually. Crying and carrying on when the coroner loaded Barbara into the ambulance." Mr. Brown shook his head and scrunched his eyes tightly. "Just terrible, it was."

"It must have been," I whispered.

A shrill, annoyed voice said, "What's taking so long?" from inside the Brown's RV. Mr. Brown's face reddened. He shrugged an apologetic goodbye as he hurriedly climbed the steps and disappeared inside. Mrs. Brown might be a princess, but she was still the one who wore the pants in this relationship.

I looked down the lane. Lottie's trailer remained quiet, but I took the chance that she might be inside. Walking in that direction, I thought about Mr. Brown's comment about running away in the night. Not only had the Browns stayed, all the long-term residents had done the same. Didn't that give credence to *their* innocence as well?

I knocked on Lottie's door, listening. No sounds of vacuuming or music today. I glanced around and spotted her across the grassy expanse. She had come out of the laundry room, juggling a large basket of clothes and a jumbo jug of detergent. I hoofed it towards her. "Hi. Looks like you could use a hand."

Lottie said, "Laundry day. What brings you here, Chloe?"

I returned to my original excuse, displaying a sheepish grin. "I got worried that you'd tell the police that I came out here asking questions. Please don't say anything, okay? I don't want to get in trouble."

I took the detergent container while Lottie jostled the full clothes basket on her hip. We went toward her trailer. "I won't tell on you."

"Gee, thanks." I glanced sideways at Lottie. She stared straight ahead, her mouth set. "Can I ask you something?" I said.

She shot a look at me. "I guess."

"Do you know that Daniel Duvall thinks you were stealing from the RV park?"

Lottie made a noise halfway between a cough and a laugh. "That's a lie!" She stopped walking and turned to face me. At first, her expression was unreadable. I couldn't tell if she was angry that I would suggest such a thing, or scared at the idea of being found out. When I didn't look away, Lottie's face grew red. "It was just once—when my daughter was expecting she needed an expensive medication. I felt terrible. On my next payday, I gave it all back and told Barbara what I'd done."

"And she let you keep your job?"

"Like I said, I paid her back. It was between me and Barbara. Her son is barking up the wrong tree." Lottie bounced the heavy basket against her hip to get a better hold on it. "Ugh, this thing is about to break my back. Thanks for your help. Set that soap down anywhere."

I put the heavy jug near her trailer steps and bid Lottie goodbye.

I was several steps down the gravel pathway before she called out to me again. "Hey, Chloe. I'd have an easier time covering for you with the cops if you'd stop coming out here harassing us." She didn't wait for me to consent or argue before slamming her camp trailer door.

That stung. I wasn't trying to harass anyone. I only wanted to find out the truth. I went to my truck and sat down heavily behind the wheel. None of these people seemed like a key suspect to me. They certainly would not benefit from Barbara Duvall's death. In fact, they were all going to lose their long-term living arrangements if Daniel really sold the park. And as far as I could tell, none of them were near the house or the pool at the time of her drowning.

With no motive and no means from the RV park residents, I was back on the trail to uncover the connection between Barbara's death and her recent discovery at city hall.

25

Laying it on Thick

I KNEW BY THIS TIME Grandma Lily would be home after her morning exercise and matchmaking excursion. I figured it would be a good time for us to go over our plan of attack for the evening. If we were going to split up (her taking the Poison Pen Book Clubbers and me taking Chief Garner) we'd better know exactly which questions we wanted to ask and what information we needed most.

I drove through downtown at the prescribed 20 miles per hour, giving me ample time to check out the activity on Main Street. A woman dressed as a can-can dancer polished the glass door of the Saddles and Spurs Saloon, a sure sign that tourist season was almost upon us. All winter, the waitresses at this establishment wore blue jeans and t-shirts printed to look like corsets. The waiters did too. Pretty funny. But now since more out-of-towners were showing up, the gals became can-can dancers, and the guys switched to donning cowboy shirts and hats with (empty) gun belts. Bree was open for business, too. Her sandwich board on the walk announced, "BOOK NOW FOR SPRING BREAK."

On a whim, I took a left at the end of the block past Bree's salon to reach the jig-jog street in front of city hall. I hoped to catch a glimpse of Garner, because, well, Garner. Or Blake, because I wanted to check on how he was holding up. Neither of them were outside the building or in the adjoining parking lot. I did spy Blake's oh-so-efficient secretary, Missy. She was carefully climbing the tall front steps of the building, precariously balancing a coffee carrier in each hand filled with the Golden Grind's recognizable bright yellow paper cups. I circled the next block to get back on track for home.

I parked in the shade of the cottonwood tree and went in the front door of our house. Grandma Lily stood in the library to my left, leading a home tour for a young couple with two small children. I could tell in an instant that she had chosen the abbreviated Jericho House spiel, which she switched to whenever there were squirrely kids or bored looking visitors present; everyone still got their money's worth, but there was no dilly dallying or extra anecdotes. I slipped into the kitchen for a tall glass of water and a chance to think.

I took the magnetic notepad from the fridge again and grabbed a pen from the junk drawer. With the RV park residents in the clear, I needed to make new notes—things felt all jumbly in my head. I wrote out my thoughts:

-Grandma Lily and I were watched, then burglarized. I think the guy was after Christy's diary.

-Jeannie said she stole the diary because she didn't want me to know she'd been mean to Christy.

-The mayor of Jericho Falls was blackmailed during the investigation of Christy's death.

-The blackmailer thought one interview was b.s.

-Barbara Duvall was found dead the same day she told Blake about a necklace she found in the old cases' evidence files.

A necklace. *A necklace?* Unconsciously, my hand went to my neck. The memory of that shiny object at the bottom of the pool came to mind. *Could it be?* Had I actually seen the necklace Barbara told Blake about in her phone message? I felt like I was spinning in circles, getting dizzier and dizzier by the second. Instead of things coming into focus, they were only getting more wobbly to think about.

SOON, I HEARD GRANDMA saying her goodbyes to the tourists and then the front door opening and closing. I also heard her turn the deadbolt. The distinct click echoed in the foyer and down the long hall. I glanced at the clock on the microwave. It was only two o'clock; it wasn't like her to close the house early. Still, her footsteps came quickly towards me.

"I finished up as fast as I could," she said. "I'll pour some iced tea. Tell me what you've been up to."

I went over the ins and outs of the information I had gathered that morning. I relayed each of the conversations that led me to believe that Daniel Duvall and the residents at Pioneer RV Park were in the clear. I told her I felt more sure than ever that the solution to the case hinged on whatever Barbara knew about the blackmail letter.

"But how, Chloe? It seems so far-fetched." I could see her point, but thankfully, in the process of reciting everything aloud to her, I formed a hazy theory.

After a deep breath, I said, "This is probably going to sound crazy, but here's what I think happened. Someone at city hall overheard Barbara Duvall's call to Blake. Whoever it was knew that the necklace she found was vitally important, and they wanted to keep it where it's been for fourteen years... buried. I think that person went to Barbara's house to retrieve the necklace. Somehow, before it was all over, Barbara ended up dead. It makes sense too, because remember the shiny object I saw in the pool? That could have been it!"

Grandma Lily had her eyes narrowed in thought. "Hmmm, how would someone get to the RV park and leave again without anyone seeing them? You told me everyone was outside listening to that man ranting about the broken change machine."

I shrugged and said, "I haven't figured that part out yet." I twirled a piece of my hair for a moment. "But whoever it is, he's also worried that there might be clues in Christy's diary. So, he broke in to find it."

Grandma Lily didn't look convinced.

I raised my hands in concession. "I know, I know, there are a lot of 'what ifs' and 'maybes' involved, but it's the only thing that makes sense. No one else in Barbara's life had the motive and means to take her out of the picture."

"You're sure it wasn't her criminal son?" Grandma said, raising her eyebrows.

I said, "I'm sure. He's got an airtight alibi for Friday night. Plus, he's gone straight. He's a successful artist now."

Grandma Lily sighed. "If it's true that Barbara was murdered because she'd discovered the truth about Christy's death, it means there's a long-standing secret being kept by some pretty powerful people. We're traipsing around in a minefield, Chloe."

"I know." Fear bubbled up in my belly. I figured Grandma was feeling the same way. She was probably gearing up to convince me to stop meddling and tell Chief Garner everything—to let him handle it. It would be sound advice.

But she surprised me. "Well, then," she said, "we're going to have to work extra fast. What are my instructions for the Poison Pen Book Club meeting?"

I smiled. *How I loved this woman.*

"Okay," I said, "We need to find out if any of them remember anything about secrets or scandals surrounding Mayor Luna. If we find out what he was involved in, we might learn who was blackmailing him."

Grandma Lily nodded while gently tapping her bottom lip with her index finger. "And let's see if they remember Governor Finney having ties to Jericho Falls. That photograph of her with Mayor Luna has to mean something."

"Right. Then I'll get the status of the police investigation from Chief Garner and see if he's still convinced Barbara's death was an accident." I rolled my eyes.

"Tread lightly, dear." Grandma looked over the top of her glasses at me. I knew she meant to be cautious when asking about this case, but also not to mess things up with the chief again.

"Believe me, I *will.*"

We were interrupted by the sound of the hand-turn doorbell. Grandma jumped up while checking her watch. "I should open back up. I might get one more tour in for the day. Maybe that's a customer now."

She scurried down the long hallway. I took a moment for some cuddles and love from the animals. In times of stress, some furry nuzzles always made me feel better.

Even though Elliot wasn't usually one for being held, I forced him into my arms and squeezed him close. I knew from experience that he'd tolerate this for just a moment, and *only* if I didn't turn him onto his back to rock him like a baby. While cats in general don't enjoy being on their backs, Elliot, in particular, detests being treated inferior in any way. The one time I'd tried the baby-kitty routine with him, it ended in a howl, a hiss, and a deep, jagged scratch on my forearm.

So today, I simply held Elliot upright and scratched the place he liked the best underneath his right ear. I spoke in normal, adult tones and told him he was a good, wise kitty. He let out a short meow, letting me know he agreed and was ready to be set down. He trotted off to the corner and quickly began washing off any traces of my hugs.

Jed, on the other hand, loved to be babied. I sat down on the kitchen floor beside him. He immediately rolled over onto his back for a belly rub. His pink tongue fell out on one side of his mouth while he panted joyfully. I scratched his chest and told him what a big boy he was turning out to be. That's when I tuned into Grandma Lily's conversation going on in the foyer. She wasn't talking with a potential home tourist. She was talking with Bree. I gave Jed's ears a final ruffle and went to see them.

I heard Bree ask, "Oh, Lily. What should I do?"

"I say get back on the horse, dear," my grandma said with gusto.

They both looked my way. "What's up?" I asked.

Grandma Lily turned fully towards me, her face hidden from Bree. She made her eyes as big as silver dollars as she spoke. "It seems that the new opera house manager has invited Bree out to dinner." Grandma's face changed to a look of confusion as she glanced back at Bree. "What did you say his name is again, dear?"

Oh, my word. This was laying it on thick, even for Lily Martin.

"Stan," Bree said obediently, playing right into Grandma Lily's ruse. "What do you think, Chloe? Should I say yes?"

"I think you should accept as long as *you* really want to. Don't let Stan, or anyone else," I cleared my throat, "influence your decision." I glanced at Grandma. She was smiling sweetly.

Usually bubbly and bright, Bree's affect seemed flat and rather dull.

"What's bothering you?" I asked.

Bree blew air up through her blond bangs, then she lifted and dropped her shoulders with a pouty frown. "I don't want to have my heart broken again."

There it was. Complete and utter honesty. That's something we could always count on with Bree. Sure, you might have to cut through a hefty dose of optimism and bouncy enthusiasm, but when it really counted, she revealed the truth with the innocence of a child. I envied this about her. While I, in the aftermath of pain, used skepticism and stand-offishness as a defense, Bree fell face first into utter despair for everyone to witness. With her heart on her sleeve, she let the people of Jericho Falls shore her up, like she needed them to, until she healed. Bree didn't want to get hurt again. I knew exactly how she felt.

Grandma Lily guided Bree into the parlour. They took a seat on the couch and I went to the wingback chair nearby. "Bree, dear," Grandma began, "I'm sure the idea of dating again is scary. But you are in the prime of your life. There's no reason not to at least make a new friend. No one says that this has to be serious."

Bree looked at me for my opinion, her eyes filled with worry.

"Grandma's right, Bree. Just think of this as making a new friend. You're great at that."

Grandma Lily nodded. "And Stan could use a friend. He hardly knows anyone in town yet."

A wry smile twitched at the edge of Bree's lips. "I would have fun showing him around. I mean, I know absolutely *everyone*."

"You do," I agreed.

Bree bounced into a standing position. "Alright, I'll tell Stan I'll go out with him. But to lunch, not dinner. That's more *friendly*. Maybe I'll suggest The Vintage Grill."

Grandma Lily and Bree chitter chatted about their favorite menu items at Jeannie's restaurant. But the mere mention of her name made my mind wander back to the diary and wonder about her reason for stealing it. Did I dare press Jeannie any more on the topic? She might know something to help me figure out who had blackmailed Mayor Luna. That's when I got the idea.

"Bree," I said, interrupting them, "do you think you could get some information from Jeannie while you're at lunch?"

She tilted her head to the side. "Sure! What do you need me to ask?"

A variety of things went through my head...*Why'd you lie to Chloe? What did those pages of the diary really say? Who else have you told about Christy's stuff?* I wanted answers to all of these questions from Jeannie, and sooner or later, I'd get them. For now, though, I had to be strategic.

"Ask Jeannie if she has an alibi for the evening Barbara Duvall died."

26

So Sorry

GRANDMA LILY AND BREE gasped in unison, then cried, "What?"

I shook my head with a shrug. "Jeannie is tied up in Christy's story just as much as Blake and I are. She was at the falls that day, too. Then she stole and vandalized the diary. Plus, Jeannie doesn't want Eric knowing about any of this. We have to consider the possibility that she's the one who has something to hide. That she paid a visit to Barbara to keep her quiet."

Grandma Lily's eyes brightened. "And maybe she's been the one who's been lurking around and broke in. If she dressed up like a man..."

Bree wasn't buying it. "Wait a minute girls, are you actually saying that Jeannie Smythe is a killer?"

I sighed. "Probably not. But she could be involved. Ask where she was on Friday night and get her reaction. Her face will give her away if she's got a guilty conscience."

Bree swallowed hard. "But what do I say, exactly?"

"Catch her off guard," I suggested. "Chat like you normally would...order your food. Then, nonchalantly add, *Hold the nightshade*."

Bree's mouth gaped open. Her eyes bulged in disbelief.

"You can do it, dear," Grandma Lily told her. "Remember to watch for Jeannie's response. Then, after a moment, just giggle. Trust me, she'll take the opportunity to get away from you and you can play it off as a little joke with Sam."

Bree looked quickly at my grandma and frowned, "It's *Stan*."

"Oh yeah," said Grandma Lily, swiping her hand in front of her, "silly me."

The little liar.

We role played with Bree a few times to help her feel more comfortable with her mission. In the end, we came up with a less abrasive, but equally surprising, way to pose the question to Jeannie. I hoped her reaction would prove one way or the other whether she was involved in all this.

With Bree prepared, she bounced out the front door. She really seemed excited about the prospect of a casual date with Stan Duncan—even if it was going to include a little sleuthing on the side.

Next, it was time for Grandma Lily and me to go over our plan one more time. "I'll send you a text when the book clubbers have left, and the coast is clear," she told me. "In case you want to invite the chief over."

I sighed, "We'll see. He's been so upset with me lately."

"Rightfully so, I'm afraid."

Ouch.

But Grandma was right. I had handled things poorly.

Grandma went on, "You must remember, dear, that Lance Garner is still in a lot of pain. Oh sure, he's the tough guy around town—everybody's hero whenever we need one. But inside? I'm not sure he's ever truly dealt with losing Rachel. Our hero could use a little help."

A sensation like a flame flickering to life fluttered in my chest... a realization. It was really no wonder that Garner and I found each other easy to talk to, or felt so comfortable with one another. We were the same. Wounded, but stoic. Hurting, but hiding it by coming to everyone else's aid.

I suddenly felt exhausted.

"Do I have time for a nap?" I asked.

Grandma Lily flicked a look at her wristwatch. "Of course, it's only three o'clock." She shooed me up to my old bedroom, with Jed following closely behind. When I reached the second-story landing, I turned, sensing that she was watching me.

"What?"

Grandma's eyes looked sad. "I'm so sorry about Christy," she said. "I'm still so sorry that things turned out this way."

MY OUTFIT FOR MY DOG park meet-up with Chief Garner consisted of a comfy pair of old jeans and a long-sleeved t-shirt I sometimes wore when cleaning the mansion. I was going for buddies, no pressure. But as we drew closer to the park, Jed barking happily from the bed of my truck when he guessed our destination, I looked down at myself and felt rather messy. I hoped I looked 'care free' and not that I 'didn't care'. At the bottom of Gold Mountain, I slowed to a stop. I undid the long braid I'd worn all day and shook out my golden brown tresses, now in perfect waves. I wound the band back around my hair to make a ponytail. I flipped down my visor mirror and pulled thin tendrils out in front of each ear, just the way I liked. There. At least my hair looked nice.

The Jericho Falls Dog Park had been constructed and dedicated a few years before. It had been an empty lot since the 1970s, after an original building burned down. In pioneer days, fire could mean the ruin of an entire town. Thankfully, the blaze had been caught early and did not spread to any of the adjoining structures. But the empty space was unsightly, like a missing tooth in an otherwise healthy mouth.

A dog park was the perfect solution. It only required fencing on each end, as the buildings on each side provided boundaries there. An awning was erected on one side of the yard for shade, and benches were added here and there. Town volunteers took turns scooping doo-doo, buying new toys, and mowing the lawn. The result was a perfect off-leash area for local and visiting pooches alike.

When I arrived, I parked behind Garner's SUV at the curb. I knew when I opened the spring-loaded gate he'd be inside, probably tossing a tennis ball for Mandy and looking attractively relaxed. I was correct. He was mid-throw when Jed and I went through the creaky gate. The evening sun caught his blond hair and his heather gray t-shirt gave me a pleasant view of his tan, muscular arms. I gave myself one more quick reminder to *think before speaking, Chloe.*

"Hi," Garner turned to greet us. He gave me a huge smile that made my heart go pitter-pat.

I waved and returned a grin, then went in his direction with Jed, doing his excited galloping/jumping routine. When it was time to unhook Jed from his leash, Garner came to my aid. He pet Jed's head and shoulders, to hold him steady. As I went to unhook the clasp to set Jed free, I looked into Garner's eyes.

"I'm glad Jed invited Mandy out," he said.

"Me too."

More pitter-pattering.

But apparently, with Jed yanking and pulling towards Mandy, I hadn't been successful at unhooking him. I let go of the leash and saw it fall to the ground between my feet. Then I watched Jed sprint away, noticing for one surprised second that he was taking the leash with him. The tail of it whipped and twirled around my ankle, jerking me off balance. I stumbled and my right foot sunk into a deep, dog-dug hole. The next thing I knew, I was going over backward. The dusky evening sky came into view as I tumbled and I came to a jarring stop flat on my derriere...in a dense pile of dog poo.

I sat there on the ground, completely frozen with my arms in a 'don't shoot' position, trying to comprehend what had just happened. In his defense, Garner tried not to laugh. He went through a series of facial expressions certainly meant to hold in laughter. Finally, it was too much. He threw his head back, put a hand to his stomach, and roared.

After the initial shock wore off, I giggled too. Our theatrics interested the dogs, and I now had one on each ear, sniffing and nuzzling me as if to say, "What are you doing down here, Chloe? You wanna play too?"

Garner eventually gained enough composure to help me up. He took my hand and pulled me to my feet. A strong whiff of doggy doo filled the air. "And there we have it," Garner said with a smirk. "I have been wondering where the real Chloe Martin's been."

"What's that supposed to mean?" I asked, continuing to hold my arms away from my sides, feeling as if my whole body was somehow contaminated.

"You haven't had any silly accidents lately, that's all," Garner explained. "I was worried that you'd become graceful and composed." Another burst of laughter.

"Hey," I frowned.

"Ahh," he said kindly, pulling me into a side hug, "I like your clumsiness."

I turned my face in his direction and raised my eyes to meet his. "Thanks. I think?" I let out another laugh, shaking my head and chalking up yet another cringeworthy episode with this guy.

As he let go of our hug, Garner turned me around to inspect the damage. "Lucky for you, that pile had been there awhile. Dry as a bone. Nothing stuck."

"Well, thank goodness for small blessings," I said with a sigh.

"Did you get hurt?" he asked.

I shook my head no. "Only my pride... what's left of it, anyway."

Garner looked to the ground and kicked at a tuft of grass. "About that," he began, "your grandma explained why Blake called you the other day. Lily and her schemes, right?"

I gulped. "You know my grandma."

"So, as I was saying yesterday, Chloe, I never meant to hurt you by keeping Rachel a secret."

"I know," I blurted.

He looked up, "You do?"

"You didn't want to talk about her. Not with me, or anyone. I've felt the same way about Christy all these years. But being back in Jericho Falls has *forced* me to think about my friend and everything that happened. It's been..." I couldn't find the right words.

"Challenging?" Garner suggested.

"Yeah, of course it's been hard. But it was also exactly what I needed. I've been stuck, Garner. Stuck at age sixteen filled with grief and guilt." A moment went by without either of us saying a word. "And sometimes I guess I still *act* like a sixteen-year-old." I raised my eyebrows and smiled sheepishly at him.

This made him chuckle again and kick at a new spot in the grass. "Nothing has forced me to deal with losing Rachel. Until now."

"Wait, I'm not forcing you to do anything."

"But it's like you said," he spoke in almost a whisper, "I'm stuck."

When Garner looked at me, his eyes were filled with savage sadness. I wanted to rush to him and hug him tight. To tell him everything was going to be all right. *Should I?* I almost took the first step in his direction when I heard the creak of the gate opening behind us.

27

Cautiously Optimistic

"CHIEF!" A CHEERFUL voice called out. "So nice to see you. And Miss Martin, how are you this fine evening?"

It was Mr. Cooper, the grocery market owner, with his two portly pugs. Our retrievers trotted over, tails and tongues wagging to greet them. The two little dogs waddled off with the big ones to play.

Mr. Cooper was shaped a lot like his pets with a ring of salt-and-pepper hair around an otherwise shiny, bald head. He looked strange to me without his usual calf-length white apron he wore at his store every day. Mr. Cooper chatted with us about the weather, the upcoming summer rush, and the recent variety show. I congratulated him on his excellent juggling skills I'd heard about through Grandma Lily. Then, the conversation turned to Barbara Duvall.

"What a horrific accident," said Mr. Cooper gravely.

I started to correct him, but Chief Garner beat me to it. "Yes, it was," he said. "We'll certainly miss Barbara."

I grit my teeth. *Apparently Garner's accident theory was going strong.*

When Mr. Cooper attempted to get more details, the chief tactfully explained that he couldn't discuss an ongoing investigation. "Well, can you tell me what will happen to the RV park now that she's gone?" Mr. Cooper asked. "I like to stock my shelves a little heavy when I know the campers will be arriving. The extra sales are sure nice. If the place shuts down..."

Garner was already shaking his head. "I don't think you have anything to worry about, Mr. Cooper. The Duvalls have a son."

"He'll take the park over, then?" asked the shop owner.

Again, I went to speak, but Garner interrupted. "Quite possibly," he said.

Mr. Cooper seemed relieved, so I hesitated to burst his bubble by relaying the drama I heard from Lottie and then Daniel. In fact, I was hesitant to share *anything* in front of the grocer. Instead, I opted to let the two guys finish their chat while I went to play with the dogs.

I tossed a well-loved tennis ball, and they all tore off to get it. The pugs waddled quickly, trying to keep up with Mandy and Jed, but they were no match for the retrievers. I found a nice seat on a park bench and called the panting pugs over to me. I pet them while continuing to throw the ball for Jed and Mandy. Every pup was happy.

It wasn't long before Mr. Cooper used the shovel provided by the park to clean up after his dogs (a nicety I felt especially thankful for after my fall earlier) and said good evening to us.

"Sorry about that," Garner said, walking my way. "Whenever I'm looking for some time off, that always happens."

"I understand," I told him. "It's your job."

"Yeah, but sometimes I wish I could get away from it all, just for an evening, at least. You know?"

I guessed it must be hard for him to live in a small town where, even when off duty, everyone knew him as "the chief." Heck, that's what we all called him. As if it were his first name.

I went to stand near him. "Well, while you're on the topic, mind if I ask you something about Barbara's case, too?"

He gave me a side glance with a look of suspicion. "What?"

"What was at the bottom of the pool?" I asked.

He let out a slight huff and pinched the bridge of his nose. "Don't ask."

"What does that mean?"

"Officer Meyers swears he bagged and tagged a necklace, but it disappeared somewhere along the way."

"You *lost* evidence?" Immediately, I realized the harshness in my tone. *Think before speaking, Chloe.* "I mean, it disappeared?"

He tightened his lips and nodded microscopically. Clearly, he wasn't proud of this. "But," he explained, "in talking with Meyers, we're assuming it was the necklace Barbara had been wearing when she went into the pool. We're asking the family to corroborate that with photos of her wearing it."

They weren't going to find any photos of Barbara Duvall with the necklace. She hadn't been *wearing* it. She'd been *protecting* it. A heavy weight of disappointment settled onto me. Without the necklace, would we ever find out what happened to Barbara and learn what the blackmailer really meant?

Mandy dropped the now slobbery tennis ball at Garner's feet. He bent to pick it up and threw it for her.

"Anyway, like I told Cooper, I shouldn't be talking about the case," he said.

"At least tell me this. Are you really still convinced it was an accident?"

He held my gaze for a long moment, then narrowed his eyes in mild frustration. "You need to trust me," he said. "I know what I'm doing."

"I just can't believe it. You saw her wrist and the bump on her head. You saw the photos I took—the chair was tipped over and there were two wine glasses. Which reminds me, why don't you have your *own* pictures?"

"We do have crime scene photos. I wanted yours too, for comparison."

"Comparison of what?"

Garner pressed his lips together again and shook his head. He came closer and softly took my shoulders. Looking at me with his cool green eyes, he said, "Leave the investigation to me. It's my job, remember?"

I would have been infuriated by his dismissive tone if he didn't smell so darn good. I started to say something else, but Garner shut his eyes lightly and shook his head. I rolled my eyes in obedience—for the moment.

This time, it was Jed who dropped the ball near us. Garner and I took turns throwing it a few more times. Finally, the dogs slowed down, getting worn out. Mandy went over to lie in front of the water dish, a paw on either side. She lapped at it until it was almost dry. Jed helped her finish it.

We cleaned up after the hounds, returning the toys they'd spread out to the laundry basket left for that purpose. Garner refilled the water dish while I easily put each dog on their leash. They were a lot less rambunctious than an hour before.

My time with Garner was winding down. I knew that any moment he was going to thank me for the visit and say goodbye. And, while this had been the most successful interaction we'd had in a week—it felt unfinished somehow. Was there still something I wanted to discuss with him about Rachel? Barbara? Probably both.

"Want to walk them along the river?" I asked him.

"Sure, I don't have anywhere to be."

Main Street was quiet. Only a few cars were left parked along the street. We easily crossed the road to Riverside Park and walked along listening to the jingle of the dogs' tags against their leads. This was something I enjoyed about spending time with Garner. He felt comfortable with silence.

The greenbelt was such a beautiful stretch of the Jericho River. It ran slowly here, with both large boulders and smaller rocks situated perfectly by mother nature to create scenic ripples, waves, and beautiful sounds. It was mesmerizing in its serenity.

"I love it here," Garner said as if reading my thoughts.

"I do too."

"I don't just mean *here* by the river, I mean Jericho Falls in general. Sure, I wish I could be a little more anonymous sometimes. But if it hadn't been for this town—these people—I'm not sure what would have happened to me."

A pang of jealousy surprised me. "I'm envious of you," I admitted.

The chief stopped walking and turned to look at me. "Why?"

"I didn't get their help after Christy's death. To be honest though, that was my fault." It felt good admitting this. "No one banished me or drove me away from here, as I liked to pretend. I went away and stayed away on my own accord."

"We all make bad choices when we're hurting," Garner admitted. "For instance, I have this really great friend and I kept a painful part of my past a secret from her for almost a *year*—just so I wouldn't have to face talking about it."

"Did she forgive you?" I asked.

"I don't know yet, but I'm cautiously optimistic." He tilted his head to one side.

I smiled, feeling tingly. We walked again in peaceful silence. It wasn't long until we reached the end of the pathway and arrived at the Jericho Falls Opera House parking lot. The lights were on, and there were a few cars in the gravel lot.

"Grandma says they're having extra rehearsals to get ready for their big spring show," I told Garner.

"I'll buy us tickets," Garner said, as naturally as could be.

We turned a wide circle and began slowly making our way back to where we started. The lampposts in the park blinked to life. Their soft glow attracted a few night bugs. Everything made for a perfect spring night.

Once through the park, we again jaywalked across quiet Main Street and loaded the dogs into their respective vehicles. Jed immediately laid down with a groan. He was satisfied and tuckered out.

"Tonight was great," Garner told me, standing beside my red truck with me.

I nodded. "It was."

An awkward moment followed. *Was he going to hug me? I definitely didn't want him to feel obligated. Should I just say toodaloo and skedaddle?* Thankfully, the chief spoke before I did something dumb like punch him in the shoulder or give him a high-five.

"Listen, you mentioned those photos earlier," he said.

"Yeah?"

"If you haven't already, please delete them from your phone. I should have instructed you to do that right away. They're evidence that shouldn't be in the hands of a civilian."

I cocked my head to the side and raised one eyebrow, trying to look cute. "Do I have to?"

Except Garner was officially back in cop mode. He didn't find this funny. "Either that or I'll confiscate the device."

I threw my hands up in surrender. "Okay, okay, I get it. I'll erase them."

"Good. Thanks."

With that, he stepped towards his SUV. "See you soon," he smiled and waved while opening his driver-side door.

I did the same while thinking, *I'll erase those photos all right, but not until I have another good look at them.*

28

Intricate Pieces

AS I PULLED THE DOOR of the truck closed, my cell phone rang. I flipped it over and found the screen displaying BLAKE WHITE. Thank goodness for better timing tonight. If Blake had phoned again while I was with Garner, that would have done it. I would have to give up, ride out into the sunset, conceding that Garner and I simply weren't meant to be.

I swiped my phone's screen to answer. "How's it going?" I asked.

"I'm freaking out! Did you find anything else because we're running out of time."

"Actually, I'm only one day into my 48-hour deadline," I reminded him.

He replied with an audible sigh.

"It's fine, Blake. I met with the chief tonight."

"Did you tell him about the letter?"

"No, I didn't *tell* him."

"Why not?"

"Because I don't want him to sweep our sketchy theory under his it-was-just-an-accident rug. He still believes Barbara accidentally fell in and drowned. He just keeps saying to *trust him* because this is his job. It's so infuriating!"

"And most likely true," Blake said. "He's the top cop, Chloe, with years of experience."

"24. More. Hours," I said gruffly before hitting the button and ending our call. I stared at my phone's dark screen. I worried about what Blake would do if he found out the necklace was missing. The longer I kept it a secret from him, the better.

I COULDN'T WAIT TO get home to find out how the Poison Pen Book Club went. There were still guests' cars in the circle drive when I got home, so I went alongside the mansion to park in front of the garage. Jed yawned at me over the tailgate and then gave a big stretch after hopping out of the truck.

I patted his head. "That's my good boy. You were a terrific wingman tonight. You deserve a good night's rest and a fancy dog treat tomorrow." He trotted through the gate and into the backyard with a wag of his tail.

Once inside, I tossed my keys onto the kitchen counter and listened to the sounds of the house. Where were Grandma and the others? I didn't hear any voices.

"Hellooo," I called, going down the wide hallway to peek in each room. I found them all in the parlour, huddled together in chairs near the fireplace. The group did not have its typical casual, friendly feel. They seemed pensive, worried even.

Grandma looked up with a start when she realized I had entered the room. "Oh, thank goodness," she said. "Come here dear, you can help us."

As I drew nearer to them, I finally understood what their concern was about. An intricate jigsaw puzzle made up of miniscule animal-shaped pieces was spread out on the table before them. They hunched over it in deep thought.

"Eureka!" called Dr. Dunning. "I found one."

"Oh my gosh," I sighed, "I thought you were poring over some juicy bit of evidence or something."

Grandma Lily didn't look up from the puzzle but said, "Silly girl, we made a plan to tackle your problem in nothing flat. So, since we were all together, we decided to have a little fun."

"Can I hear your plan?" I asked.

Grandma Lily finally tore herself away from the addictive puzzle, poured me a cup of tea from the nearby tea cart, and told me to take a seat on the couch.

I shook my head. "Better not. I took a spill at the dog park and fell into it. Literally."

Grandma made a gruesome face while handing me the teacup. I sipped as she explained. "Leonard will look through the government archives at Lakeview Community College for information on how Mayor Luna and Governor Finney were acquainted."

Dr. Dunning nodded in agreement. "He may have served on a state committee or something. If so, I'll find out."

Grandma went on, "Anna is going to learn about the specific effects of Cut-throat Nightshade when mixed with alcohol, and find out if Barbara was taking any medications that may have furthered a reaction. It's a long shot. Everything's so protected these days. But if anyone can get the details from the pharmacist, it's Anna."

"How?" I asked. Anna Dunning was about the least charming person I knew.

"Womanly wiles, Chloe," Anna said, with perfectly erect posture and mildly flared nostrils.

I flashed a 'what the heck?' look at my grandma. "Anna and the pharmacist? Isn't he married?" I whispered.

Anna heard me. She turned sharply; her black, blunt-cut hair framing the perturbed look on her face. "Innocent flirtations when one's getting her thyroid medication filled do not constitute infidelity, Chloe. Felix and I go way back."

"High school sweethearts," Grandma said under her breath with a wink.

Bree clapped her hands quickly. "Yay! I found one!" She jumped up from the table and came bounding my way for a high-five. We slapped hands with a crack before she pranced back and began searching once again.

"Anyway, you're familiar with Bree's mission at The Vintage Grill," Grandma noted. "That just leaves Karen and myself." A dramatic silence hung between us, and a look of delightful anticipation played on her lips.

"Are you going to tell me?" I asked.

"You won't believe it! Bree has Mrs. Brown from the RV Park scheduled for a hair appointment tomorrow morning."

My eyes felt like they might pop right out of my head. "You're kidding me."

Bree looked my way from across the room. "Nope! It's an amazingly happy accident," she cried.

"But what's *not* an accident is our plan," Grandma Lily explained. "Karen and I will be in the waiting area as if we have upcoming appointments. That way, we can all have a friendly little chat and see what Mrs. Brown can tell us about the happenings at Pioneer RV Park."

I was lost for words. They'd made a genius plan together.

"You're the best!" I said, shaking my head in disbelief. "I don't deserve friends like you."

All at once, the entire group's attention was averted from the puzzle. One by one, they looked at me with identical, quizzical looks. Dr. Dunning spoke up, "Whatever do you mean by *deserve*? Friendship isn't about deservedness. It's about..." he paused, searching for just the right word. "It's about love, Chloe. We love you and want to lend our assistance."

I wasn't prepared for the tears that sprang to my eyes. It must have been the relief of having made things better with Garner mixed with the support of these fine people, because I was taken over by a rush of thankfulness. For once, I didn't hold my emotions in, either. I wiped a tear from my cheek and simply said, "I love you guys, too."

Grandma Lily squeezed me lightly around the shoulders, looking at my face sweetly. "We're all in this together, dear. Tomorrow afternoon, we'll meet back here to go over what we've found. Now, we need to get this puzzle finished or I'm bound to stay up too late. Again." She giggled and went back to join the others.

I watched them, sitting together having such a good time. It was simply amazing having a real circle of friends again. And at that moment, I truly believed that with each of our missions in place, we would put all the intricate pieces together and discover what really happened to poor Barbara Duvall.

29

Stop Pretending

IT RAINED ALL NIGHT long. At first, I found the sound soothing. Memories of lying in the same bedroom as a kid, in the same wrought-iron bedstead, listening to a storm, made me smile. But after an hour or two, the raindrops on my window and the wind in the trees gnawed at me. I buried my head under the pillows to escape the dripping and blowing. When I finally slept, I had an eerie dream.

*Garner stood on the far side of the Jericho River; the dogs, Mandy and Jed, were at his side. With a terrible urgency, he beckoned me to come across. His face was filled with distress as he made 'come on' movements with his arm. I searched frantically, but there was no bridge to be seen and the river raged between us. I felt confused—how did Garner expect me to get to him? Suddenly, his eyes widened as he saw something coming up from behind me. I spun to look...*that's when I awoke.

AT BREAKFAST, GRANDMA Lily informed me that the handyman would be by again later to fix my apartment door and install a security system around the property. I pumped my fist in celebration of winning this ongoing debate between us. Grandma Lily rolled her eyes.

"I still think it's an unnecessary expense," she said, "and what if I can't work the darn thing?"

"It's going to be easy," I reassured her. "We can probably put an app on our phones."

Grandma made a sorrowful-looking face at me. "Not long ago, I didn't even bother locking the front door of Jericho House. I'm disappointed that things have come to this. It reminds me of that mishap last Christmas, with the car break-in at the Lakeview Mall."

"Jericho Falls is still a safe place, Grandma. But with visitors coming in and out of our house, a few cameras and an alarm are good ideas."

A sinking feeling came over me. If we'd had cameras last summer, maybe that sneaky Jeannie Smythe wouldn't have attempted to steal Christy's diary. Then, it would still have all of its pages and I'd know everything the book had to tell me. I clenched my jaw, thinking about her.

"What is it, Chloe?"

I shook my head, not wanting to bother Grandma with this again. "It's nothing." I got up from the kitchen island quickly to distract both of us from my rumination. "Except that Jed and Elliot think they're starving to death."

I went to the pantry to get their food. Elliot meowed melodramatically when I didn't fill his bowl clear to the rim. He sat beside it and narrowed his yellow eyes at me. "All right, all right," I told him while adding another dash of cat food.

Jed was already three quarters of the way through his bowl of kibble by this time. I stroked his back while he ate and urged him to go slower.

"What time are you going to the salon?" I asked Grandma Lily.

"Eleven," she said. "Mrs. Brown's appointment begins at 10:45, so we'll give her some time to get settled in with Bree. I'll arrive and then Karen will coincidentally show up a few minutes after." Grandma gestured quote marks around the word coincidentally and gig-gled. *Had I created a monster?* She seemed to love this kind of stuff. First her clandestine match-making, now 'Lilian Martin Girl Detective.' *Geesh.*

"Remember to be nonchalant," I instructed her. "Bree does a great job of getting people to talk while she works. You can mostly just listen, interject a question now and then—but not too often."

Grandma waved a hand at me. "Chloe, dear, stop worrying. Mrs. Brown's not going to suspect a thing from two old gals like Karen and me. Speaking of today's plan, what are you up to?"

"Loose ends," I said thoughtfully.

"All right, that's enough. What's going on?" asked Grandma Lily. "You're making the same broody face as a few minutes ago when you purposely changed the subject."

I rolled my eyes at her. "I can't get away with anything around you, can I?"

"Nope. Now spill it."

"It's the diary. I'm so miffed that Jeannie ruined it and now I'll never know what else it had to say."

"If I remember correctly, Jeannie denied taking those pages," Grandma said sharply.

I gave her a skeptical look. "And we're going to believe that thief?"

Grandma turned her palms to the ceiling. "Try it on for size. Assume everything she told you the other night is God's honest truth and see where it takes you."

I groaned, still completely irked at my so-called friend. "I'll try."

Grandma did a quick sweep of the kitchen while I tidied up our breakfast dishes. Then she was off on her daily walk. The rain had finally stopped, but Grandma carried her umbrella in one hand just in case. I called Jed to follow me upstairs for what was hopefully going to be my last morning shower in Jericho House for a while. I was looking forward to having my apartment back in safe, working order by that evening.

When I went back downstairs, Elliot paced the hallway and me-owed loudly over and over. The hair on the back of Jed's neck rose as he sniffed around the front door. They seemed to be trying to tell me something. *Oh no,* I thought, *the handyman probably arrived.* I hoped he hadn't left when no one answered the door.

I checked the front porch, but when I didn't find him, I hurried down the driveway towards the garage and backyard. There I found the jeans and flannel-clad handyman unrolling a line of black cable and whistling to himself. "Oh, thank goodness you're here. I was afraid you took off when I didn't answer the door," I said.

"Oh, I didn't bother to knock," he said. "I have lots to do out here first. I told Lily I'd finish up inside whenever she returns from her walk."

"You're sure you didn't knock?"

He looked at me, puzzled. "Not me."

I had goosebumps on my arms when I went back inside. *Had someone been prowling around again, upsetting the animals?*

I went back in to sooth Elliot with a few pets and pats (and a tuna flavored num-num). His hair smoothed back to its usual black gleam and he finally purred a bit when I scratched behind his ears.

"Are you going to be all right now?" I asked him. He nuzzled my fingertips and gave one yowl in response.

GRANDMA'S SUGGESTION to take Jeannie at her word made me think. If Jeannie really was telling the truth about not taking pages from the diary, then who had? I was going to have to inspect the source, the diary itself, and hope that it lent me a clue.

I went to retrieve the box from my favorite third floor hiding spot. As I climbed the stairs with Jed, I got a little anxious. A lot was riding on today's findings—my own and those of my Poison Pen friends. If we couldn't put the pieces together today, I'd have to keep my promise to Blake and hand over everything to Chief Garner. Then, it would be a matter of praying that he took us seriously. In my head, I heard him say, *Chloe, I'm the professional here. Believe me, I know what I'm doing.*

I switched on the flashlight of my cell phone to light my way from the second to the third floor. True, there was a light switch at the top of the flight for the ballroom space once I got there. But here on the dark cherry wood steps, only the light from a small octagon window at the turn of the stairs lit my way. Jed didn't follow me on this last set of steps. He never would go up there with me—something about the third floor bothered him. Instead, he obediently curled up and waited for me at the bottom of the stairs.

The ornate brass doorknob felt cool in my hand as I turned it to open the double doors and enter the ballroom. I walked across the space where Grandma now stored various boxes of holiday decorations and family heirlooms. In the center of the room, there was a fireplace on one wall with a built-in buffet cabinet, including the dumbwaiter.

In the old days, the servants used this mini-elevator to send delicacies up from the kitchen for service at the festivities, and then sent the dirty dishes back down for clean up. Unfortunately, the dumbwaiter was now defunct, since its counter-weight system had fallen into disrepair. My father assured me this had nothing to do with him and his friends playing hide-and-seek in it, trying to hoist one another from floor to floor when he was young.

When I was a kid, I feared the dark staircase, but loved being in the ballroom imagining what the lavish parties hosted by my ancestors must have been like. Even now, I enjoyed looking around the vast room, knowing that many of the Jericho Falls' founding families spent time here socializing. But I could save these reminiscent thoughts for another day.

I lifted the door of the dumbwaiter and reached inside for the shoebox full of Christy's belongings. Once in hand, I tucked it under my arm and headed downstairs for another reading of the now infamous diary.

After a brief stop in the kitchen to warm my coffee, I landed on the couch in the parlour. I tucked my knees up under me and sat the shoe box on my lap. I placed a hand over the knee of my jeans where my scar was. I didn't remember getting the gash on my leg that led to this large, jagged scar I now bore. But somehow, during my panicked search for Christy, I'd become injured. This raised flesh on my knee was my permanent reminder of that day. "Help me understand," I whispered. I wasn't sure who I was talking to. God? Christy, maybe? Whoever was listening, I hoped they heard my pleas.

The diary was nestled in between the old friendship bracelets, the red sunglasses, and the CDs. I lifted it out, setting the box beside me. With a deep breath, I opened the book directly to the spot where the pages had been removed. If I read what the diary contained right before and right after, it might give me a hint about what was missing.

I read Christy's cursive writing in bubble-gum pink ink:

Dear Diary,

School was miserable today. I wish Chloe went to my school with me. Then, it wouldn't matter that the popular girls seem to hate me. Chloe would have my back.

I'm so glad the year is almost over so I can hang out with Chloe and my REAL friends. When summer comes, we won't have to pretend anymore.

Why had the popular girls turned on her? And what did she mean by 'pretend'? Those were her last words before the missing pages began. I guessed four or five pages had been torn out complete-ly from the book's spine.

The next page was written in purple pen and dated April 5th:

Dear Diary,

I'm almost certain my dweeby little sister has found my hiding place and is trying to read this. If I'm right, I'll have to make some changes. She's such a blabbermouth.

The girls at school are still being super mean to me, but it will be over soon.

Then the next day:

Dear Diary,

Ellie said she didn't read my diary, but I don't trust her. I'm going to make sure there's nothing good for her to find here, just in case.

I felt a tingle at the nape of my neck. How, exactly, could Christy "make sure" there was nothing for Ellie to find? Would she have tak-en pages out in order to hide them? I gulped. Maybe Jeannie was telling the truth—and Christy ripped the missing pages out herself.

Another close reading of the book would be wise, but I didn't have time today. I flipped rapidly through the pages, watching Christy's rounded handwriting flit by in various colors. When I reached the back, those mysterious numbers scrawled on the end pa-per caught my eye again. There were three sets of double digits—or was it two sets of triple digits written in columns? I wasn't sure. It could either be 11, 22, 68 stacked up, or 126 beside 128. I rolled my eyes at myself, hoping I wasn't putting way too much thought into a teen-age girl's math notes, or where she scribbled down her locker combo so she wouldn't forget it.

A combination.

My heartbeat picked up speed as a childhood memory resur-faced... a little red safe with a spinning combination lock on the front. Christy and I used to play with it when we were girls. We'd pretend that it was the safe in an old west bank just like the one in downtown Jericho Falls. When we got older, I recalled the red safe being pushed underneath Christy's bed—dusty, unused, and forgotten. I remembered the combo too, 11, 22, 68. Christy told me I'd never forget it if I thought of the cheer, 'two, four, six, eight who do we appreciate', because 1 plus 1 is 2, and 2 plus two is 4 and then, 6-8. *Did Christy hide the pages from her diary there?*

I laid the little book on the couch and began pacing the hallway. My footsteps reverberated through the massive emptiness of the house. This woke Jed from the rug in the parlour, so he fell in step behind me. We walked single file to the front door, did an about face, went down to the kitchen, turned around, and did the whole thing over again. Suddenly, Elliot appeared in the parlour doorway. He didn't join the parade. Instead, he stared at us, looking peeved. He yawned, showing his white, sharp teeth and then walked away with a swish of his elegant black tail.

But since Jed seemed interested, I decided I might as well talk it out with him. "I suppose it's possible," I said as we walked, "that Christy tore the pages out of her own diary in order to hide them from her pesky sister, Ellie. And she probably wouldn't want to destroy them if they meant something to her."

I turned around to look at Jed, who was still following me closely. His big, soft eyes looked concerned. I clicked my tongue. "I know. It's nothing more than a shot in the dark."

I thought in silence for a few steps, then halted. Jed's nose jabbed into the back of my leg. "Oh no," I said, realizing what I must do. "Jed, I have to go ask Ellie Porter what happened to that little red safe."

Jed whined.

"My thoughts exactly."

30

Painful Memories

AFTER MORE PACING TO make a plan of attack, I went out the back door with my trusty BFF, Jed, to see if Officer Ellie Porter was on duty at the police station. I sure hoped so. She was less likely to:

A) chew me out

B) knock my block off

or C) arrest me for no good reason, in the presence of her fellow officers.

When I made it outside, the handyman and Grandma Lily stood together in the backyard chatting. He seemed to be explaining the best places for exterior security cameras. She listened intently, hands on her hips. Neither of them noticed me as I passed through the yard for the driveway.

But dang. When I got there, I realized Grandma Lily had parked her Subaru behind my truck. Rather than play the vehicle shuffle, I simply went inside, traded my keys for hers, and went back out. I waved to her with her gigantic jangly mess of souvenir key chains. She got the picture—I was taking her car into town.

Unfortunately, this meant Jed was staying behind. Grandma hated it when he put nose prints all over her car windows. Jed literally frowned when I shut him inside the gate. "I'll be back soon, boy, and we'll take a walk or something. I promise."

Down Gold Mountain, I drove in a mild mental fog. I knew this feeling. It meant I had seen or heard something over the past few days that would help me unravel this whole thing, only I hadn't caught on to it yet. It was like trying to remember someone's name, having it on the tip of your tongue, but not being able to spit it out.

I parked along the curb at Jericho Falls City Hall, locked the car, and did my best to fit Grandma's outrageous key chain into the front pocket of my jeans. Several blingy pieces spilled out over the front and it created a weird bulge. Better here though, than in my back pocket—giving brand new meaning to the term junk-in-the-trunk.

I jogged up the front steps and opened the door to find Missy Bray at the reception desk once again.

"Hi," I said cheerfully, "how are you today, Missy?"

She held her lips in a tight, fake grin. "You again? Here to play another trick on me?"

I raised my eyebrows and shrugged.

Her eyes contracted into tiny slits. "There was no emergency."

"There sort of was," I said.

"There's no such thing as a *sort of* emergency. I'm ashamed of myself, too. I've had this job way too long to be duped by hysterical patrons like you."

"I wasn't hysterical," I defended. "I was just...really worried."

Missy sat staring at me, blinking slowly. "Anyway," she said, "what can I do for you *today*?"

I took a deep breath and pasted on a new smile. "I was hoping to speak with Officer Porter."

Missy rolled her eyes, but took up the receiver of her phone, pressed one of the myriad of buttons on her large phone panel, and spoke sweetly, "This is reception. I have someone who'd like to speak with Ellie."

Missy paused, her eyes cast down as she apparently waited for Ellie Porter to come to the phone. "Yes," she said, "it's Chloe Martin."

Shoot. I was hoping Missy didn't remember my name. And I definitely hadn't wanted her to spout it off to Ellie, who might easily refuse to see me considering our contentious relationship. But then Missy's eyes met mine and I could tell that Ellie had agreed. Within seconds Missy said, "Okay, I'll tell her to wait."

Missy asked me to take a seat in one of the jury style arm-chairs lining one wall. Officer Porter would be right with me. Missy busied herself with typing, dashing off information on post-it notes, and generally pretending I didn't exist.

Sooner than expected, I heard footsteps coming down the hall towards me. I stood to ready myself for this exchange. When I saw Ellie, it surprised me that her ashy-blond, curly hair was free from its usual low ponytail. She seemed younger somehow, like the little girl who used to love bothering Christy and me.

"Hi," I said, speaking first, "could we talk? Somewhere private?"

Ellie's brow furrowed briefly. "What for?"

"I'll explain everything." I glanced at Missy, who was likely eaves-dropping. I lowered my voice to a whisper. "If we can talk alone."

Ellie continued to look at me with suspicion, but motioned to me indicating I should follow her. We went down the long corridor. A heaviness fell over me as we approached the wooden double doors marked JF POLICE DEPARTMENT in swirling painted script. This is where I had been questioned after Christy fell and died at the falls. I willed myself to keep composed, to breathe deeply and ward off an anxiety attack.

When we went in, I clearly remembered this expansive room where each officer had a desk designated to them. Today, Officer Meyers sat at one, completing paperwork. He glanced up and gave me a quizzical smile. To our left was the chief's office, surrounded by a wall of windows so he could keep watch over his staff. He hunched over his desk, apparently reading something.

Ellie noticed me studying him. "He's busy."

I shrugged. "That's okay, I came to talk to you."

"Uh, huh," she said, rolling her eyes.

Ellie led me to the other side of the room where two separate doors were marked INTERROGATION. I swallowed, rubbing my palms on the front of my jeans. *Relax, today you're the one asking the questions,* I told myself silently.

Ellie closed the door behind us and we took chairs across from one another at a table that was bolted to the floor. "So," she said, "what's up?"

I drew in a long breath before I began, "This is going to sound weird, but do you remember the little red safe Christy had when we were kids?"

At first Ellie frowned, but then she sniffed a laugh and broke into a sad smile. "Oh yeah, we used to play old-west bank. It always ended with a robbery—one of us wearing a bandana around our face as the bandit."

I nodded quickly. "Yes, you remember."

"What about it?" she said, going serious again.

"Do you know where it is now? I'm feeling a little sentimental and hope to see it again." *Sentimental about a toy safe? I was treading on some very thin ice.*

Ellie shook her head. "I think Mom finally cleaned out Christy's room last year. I don't know what she did with her stuff, though."

Gulp. Some of it was at Jericho House right now.

According to Chief Garner, Ellie didn't communicate with her mother anymore. After Christy's death, the family crumbled. Their parents eventually divorced. Their father declined into fatal alcoholism and their mother became nothing more than a depressed hermit. I understood on some level why Ellie would resent her mother for this. Still, estrangement only added another layer to an already tragic family saga.

"Did you want any of it?" I asked Ellie. "Chrisy's things, I mean?"

She twitched one shoulder and tried to seem uninterested. "It's not a big deal. I hardly remember her."

I knew that was a lie. Ellie was almost eight years old when her older sister died. Plus, she'd just relayed a vivid story of them playing together. No, Ellie was simply using a skill I had perfected myself—pretending like she didn't care as a defense mechanism.

I had a choice to make. I could either leave Ellie in the dark about what was going on and visit her mother to see if the safe still existed. Or I could let Ellie in on some of it and ask for her help. Maybe, if I brought her in on this, she'd face some of the feelings she was obviously hiding from.

It was probably only a few seconds, but deliberating between the two options seemed to take me forever. Mostly because I really didn't like Ellie. She had been Christy's bratty little sister when we were young, and then pivotal in pointing the finger at Grandma Lily for Art's murder last summer. Did I really *want* to help her? I touched the thick scar on my knee through my pant leg. Christy would want me to. She'd want her little sister to move on, not stay trapped by painful memories and regrets.

"Ellie, I need to tell you something," I said. "Your mom sent me some of Christy's things last summer."

Her face stayed unreadable, but the feisty young police officer reached into her pocket and took out a rubber band. She said nothing as she pulled her curly tresses into a tight, low ponytail. This reminded me of how Garner would suddenly go into cop-mode sometimes.

I went on, "I'd be happy to share some items with you—if you're interested."

"I don't see my mom much anymore," she mumbled. "What did she give you?"

I told her about the odds and ends that her mother mailed to me, naming off all that I could think of. But I skipped mentioning the diary, for now.

Ellie seemed confused. "So, what made you think about the red safe?"

I bit at my bottom lip, trying to think up a good excuse.

Suddenly, there was a knock on the door. It opened up before either Ellie or I could respond. Chief Garner stood there gripping the doorknob, his jaw set tight.

"What's going on in here, Porter?" he barked. "Explain to me why you've detained this witness. Now!"

Ellie immediately told the chief that *I* was the one to call this meeting—she wasn't questioning me. So it was up to me to tap dance my way out of this. But how? I couldn't tell Chief Garner what I was really up to.

"Ellie's telling the truth. I came here to talk to her about old times," I said. "I've been reminiscing a lot about Christy lately." *Not a lie, at least.*

Garner glared first at Ellie, then at me. He was thinking, and it didn't look like he was buying my easy excuse. After all, he knew that Ellie Porter and I were far from chummy. But, after another suspicious look around the room, he let it go. He instructed Ellie to show me to the front door. Before we left the room, he issued me a warning, "We'll discuss this later, Chloe."

As Ellie and I made our way back to the reception area, with only the sound of our footsteps on the shiny tile floor, I restrained a smile. Garner had come to my rescue. Again.

I was wondering how to get in touch with Christy's mom to discuss the whereabouts of the safe when Ellie surprised me. "Listen, I'll call my mom later to ask about the little lockbox."

I nodded in appreciation. "You will? Thanks. Thanks a lot."

She waved goodbye before disappearing back down the hallway. I stood there in the lobby, a bit dazed at how well this had gone. *Were Ellie and I calling a truce?* And was the excuse to contact her mom about the red toy safe enough to get the two of them on speaking terms again?

Well, shucks. I just might solve a mystery and reunite a family before this is over.

31

Wasting Time

WHEN I GOT INTO THE car, I remembered I owed Jed that swanky dog treat for his help the night before. Maybe he wouldn't be as mad at me for leaving him at home today if I returned bearing a gift.

I eased out of my parking spot and went down Main Street to Blue Bonnet Bakery. This den of delicacies was just one block south of Bree's salon and owned by Jill Owens, who'd loaned me a pair of strappy heels for the Founder's Day Ball last year.

The building was originally a hardware store. In fact, it remained one through the 1950s. But the '60s and '70s were a time of decline in Jericho Falls and the store eventually closed. The final death throes of the mining boom were over by that time, and the notion of becoming a tourist town hadn't yet begun. The town nearly dried up completely. The few residents that remained got by with only the bank (still in the original building), a gas station on the outskirts of town, one saloon, and one church. Residents drove to nearby Lakeview for groceries and other shopping needs. Even the legendary Jericho Falls Opera House fell vacant and in disrepair.

By the 1980s, Americans became interested in preserving and commemorating old mining towns. Funding poured in and businesses began opening up again. Sure, most of them were geared toward tourists; refurbished hotels, gift shops toting themed souvenirs, museums filled with antique mining items, and the like. But the town also expanded with shops like the hair salon, Sarsaparilla Sally's Candy and Soda Shop, and Jill's wonderful bakery. A few more saloons popped up, too.

I pushed open the robin egg blue door to Blue Bonnet Bakery and breathed in the scent of sugary goodness. Glass fronted counters displayed Jill's handiwork; brightly frosted sugar cookies, chocolate cupcakes with tall twisted spires of icing, and loaves of beautiful artisan breads. To one side was a smaller cabinet filled with tasty treats for patrons of the canine variety.

"Well, hi, Chloe," Jill said from her large worktable in the center of the room. "What can I help you with? Not dress shoes today, I'm guessing," she said with a laugh.

I made a frightened face and shook my head dramatically. My days of strappy, painful heels were over. From now on, if an outfit requires anything but Converse tennies, I won't be wearing it. "Thankfully, no. I promised the big guy a special treat."

"I'll be right there," she said, moving toward her stainless steel sink to wash up.

I studied the glass shelves displaying dog bone-shaped cookies in several colors. There were also mini 'pupcakes' topped with paw print decorations, and cellophane packages of training treats that looked like chocolate chips.

"It might not seem like it, but everything in this case is 100% pet-friendly," Jill said. "What would Jed like best?"

I chose a peanut butter flavored cookie for him to eat when I got home, and one of the pupcakes to give him after dinner.

"I heard you were there when they found Barbara Duvall," Jill said while bagging up Jed's goodies.

"I was. How did you hear?"

"Bree told me. She stopped in with Marilyn yesterday. Was it awful?"

I cast my eyes down, remembering the pallor of Barbara's skin, her ripped stockings, the shiny object at the bottom of the pool—probably the vital clue, now missing. "Yes," I finally said in response, "it was."

Jill rang up my purchase. As a bonus, she threw in a sampler bag of broken cookies. She said Elliot would probably even like the salmon-flavored ones.

On my way back up the block, I spied Grandma Lily entering Bree's Beauty Salon. I could have sworn she noticed me too, but like any good sleuth on a secret mission, she kept an innocent, nondescript expression on her face as I passed by.

JED STOOD AT THE BACK gate, wagging, as I entered the driveway. He gave his usual one big bark. "I have a surprise for you!" I sang, going into the backyard. He spun a full circle in excitement.

I reached into the white paper bag and asked Jed to sit. He obeyed, so I showed him the special cookie and tossed it to him. He barely chewed. Still, he seemed to enjoy it. "Thanks for breaking the ice with Garner last night, boy." I stroked his soft head gently and gazed into his dark eyes. "You were great, as usual."

Inside on the kitchen counter, I found our invoice from the handyman. He'd detailed his work, listed the total for his services, and left us two shiny new keys to my apartment. There was also a brand-new electronic keypad on the wall near the back door, right below the line of hooks where we hung our car keys. He'd left a note with operating instructions.

I couldn't wait to see the result of my repaired door and move back into my cozy space. I'd barely spent any time out there since that intense talk with Chief Garner over lemonade. I shivered, thankful that we'd gotten past our argument. Thinking of Garner also reminded me I'd never deleted the photos of Barbara Duvall's kitchen as he asked me to. I'd never studied them again, either.

I took my phone out and leaned back against the kitchen counter. *What did Garner mean by 'comparing' my pictures with his?* I snapped my photos first. Did he suspect something had changed by the time the police photos were taken?

I scanned the images of Barbara's table, the half bottle of wine, the flowers which I now knew were trouble with a capital 'T', her slippers stashed in the corner, the tipped-over chair. None of these things could have possibly changed on their own. If Garner's photos differed from mine, someone must have gone in there and disturbed things before the techs got to it. *The killer? An accomplice?*

I let out a huff and began deleting each image. I'd gathered all I could from the photos. Without knowing what the chief was looking for, all this guessing meant nothing. I was only wasting valuable time.

I was about to go upstairs and gather my things to move back into the apartment when I heard Grandma Lily at the front door. I glanced up at the clock on the wall. It was only twenty after eleven. *What's she doing back so soon?* As I went down the hall, I could hear her muttering to herself. She was upset.

"Hey," I said, "how'd it go at Bree's, with Mrs. Brown?"

Grandma Lily looked at me and frowned. "She was a no-show. I should have known not to open my umbrella in the house this morning. It was a little damp, so I set it out to dry on the rug. Now look at what's happened."

I laughed. "I'm sure this has nothing to do with your umbrella superstitions, Grandma. Something probably came up for Mrs. Brown."

Grandma Lily rolled her eyes, peeved. "If you say so. But anyway, Karen and I didn't find out anything to help you. I'm sorry."

"It's all right," I assured her. "We still have Bree on her lunchtime mission at The Vintage Grill, Dr. Dunning scouring the college archives, and Anna working her *womanly wiles*." I added air-quotes and made a funny face for effect. This, at least, got a smile out of Grandma.

I suggested we make some lunch and take it easy before our friends arrived later to fill us in on their discoveries. And so, we were just cleaning up the kitchen from our tomato soup and grilled cheese sandwiches when there was a brief knock on the front door. It was Dr. Leonard Dunning.

"You're here earlier than expected," Grandma Lily said.

The history professor gave us a sad smile. "I'm afraid I don't have much to share with you."

Grandma herded us into the library. We each took a seat so Dr. Dunning could continue. "I can't find any record of Mayor Luna serving on state committees or the like. In fact, I didn't find proof that he and Governor Finney were connected at all."

Grandma looked at me. "Perhaps only socially?"

I nodded. "Maybe so."

Dr. Dunning went on, "I checked the human resources files too—at least what is available in public record. There's nothing to suggest the Governor was ever suspected of wrongdoing. She seems clean as a whistle."

I bit at my bottom lip. "Well, thanks. You did what you could."

Dr. Dunning removed his wire-framed glasses to clean the lenses. "I only wish it were more."

"I'll make us some..." before Grandma could get the word 'tea' out, there was another knock at the door. This time, Bree stood in the doorway looking defeated.

Grandma tilted her head in sympathy. "Dr. Dunning and I struck out...don't tell me you did too."

Bree dragged herself into the library and plopped onto the brocade fainting couch with a pout. "Jeannie had the day off."

"I told you Chloe, it was the umbrella," said Grandma Lily.

"Oh, for crying out loud!" I griped.

This made Bree start to cry. I hurried to her side and put my arm around her. "I'm not mad at you Bree, it's just that our entire plan has been a bust and Grandma keeps blaming it on a stupid umbrella."

She sniffed and looked into my eyes. "That's not all."

"What is it, dear?" Grandma Lily landed on the other side of Bree, patting her knee.

"I'm not Stan's type," Bree sniveled.

"Oh, I'm sure that's not true," said Grandma. "Why else would he ask you out?"

I looked at Grandma Lily over the top of Bree's bowed head and sent her a brief glare.

"It *is* true," Bree went on. "He was thrilled that I knew everyone in town because... because... he's hoping I'll put in a good word for him with Nick Newsom."

"Ohhh," said Dr. Dunning, nodding with realization.

"Oh!" said Grandma Lily.

"And that's okay," I said quickly to Bree. I squeezed her tight. "Like we told you, today was all about making a new friend."

Bree sniffed again. Grandma Lily handed her a tissue, and I noticed her cheeks had grown a little pinker than usual. I hoped my Grandma felt embarrassed after putting Bree and Stan through this mismatched matchmaking.

"You're right," Bree tried on a smile, "and he *is* a great guy. I think we'll make super friends. He even asked me to help with hair and makeup for the play they're rehearsing. I missed auditions, but maybe next time."

I smiled at her. "See, that sounds like fun."

We were interrupted by another knock at the door. "That must be Anna," Grandma Lily remarked as she went to answer.

She was right. Anna Dunning stood straight as a stick at the front door. A box-shaped black handbag hung on her elbow. She looked unhappy. But that meant nothing. Anna always looked mildly perturbed.

Grandma welcomed her inside, and we caught Anna up on our lack of progress. She rolled her eyes, made a tsk-tsk noise with her tongue, and said, "Well, at least one of us understood the importance of their assignment." She opened her purse and withdrew a piece of notepaper. She reviewed it and explained, "Barbara Duvall has been taking a prescription SSRI for depression since the death of her husband. SSRI stands for Selective Serotonin Reuptake Inhibitor." She looked down her nose at the rest of us.

"And?" I said.

"SSRIs are known to cause drowsiness in some people. Combined with wine and Cut-leaf Nightshade, Barbara would have likely been extremely impaired."

"Which is why she couldn't save herself from drowning," Grandma Lily surmised.

"And why she'd be easy to push in," I added.

Dr. Dunning and Bree cringed in unison.

"That's not all," Anna continued. "I also learned something regarding Jeannie Smythe. Lily tells me she may be involved..." Anna looked at me, letting her words trail away.

"It's possible," I said.

"Felix writes his voice messages on a pad he keeps by his phone. When I saw Jeannie's name, it caught my eye. It seems Jeannie called on Sunday evening requesting a refill on her anxiety medication. Something must be bothering her."

"Sunday was when I dropped in at the restaurant to see Jeannie," I explained. "Felix must have been who she called after I left and watched her through the window. She'd searched for something in her purse before making the call. She must have looked for her medication and when she didn't find it, she called him. So much for my suspicion that she phoned a partner in crime."

We exchanged concerned looks.

"Anyway, thank you, Anna," I said after a moment. "I really appreciate your help."

"We all do," said Grandma Lily.

Anna didn't reply, only gave us a curt nod. The group mingled for a bit longer. But the letdown of the day weighed on us all. There were no takers when Grandma offered to make tea. Instead, the Poison Pen Book Club members noted the date of their next regular meeting and took their leave.

THAT EVENING, I FELT like I could use a dose of SSRI. My time was effectively up and I didn't have enough to go on; not to make a solid case with the PD, anyway. I didn't have the pages of the diary; I didn't know if Jeannie was involved, and the necklace was missing. I spent the evening pouting, moping, and pacing. I even turned off my cell phone, hoping to avoid a call from Blake with pressure to go to the police.

Around eight o'clock, I came downstairs with my duffle bag packed. I went into the parlour to find Grandma reading in front of the fireplace.

"And where do you think you're off to?" she asked, her glasses slid almost to the tip of her nose.

"I'm moving back to the apartment. It's all fixed now and the security system is in place."

"I don't think so." Grandma closed her book and set it on the arm of her chair. "You're not going anywhere until we settle this whole mess. I'd be worried sick about you."

I let the duffle bag thump down onto the dark hardwood floor. If I was honest with myself, staying alone out there with the burglar still at-large made me uneasy, too. Rather than admit my fear, I'd let Grandma's worry be my excuse for remaining in the main house.

"All right, if you say so."

32

Like a Locomotive

THE HAND-TURN DOORBELL made its familiar 'brrring.' *Who could that be at this hour?* My bare feet were silent against the wood floor on my way to the front door. I switched on the porch light. There stood Ellie Porter. I unlocked the door and pulled it open, now only the screen door dividing us. She wore joggers and a hoodie.

"Uh, hi," she said with a sheepish grin. "Sorry to bother you so late, but I wanted to bring you this."

That's when I noticed Ellie was holding the small red safe under one arm. She held it out in front of her now. I pulled the door open wide and asked her to come inside. She handed the safe to me on her way past. It was funny how little it seemed now that I was older. No bigger than a toaster, really. Sizes of rooms, streets, and apparently toys always seemed bigger in my memory. I set it on the hall table and worked to contain my excitement. *I had the safe!*

"Again, sorry to drop by so late," Ellie repeated. "I stayed at my mom's place longer than I expected."

"That's great," I said.

Ellie's face softened. "Yeah. Anyway, that's all yours if you want it," she said, motioning toward the locked box.

"Any idea if there's anything inside?" I asked her. What I really meant was, *did you empty it before you brought it over?*

Ellie only shrugged, "No idea. I doubt anyone remembers the combo anymore."

I felt a sharp pang. I wished for just a moment that Ellie Porter wasn't a cop. Because I wanted more than anything to reveal to Christy's kid-sister that *I did* remember the combo. Then, I wanted to invite her into the library and have her watch while I opened it up and see her face when we read through the missing pages of her sister's diary. I wanted to include her. However, that wasn't possible. Because Ellie *was* a cop and that meant I couldn't let her in on this... not yet.

I gave her a half-smile. "You're probably right. Thanks for bringing it over, anyway."

"You bet," she said. Her expression told me she wanted to say more. I stayed quiet, giving her the chance. "Maybe sometime we can look through Christy's things—the stuff my mom gave you," Ellie finally said. There was a catch in her throat.

I nodded. "Of course, I'd like that. But... darn it, it's upstairs and Grandma Lily is sleeping." This was a lie. The shoe box had been in the parlour since I went through the diary again. But now was not the time for a walk down memory lane with Ellie. I was dying to be alone with that little red safe.

"Some other time then," Ellie said, awkwardly reaching out to me for a handshake. And so Ellie Porter and I 'shook on it' before saying goodnight. Whether we were simply agreeing to meet again to look through keepsakes or if that handshake meant more, I wasn't sure. Either way, I locked up Jericho House for the night, feeling hopeful about our future.

My feelings about Ellie were not the top priority at the moment, though. I rushed to the table, nabbed the toy safe and ran to the kitchen where I placed it on the center island. Then I padded back to the parlour for the notorious shoe box and back to the kitchen. All this rushing around convinced Jed that I wanted to play. He juked and jived ahead of me, then made a dash for Elliot, who promptly dove underneath the island for safety.

"Shhh, Jed," I whisper-yelled, "Grandma is sleeping." That much I'd told Ellie wasn't a lie. Jed thwacked the cupboard repeatedly with his big tail and 'grinned' at me. "Seriously, stop the drumming." Finally, when I took a seat on an upholstered bar stool, he laid down with a "harrumph".

I arranged the safe and the shoe box on the counter in front of me, just staring at both of them for a moment. *Was this it? Was I about to find what the missing pages of Christy's diary had to say?*

I turned the little dial of the safe first one way and then the other, testing it. It still turned well. That was a good sign. I repeated the rhyme to myself, *two, four, six, eight,* then rotated the knob accordingly. 11-22-68... the small lock made an audible click and when I let go, the door popped open a bit. I swallowed hard before pulling it open the rest of the way.

A heaviness filled my chest when I saw what was inside.

There were no diary pages. I had been all wrong. This failure was enough to bring tears to my eyes. *I thought this would explain everything.* I tilted my face toward the ceiling and scrunched my eyes shut. *Now what?*

However, even though the diary pages weren't inside. The safe wasn't empty. There was a piece of lined notebook paper inside, folded in the complex way I remembered doing as a young teen. The last fold tucked back inside so the whole thing made a little origami-like packet.

I carefully unfolded it. Never could I have expected what I was about to find. It was a pencil drawing of a heart. Inside the heart was the familiar message, *B+C4ever.*

My heart banged in my chest. I turned the paper over, inspecting every inch for something else, some explanation. But other than the sketch of what ended up on that tree in the field, there was nothing more. One thing was certain. Christy didn't want anyone to see this—she'd hidden it away in a very safe place. So, if *she* was the "C" mentioned in the carving...

My hands shook so badly I could hardly manage my phone. I switched it on and waited an excruciatingly long time for it to come to life. I fumbled around, having to try several times and correct multiple typos, but I finally managed to send a text to Blake.

I attached the photo of the carving on the tree I'd taken along with the message:

ME: Care to explain?

While I waited for Blake's response, I paced around and around the kitchen island, stepping over my sleeping golden retriever on each lap. I took slow breaths through my nose and exhaled even more slowly through my mouth. Even so, my heart still pounded like a locomotive.

BLAKE: Explain what? Where'd you find that?

I tried to type a response, but found my shaky fingers too difficult to control. Instead, I pressed the call button.

"Chloe, it's almost midnight. What's this all about?" Blake sounded groggy.

"Were you seeing Christy?"

"What? No! Wait...*what?*"

"You saw the initials in that photo. So I'm asking you one more time. Were you dating Christy while I was away in Idaho?" I kept my voice quiet, so I didn't wake Grandma, but I knew my fury and suspicion showed through.

"Absolutely not. Wait. Is this the carving on the tree you asked me about last summer? At the Founder's Day Ball?"

"Yeah."

"I told you then. I didn't carve that. Not for us, and certainly not for Christy."

"Then who did?"

"What makes you think it has anything to do with her? A lot of people's names start with C. Plus, that could be a guy's initial for all you know."

"Trust me. I have proof."

Blake's end of the call went silent. I wasn't sure if he was busy thinking or if we'd been cut off. Finally, I heard him breathing. "Maybe it was Brian," he whispered.

"Brian Simmons? As in *Jeannie's* boyfriend back then?"

"Yeah," Blake said.

I heard rustling noises, like he was holding his phone between his shoulder and chin while moving around.

He said, "I'm getting dressed. I'll be right over."

The line went dead.

Blake couldn't possibly be serious. Jeannie and Brian were tight; they'd been a couple since eighth grade or something. Brian wouldn't two-time her with Christy. And then there was the fact that Christy was way too nice of a person to be "the other woman". Right? And yet, when I considered Christy's diary entries, there was the issue of the popular girls suddenly being mean to her. Beautiful and exotic-looking Jeannie was most definitely in the popular sect; head cheerleader, homecoming queen, you name it.

Was this really possible?

33

By Heart

WHILE I WAITED FOR Blake's arrival, I lifted the lid from the shoe box yet again to find the diary. I scanned the pages as quickly as I could, searching for names Christy might have mentioned—specifically Brian or Jeannie. I found no mention of either of them. In fact, the only names written in the diary were mine, Christy's, and Mr. White (for Blake). She referred to her 'mom' and 'dad' and her 'little sister' preceded by a variety of adjectives such as 'dweeby,' 'dorky,' and 'dumb'.

An odd teacher's name popped up once in a while. Oh, and her gerbil, Geraldine, showed up quite a bit. Good old Geraldine was Christy's faithful companion until the spring of that fateful year. Christy woke up one morning to find the poor little thing dead in her cage. On April seventh, she wrote in the diary:

Dear Diary,

Geraldine the Gerbil died last night. I'm so glad I gave her a carrot and played with her before bedtime. I'm sad, but we'll bury her in our special spot later today, so I'll always know where she is.

In previous readings, I always assumed the "we" Christy referred to was her family. I figured they had a spot in their backyard or the local hills where family pets were traditionally laid to rest. But maybe it wasn't her family Christy was talking about. *Who was this we, and what special spot?*

A quiet rapping on the backdoor startled me away from these questions. Jed lifted his head and cocked it to one side, letting out a low growl. "It's all right, boy," I told him. In an odd moment of déjà vu, I ventured to the back porch, lifted the white cafe curtains to make sure it was Blake, and opened up.

Just as before, he looked rumpled and a little scared.

"You didn't need to rush over here..." I started.

Blake interrupted me. "There's something I need to tell you, Chloe."

I motioned towards the kitchen. We took the same spots we sat in when we'd gone over the message from Barbara Duvall and the blackmail letter. Blake popped each of his knuckles, then ran a hand over his head.

"What is it?" I asked. His nerves were catching.

He spoke, keeping his eyes cast down. "I haven't thought about this for years. Heck, I barely thought anything about it at the time. Anyway, this happened right before school let out the year Christy died. I was half-way home after track practice when I realized I'd left my homework in the locker room. When I went back inside the school, I heard voices in the main hallway. I wouldn't have noticed or cared, but... well, it sounded like a guy was bugging a girl. Harassing her maybe."

Blake looked away from his hands and into my eyes. "You know what I mean?"

I nodded. "You thought she might need help."

"Yeah, so I went to see. When I got there, it was Brian and Christy."

"Was he hurting her?" A flare of anger shot through me.

Blake screwed his mouth to one side apologetically. "Not exactly. I misread the sounds. They were up against the lockers kissing, laughing—just horsing around."

I sat back in disbelief. "Are you sure?" This seemed impossible. Christy had never said a word to me about being involved with anyone, let alone Jeannie's steady boyfriend.

"I'm positive, Chloe. They didn't notice me, so I left and I never told a soul."

"Oh, my gosh." I thought I might be sick. Not because my friend had kept this secret crush hidden from me. Not even because I thought she was a complete jerk for seeing Brian behind Jeannie's back. I was feeling sick because I suddenly knew that 'b.s.' in that threatening letter to Mayor Luna didn't mean bogus or fake. It stood for Brian Simmons.

And this must have been what Barbara Duvall discovered the day she died. It was the reason she told Blake that the letter didn't mean what they thought. Whoever wrote the blackmail letter wanted Brian Simmons' statement about Christy's accident to go away. Which meant Brian probably knew what really happened to Christy that day at the falls.

My face must have displayed the range of emotions I was going through. Disgust, realization, worry, interest. Blake stared at me, waiting to see what I would say.

"B.S." I said, looking at him pointedly. "Brian Simmons."

Blake's eyes widened as the pieces fell into place for him as well.

"Where's the blackmail letter?" I asked.

"It's locked away. Why?"

"Because knowing this, I want to read it. Can you get to it?"

"No need. I know that thing by heart...I've read it so many times."

Blake recited the letter to me.

Mayor Luna,

It's up to you to make sure the b.s. interview about the drowning girl gets thrown out. Otherwise, I'll make sure everyone learns the truth about you. Do whatever it takes.

I sat with my eyes closed for a moment, letting the words of the letter sink in.

When I opened them, Blake looked confused. "But we were all interviewed. What could Brian have said that was so important?"

"He could have made a confession."

"Oh, Chloe. No."

I shrugged. "Obviously, whatever he said was harmful to him or someone close to him. Otherwise, it wouldn't have mattered."

Blake shook his head, still struggling with the idea. "And apparently, whatever the blackmailer knew about Mayor Luna was bad enough to get him to comply."

"Yep. And to find a scapegoat," I said. "Me."

We shared a long look, remembering the horror of my being accused of fighting with my best friend at the top of the waterfall and causing her to fall to her death. Blake's testimony was key—but now it made sense why his parents pressured him into telling that trumped-up story. The mayor himself was working to sell it. The Whites were still snakes in my book for playing along, but maybe even *they* had been pawns.

"This ran deep," I whispered.

Blake let out a long breath. "What do we do now, Chloe?"

I held up one finger, asking him to give me a minute, and started my laps around the kitchen again. I had to think. I needed to get this legacy of secrets straightened out once and for all. I went back to that day in my mind—the day we all went to the falls together. It should have been a fun-filled summer escape, but it all went wrong. *When had it spun out of control?*

In the past, I would have said that things went awry when Christy realized I'd forgotten to bring a swimsuit for her. She lost her temper and started a fight with me that we were never able to finish. She ridiculed me for spending too much time with Blake—for ignoring her all summer. It always felt like her anger about a forgotten bikini was unreasonable and uncharacteristic of her. *What if she was actually angry about something else and simply took it out on me?*

"Do you remember whose idea it was to invite Brian and Jeannie to the falls that day?" I asked Blake.

"Not sure. I remember you, me, and Anthony went with Christy to convince her mom to let her go."

"And then we stopped at Jeannie's house to invite them along when we saw Brian's truck in the driveway."

Blake nodded. "Yeah, it was a spur-of-the-moment kind of thing, right?"

After another lap, I said, "I think Christy became angry when we found them together."

Blake's eyes searched the room as he tried this theory on for size. "That could have been why she went berserk in the parking lot and ran off from everyone."

I was already leafing through the diary to find the passage I wanted to show Blake. When I spotted it, I read aloud:

I'm so glad the year is almost over so I can hang out with Chloe and my REAL friends. When summer comes, we won't have to pretend anymore.

"Do you think Christy expected Brian to break up with Jeannie when school let out? To be with her?" Blake asked.

"Yes. But, then Christy found the two of them together that day..." A whispery kind of memory floated through my mind. That person in the woods after Anthony and Blake had gone back down the pathway, hoping to find Christy safely in the parking lot. I waited at the top, wondering if she was hiding from me—still angry. That's when I thought I saw someone running through the trees. At the time, I didn't trust myself because I was so worried, so filled with fear.

I thought I must be imagining things. But maybe I hadn't imagined it. Maybe someone else *was* up there. Brian? Jeannie?

"But come on, Chloe, could this really have anything to do with why Barbara Duvall died?" asked Blake, drawing me away from my memories.

"It's too coincidental not to. Think about it, Blake. Barbara discovered what b.s. really meant and was involved in a fatal accident mere hours later."

"That's just it," Blake said. I could tell he was getting exasperated with me. "Brian Simmons is nowhere around anymore. Last I heard, he was living it up in Florida. How would he know, and why would he *care*, what Barbara Duvall found out?"

I had theorized about this before. "I think someone at city hall tipped him off," I said, decidedly. "Who could it be, Blake? Who's been there long enough to know about Christy's case and Mayor Luna's situation?"

Blake began shaking his head before I even got my words out. "Stop, Chloe. Do you realize how crazy you sound? An inside informant in sleepy Jericho Falls City Hall?"

He had a point. My theories were spinning off in all sorts of wild directions. I had RV park dwellers, old flames, and city politics tied up in a crazy knot. If only I could find the end of the thread, to tease it loose.

When I didn't reply, Blake went on. "Listen, it's time we talk to Chief Garner. I'll admit, there is a possibility that something Barbara uncovered may have upset the status quo. But if so, it's *way* out of our league. We need to let law enforcement in on this."

"No," I cried, "please, I just need a little more time."

"I've waited long enough, Chloe. As Jericho Falls Mayor, I can't stand by and let you hide evidence any longer. It might cost me everything!"

I hung my head. *How could I convince Blake that we should keep working on this? What would persuade him?* Ego. That's what. I raised my face to look directly at him. "Or you could be the town hero."

"What?"

"If we succeed, you could be the one remembered for solving the case. Not the Jericho Falls Police Department. The mayor himself."

A twinkle glimmered in Blake's eye. I had him. That dreamy look of his vanished quickly, though. He frowned, trying to appear tough. "Okay. We'll work on this one more day. But that's it. If we're still lost by tomorrow evening, I'm calling Chief Garner."

I agreed. I felt sure that one more day would do it. We were so close, after all. But soon I learned that it wouldn't be fast enough.

34

In One Go

BLAKE AND I AGREED to meet early the next morning to begin working on our final push for the truth. He offered to stay the night again, so we could start right away in the morning. But I had visions of Garner going in for the early shift and happening to find Blake's car in our driveway before dawn. He'd certainly (and understandably) get the wrong idea and I'd be right back in the doghouse with him.

"No, go home, Blake. Let's both try to get a little sleep. We're going to need it."

He went out through the back and I locked up. Who was I fooling? There was very little chance that I would get any rest. Instead, I started a pot of coffee and laid out the evidence I had at my disposal. To represent the blackmail letter, I scrawled the gist of it on a stickynote and included it with everything else.

Before me lay the diary, the sketch of the tree carving, the faux blackmail letter along with my list of clues and theories I'd been keeping for almost a week now. I moved them around the kitchen island like chess pieces, hoping that rearranging them would make something click in my mind.

The coffee maker gurgled the last bit of water into the pot, signaling me to get my favorite mug filled. I sipped, I paced, I looked at the counter-full of information. Mostly, I thought.

What exactly did I *need*? I needed to understand what the cover up was all about, or at least who was behind it. Certainly, all those years ago an adult, not one of us teenagers, wrote the letter to Mayor Luna. Brian Simmons' mother or father, maybe? But now, the most likely culprit for continuing the concealment was Brian himself. If Brian still worried about his testimony coming out, and went to the great lengths of harming Barbara Duvall to keep her quiet, he was probably our burglar too. If he'd gotten wind that I had the diary, he'd be very interested in knowing what Christy had written about him.

Time to make a new list—this time a *to-do* list.

-Ask Jeannie if she told Brian that I have the diary. If not? Who?

-Find those darned missing pages.

What else... I thought. I took a few sips of coffee, but wasn't really in the mood for it. I laid my head down on one arm... I'd rest, just for a second.

THE NEXT THING I KNEW, I heard Grandma Lily whistling. I raised my head, wincing from the pain of a terrible kink in my neck. The clock read seven a.m. Grandma appeared in the kitchen doorway donning yellow rubber gloves and her wireless earphones. She held a toilet brush and a roll of paper towels. "Well, good morning, dear," Grandma Lily yelled, clearly not considering the volume of whatever music she was playing.

I pointed at my own ears and squinted. Grandma chuckled, "Oops, sorry. Anyway, could you give me a hand tidying up a bit? I got a call from The Ladies' Auxiliary. They'd like to pop in for a potluck brunch today at ten. Seems the church is getting sprayed for ants and they can't meet there as planned."

I couldn't say no. I felt guilty for not helping much around Jericho House lately, being so preoccupied. "Sure, what can I do?"

Grandma Lily gave me marching orders. I slugged down the rest of my cold coffee for the energy to get going and pushed my own to-do list into the front pocket of my jeans. The next hour went by in a flash as I swept, dusted, watered plants, and polished mirrors.

Back in the kitchen, I found my grandma preparing a light breakfast for us. She'd stacked my evidence into a neat pile in the center of the island. "Still investigating?" she asked, looking cynical.

"Yes, and things are only getting worse," I said with a sigh.

"How so?" Grandma sipped a cup of tea and took the stool beside mine.

I explained what Blake and I had pieced together the night before. Grandma studied my face with growing concern.

"Chloe, I want you to call the chief right away!"

"I'm not ready...not yet."

Turns out. I didn't have to call him. At that very moment, the front doorbell chimed. I went down the hall to answer, expecting it to be one of the auxiliary ladies coming to set up for their event. I was wrong. It was Garner. I groaned inwardly when I thought of him seeing me in these clothes I had spent the entire night in. What must my hair and face look like? But there was no running away to hide from him this time. I opened up.

There he stood, literally beaming. He was in his full navy-blue uniform and holding his service cap under one arm. Despite my fatigue and disheveled state, his smile was contagious.

"Good morning," I said with a grin. "What brings you here so early?"

"I thought the Martin ladies might like to celebrate with me. I assume that Lily has a pot of tea ready by now."

I ushered him into the foyer. By now Grandma had joined us. "Why, of course I do," she said happily. "Come to the kitchen."

I thought my heart might stop. *The kitchen? Where the diary, shoe box, faux blackmail letter and list of clues sat on full display?*

"Wait!" I hollered.

Both Garner and Grandma Lily turned sharply to look at me.

"How about the library?" I tried to make my face look normal.

Grandma raised her eyebrows but agreed to make up a tray and bring it in. Garner and I turned to enter the admirable, book-lined room.

"What are we celebrating?" I asked, hoping to distract him from my odd behavior.

Chief Garner stretched out on the antique fainting couch, crossed his ankles and raised his chin proudly. "I made an arrest in the Duvall case this morning."

"No!" I barked.

He shot me a look and frowned.

I corrected myself at once. "I mean...you don't say." I took a seat in the chair across from him, leaning forward and waiting intently for more details. My mouth felt dry, but my palms were damp.

Garner's face had gone back to a look of contentment. "I have to thank you, Chloe. Without your photos, I'm not sure I could have proven it."

My photos?

Grandma Lily arrived with a beautifully arranged tray. She had chosen the green Wedgewood tea set and included a plateful of oatmeal cookies. Everything was arranged on paper doilies, per usual.

"Did I hear correctly? You've made an arrest?" Grandma asked Garner.

He nodded while swinging his feet off the lounge chair. He stood to help her with the heavy tray. "That's right. I'm not at liberty to share any of the details yet, but it looks like the case is closed."

"Thank heavens," Grandma said, looking at me. "Now we can all get back to normal."

Suddenly, a realization hit me. "Wait, Garner. You kept saying Barbara's death was an accident. When did you change your mind?"

This cheshire cat grin he kept flashing was annoying me. "I never thought it was an accident. I intentionally *said* that aloud at the crime scene to make the killer, who I knew was likely present, feel safe."

"But at the dog park, you told me..."

"I only said you needed to trust me and that I knew what I was doing."

True enough. I had assumed that his words meant that he still believed Barbara's death was accidental. He'd never actually said that. The gravity of my assumption hit me hard. *What else had I been assuming about Barbara? Or assuming about Christy?* Likewise, maybe this assumption of mine that Barbara's murder was connected to Christy's long-ago death was wrong too.

"Who did it, then?" I asked Garner.

He shook a finger at me. "Ah, ah, ah, like I said, I can't discuss that until the paperwork is completed."

I huffed. "Okay, then at least tell me how my photos helped you. Was it the wildflowers? The two wine glasses?"

Garner's dark browns knit together. "No. It was the shoes. But hold up. What do you mean..."

I interrupted him. "The shoes?" I was pacing now, starting a loop around the room. "They were slippers, right?"

Garner said, "Yeah. But Chloe, go back to what you were saying..."

I felt my eyes widen when I remembered where I'd seen the dingy slippers aside from in the photograph. On Lottie! Those weren't Barbara Duvall's slippers stashed in the corner of her kitchen, as I had *assumed*. They were Lottie's slippers. And she'd been wearing them!

"Lottie was in the kitchen when I took those photos, wasn't she?" I stood stunned.

Garner sat back onto the lounge, "Chloe. Stop."

"Lottie hung out in the house until she could sneak out. Your crime scene photos didn't have the slippers in them because by that time she was gone. That's why you wanted to compare our photos."

Garner didn't say a word, only stared at me with pursed lips. He'd said too much and without meaning to, he'd revealed to me the person who'd been arrested.

"But she didn't do it." I went on, thinking aloud. "She obviously got caught up in it. But Garner, Lottie didn't kill her boss."

The chief stood and gulped down an entire cup of tea in one go. He placed his hat back on his head, adjusting it just so. He gave Grandma Lily a slight, gentlemanly bow and thanked her for the tea.

"I better be going," he said, clearly tired of me and my speculation.

I was too caught up in my own thoughts to respond or accompany them to the front door. When Grandma Lily returned to the library, she was beyond miffed. "What in tarnation are you doing, young lady?"

"Hmmm?" my mind was still elsewhere.

She swiped a hand at me. "Nevermind. You go ahead and ruin things with that fine young man if you want to." She continued to mumble to herself in frustration as she gathered tea cups onto the tray and moved down the wide hallway to the kitchen.

I wouldn't ruin things with Garner. That was the one thing I knew for sure. I'd make it right with him. That is, as soon as I fixed the mess he'd made of this case.

35

More Bones

POOR LOTTIE WAS SITTING in a jail cell right now, charged with a crime I was fairly certain she didn't commit. I could see the motive that Garner was operating off of; a scorned employee, a history of sticky fingers. Heck, I'd thought the same thing along the way. And let's face it, her standing in Barbara's kitchen with a whole "lottie" evidence spread out on the kitchen table didn't look good. But Chief Garner didn't know that there was something bigger at play in Jericho Falls. And, if the paperwork to charge Lottie wasn't finalized yet, I still had time to prove what really happened.

I dashed to the kitchen to find Grandma Lily feeding our furry friends. Still irked, she pretended I wasn't there, simply giving Elliot and Jed her complete attention. That was fine by me. I grabbed my cell phone and went outside through the back porch. Jed hurried to follow me when he realized I was headed outside. I was pressing icons before I made it through the backyard and took a seat in an Adirondack underneath the big maple tree.

Blake answered my call. "Hey, did you get any sleep?" he asked me.

"Very little and in a horrible position. I think my neck is fractured."

He laughed, "I didn't sleep much either. Now I'm at work and feel like the walking dead. Anyway, are you ready to go talk to the chief?"

"Already did."

"Well, good, it's about time."

"It's *not* good, Blake. He arrested Lottie Sloan from the RV Park."

"Oh," Blake quietly said.

"According to Garner, there's still paperwork to be done before it's official. I need to figure this thing out today. This morning even. Is there anything you can do to stall things, you know, slow down the filing process?"

"Like what?"

"I don't know, occupy the chief's time so he can't get the paperwork done... call an all staff meeting."

Blake's end of the call was silent, as it tended to be when he was thinking. "I don't know why, but I'll do it," he groaned. "I'll put the word out immediately that I want all personnel in the conference room in ten minutes. I can't keep them for long though, Chloe. You have to hurry."

"Thank you, Blake, thank you. I mean it."

"You can *thank* me once this whole thing is over and neither of us is in jail. Come to my office as soon as you can."

We wished each other luck and ended our call.

Which should I tackle first? Asking Jeannie if she told Brian Simmons about the diary, or trying to find those darned missing pages? I thought about how unhelpful Jeannie had been to this point. The chances of her suddenly becoming an open book were slimmer than me ever dating Blake again—or Bree Brandon wearing neutrals. I whistled for Jed. He hopped up from the spot of sun he'd been laying in and came to my side.

"We're on our own, bud," I told him. I rubbed his ears, both for his sake and for mine. A wave of panic was building inside me at the thought of the tight deadline I was working with—I needed this rhythmic, soothing moment stroking Jed's soft golden fur to settle me.

As I pet him, I gently tilted my head back and forth to loosen the stiffness in my neck. It sent a knife blade of pain into my left shoulder. Jed wandered away, sniffing and marking a few things. Then I heard him digging. I turned to scold him for bothering the fish's burial place yet again. But just before I spoke, an answer came to me.

"Geraldine!" I yelled. Jed cocked his head to one side as if to say, "Why you callin' me Geraldine?"

"Come on, boy," I told him. "I'll explain on the way."

I THREW OPEN THE BACK gate and ran for the grove of trees. Jed raced after me.

"That was Geraldine the gerbil you dug up out here the other day," I explained as we jogged. "I'm sure of it! Christy buried her in the special place beneath the carving. *Her* special place with *Brian*. That's what she meant in the diary."

Once there, I quickly found the tree. I took a minute to trace the lines of the heart with my index finger, finally knowing the identities of 'C' and 'B'. Sadly, I also knew that their love had not been '4ever'.

I kneeled down, unconcerned that the knees of my pants would become dirty and wet. I combed through the grass to find the spot where Jed had been digging before. I found the scattering of little bones right away. I took up a stick and gently scooted them to one side. It creeped me out both because—duh, dead animals, but also because now I had Jed. And Elliot. And I couldn't imagine how heartbroken I would be to lose either of them.

If Christy buried her pet gerbil here, might she also have buried the missing diary pages in this "special" spot? I decided to start right at the base of the tree where the young lovebirds had carved their initials. I scratched at the earth with the stick, making quick progress in the soft, wet ground. I heard Jed come up behind me, curious about what I was doing down on all fours. He sniffed at the back of my ear, tickling me and making me laugh.

"Stop it Jed, I'm busy."

With my next stroke of the stick, I bumped up against something hard. I pressed down into the ground again. Was it just a rock? I dug more intently now. No, not a rock. Something else was definitely down there.

Jed became even more interested in what I was doing when he noticed I was full-on digging. He came over and swiped a paw at the edge of the hole. "What do you think it is, boy?" I asked him.

He whined.

"I know," I said, looking into his cute face. "I'm a little worried it's something gross, too. Like more bones." He looked at me with his head cocked to one side. "Let's not think about it, 'k?" I told him.

With each swipe of my makeshift trowel, I got a little closer. Finally, I started to make out a shape—a heart-shape to be exact. It was a metal heart-shaped tin; the kind that Valentine candy comes in. Carefully, I carved around it with the stick until I could fit my fingers around the edges to pry it out. Inspecting it, I noted that at one point the tin had probably been red, but it was now more of a rusty orange shade. I turned it over in my hands. I could feel that there was something inside. The contents shifted and thumped with movement. But when I tried to lift the lid, it wouldn't budge. I'd have to take it back to Jericho House and find a tool to pry it open.

Before I left, I carefully gathered the remains of Geraldine the gerbil and placed them in the hole. I covered her with dark, rich soil and told her to rest in peace. Christy would have wanted that.

Jed and I hurried with intent for Jericho House. I looked back over my shoulder once or twice on the way with a prickly feeling of being watched.

36

A Cringy Sound

I WENT STRAIGHT TO the garage and sat the heart-shaped tin on my grandfather's built-in workbench. I dusted my hands. I hated the feel of dirt under my fingernails, but there was no use in cleaning up yet.

In the tool boxes that had been in the garage longer than I had been alive, I searched for a narrow, straight-head screwdriver and some WD-40. I applied the lubricating spray around the edges of the metal box and then carefully started to scrape and pry. The metal was soft with age and rust. Although I knew there was no real harm in ruining the container, I felt compelled to go slowly, to preserve the valentine tin. It had been special to Christy, after all.

Eventually, with even more of the oily spray and a lot more prying, I made progress. One edge of the box lifted with a squeak. It was then I realized I was finally going to find the missing pages—or not. This made me pause. If this was a bust like the locker had been, I was sunk. I was out of ideas. Out of options. Out of time. I took a deep breath to quiet my pulse and went for it.

A cringy sound like fingernails scraping a chalkboard filled the garage when I released the lid at last. I almost couldn't bear to look. But yes, tied together with an old shoelace was a stack of diary pages. Tears blurred my vision. I did it! I knew my friend so well, I was able to follow the clues to uncover her secret. I braced myself against my grandfather's work bench and let a mix of relieved and sorrowful tears flow. *Oh, how I missed her. Oh, how sorry I felt that I didn't know enough to save her life all those years ago.*

I left rusty fingerprints on the paper when I lifted the pages from the tin. I quickly dropped the packet onto the workbench to wipe my hands on my pant legs before marring any of the writing.

With cleaner hands, I hugged the little packet to my chest. "Please tell me what really happened," I whispered hopefully. Jed and I went outside and into the backyard. I sat in an Adirondack to read them.

CHRISTY HAD REMOVED seven pages from the book. They differed from her usual entries. Instead of addressing the anonymous "Dear Diary" she wrote these entries to Brian.

In Christy's recognizable hand, the first one read:

Dear Brian,

I have never been so happy. I never imagined that you and I would be a couple! But it's true, we are! Whenever I have a bad day at school, or my mom and dad are fighting, all I have to do is remember that we love each other, and it makes everything all right again. I know that after you graduate this year, you will break up with Jeannie and everyone will officially know we are boyfriend and girlfriend. I can't wait.

But this had not come to pass. Brian didn't break it off with Jeannie. What had changed his mind?

I continued reading.

Dear Brian,

I know you're stressed out since it's your senior year, but lately you seem different. I hope it's nothing.

And later,

I wish I knew who started that stupid rumor about Jeannie. I know it's not true because you only want to be with me. Like you always say, we'll be together forever. Only a few more weeks until you graduate and we can tell the world.

Aside from a few variations on the theme, that's all the pages had to tell me. Blake and I were right, though. Christy and Brian were seeing each other behind Jeannie's back, and Christy believed Brian was going to break-up with his long-term girlfriend to make it official with her. When we found Brian at Jeannie's house that day, it must have become brutally clear to Christy that *she* was the one being jilted. There was no doubt in my mind now that Christy's anger at the waterfall was because of this issue with Brian, not some stupid swimsuit I had forgotten to pack. And while she had berated me for spending too much time with Blake, it was probably only because she wanted to be spending time with the boy she cared about.

Everything about that fateful day was coming into focus. Starting to anyway, but things weren't crystal clear yet. In order for the rest of the image to become visible, I needed to talk with Jeannie. Now, armed with the information from the missing pages, I knew I could get her to talk.

I gave Jed a smooch on the head, locked him safely in the backyard, and hoofed it to town. I didn't want anyone to spy my truck on the street to know I was there. Let them believe I was being a good-girl hanging out innocently at Jericho House. *As if.*

I arrived at The Vintage Grill just as it opened for the day. A waitress was busy filling salt and pepper shakers on each table. "Hi, a table for one?" she smiled. Her expression faltered as she surveyed my filthy clothes, grimy hands, and what must be a wild hairdo.

"Nope. A word with your boss," I demanded.

"Eric just left for the bank."

"Good. 'Cause I want to talk to Jeannie."

She hurried towards the kitchen. I took a seat at a table, front and center.

Soon Jeannie turned the corner from the kitchen and halted when she saw me.

"Come have a chat with me," I said, patting the seat next to me.

"We're open for business, Chloe," Jeannie said with a worried look.

"That's okay. This will only take a minute."

Jeannie approached me warily and sat. "What do you want?"

"I found the missing pages of Christy's diary. Turns out you were telling me the truth about not taking them. Christy secreted them away herself."

Jeannie swallowed hard, but stayed still.

I went on, "So, now I know Brian was seeing Christy behind your back and at some point, you learned about it. That's why you and your friends were bullying her, huh?"

She shrugged. "Hey, she was the one in the wrong. He was *my* boyfriend."

"I agree. What they did was wrong," I admitted. "But I'm curious about what made Brian change his plan to dump you after his graduation."

She shook her head, and a flush came to her pretty cheeks. "Christy was just a fling."

"You're lying. Something changed his plans. According to the diary, there was a rumor going around about you." I waited to see if she'd explain.

We were several seconds into a verbal stand-off when a strange feeling came over me. I suddenly knew what that rumor was. Grandma Lily had unwittingly spilled the tea earlier that week. She mentioned a "rash" of teenage problems, including... pregnancies.

"Were you *pregnant?*"

Jeannie stood so fast her chair tipped over, causing a crash that brought the waitress out from the back. "You don't know what you're talking about," she whispered sharply. She leaned onto the table, glowering down at me. "As soon as I heard you had Christy's diary, I knew it meant trouble for us."

"*Us* as in you and Brian? You contacted him when you found out I had the diary, didn't you? You worried it would bring your house of cards down, right? First, you tried to steal it and lately Brian's been poking around Jericho House for it."

Jeannie's eyes narrowed. She shook her head.

I went on, "But don't lay all the blame for this on me. Blake found the blackmail letter to Mayor Luna, Jeannie. He knows someone forced the mayor to keep Brian's testimony a secret. Is that because Brian confessed to pushing Christy over the falls? And then, did he kill Barbara Duvall when she found evidence linking him to the crime?"

Jeannie's face went slack. She gave a long blink and opened her mouth to speak. But at that moment, the restaurant door opened. A change came over Jeannie's face when she saw her husband enter.

"Hi, hon. Chloe just dropped in for a cup of coffee." Jeannie said while quickly picking up her chair. She went behind the counter to fill a styrofoam to-go cup. "She's uh...gardening again today."

I looked at my blackened fingernails and filthy clothes. "Something like that," I replied. I made unmemorable but necessary chit-chat with Jeannie's country-boy husband before heading for the door.

Jeannie walked with me. "You'd be smart to drop all this," she whispered.

"And you'd be smart to come clean with Eric while you still have the chance," I said. I went out the door, dropping the full cup of coffee in the garbage barrel on the boardwalk. I wasn't accepting any favors from Jeannie Smythe today.

37

Wise Decision

I HOPED THE MEASLY circumstantial evidence I had was enough to convince law enforcement that Brian Simmons, not poor Lottie, should be charged with murder. I glanced at my phone—just over an hour had passed since Blake was going to convene his all-staff meeting. Even if he'd managed it, I doubted he could hold them much longer. I'd take what I had, and visit his office.

It was risky to meet Blake at city hall. I didn't want to run into the chief and have him assume I was on a social call with my ex, the mayor, or find out I was still investigating the case.

But since I was on foot, I'd leave no car on the curb and would go straight to Blake's office. The only person who would know I was in the building was his lobby-watching secretary, Missy.

When I reached the top of the tall steps, I peered through the glass doors. Missy's desk was empty. Hopefully, Blake had convinced her to sit in on his spontaneous conference, making it even easier for me to slip in with no one knowing.

I tiptoed through the big room, but with the glossy floor and high ceilings, my steps were still audible. I paused at Missy's desk, just to see if she'd left any interesting tid-bits behind for me to eavesdrop on today. Again, I found her workspace to be as neat as a pin. Just a computer keyboard and monitor, a cup of perfectly sharpened pencils, and her phone with switchboard-like capability. The scar on my knee tingled as a thought came to me. *Missy can listen in on everyone's calls at city hall.* The realization took my breath away.

All at once, the room felt a little spinny. Still, I managed to turn and make it down the hallway for Blake's mayoral office. The door was open, and there was no one inside. It contained a couch, two side chairs, and an executive desk in front of a tall picture window. I pulled the door closed behind me as quietly as possible, just before voices and footsteps began in the hallway. *The staff meeting must be* over. I heard grouchy mumbles and a few jabs at Blake as the employees filed by. I owed him big time for whatever fall out this created.

I stood behind the door, praying that Blake would return soon... and alone. Sure enough. After the hallway was finally quiet again, I heard a single set of footsteps approaching. Blake entered his office and sank miserably onto the couch. He jumped when he saw me standing against the wall near a bookcase.

"Holy smokes," he gasped.

"Sorry," I whispered in reply. I went to sit in a chair near him.

Blake rolled his shoulders and massaged his temples with his fingertips. "That was easily the most grueling hour of my life."

I cringed. "How did you convince them to meet?"

"I used my recent mayor's conference as an excuse. I told them I was required to go over what we learned with all my employees."

"That was a great idea." I tried to sound encouraging.

"Yeah, well, that took all of about fifteen minutes and then I had to just wing it. I'm sure they all think I'm an idiot."

I moved to the couch and placed a hand on Blake's shoulder. "What if I told you I learned some helpful information while you were in there stalling?"

He turned his head to look at me. "Yeah?"

I wiggled my eyebrows and nodded. But before I dove in to tell him what I'd uncovered, Blake's eyes traveled up and down my body. He wrinkled his nose. "Why are you so dirty?"

BLAKE WAS UNIMPRESSED with my findings.

"On a personal level, this is fascinating," he said. "Now we finally know why Christy stormed off and went to the top of the falls. But that's it, Chloe. There's absolutely no evidence that Brian Simmons harmed Christy *or* Barbara Duvall."

I winced. He was right. I'd played all my cards, dug as deep as I could. Even so, all I had were hunches and conjectures. I stood to pace the room, twirling a finger around a thin strand of my golden-brown hair. There was one more detail I hadn't yet shared with Blake. Missy's switchboard. If she was the one to listen in on Barbara Duvall's fateful phone call to Blake, she'd known that Barbara was taking a piece of evidence home with her. Was *she* the informant that got Barbara killed?

Each interaction I'd had with the professional and poised Missy Bray played over in my mind. That first time, I got on her bad side by misleading her. On my second visit, she said she was unhappy with herself for letting me trick her after working at city hall so long... or something to that effect.

"Blake," I said. I turned to find him staring into a framed mirror on the wall while straightening his tie and smoothing his hair. "How long has Missy worked at city hall?"

He shrugged. "She started right out of high school, I think. She's from Lakeview, but her parents are in politics. They pulled some strings for an internship during her senior year. The city hired her for a full-time position right after."

"Always as the Mayor's secretary and building receptionist?"

"As far as I know."

I was having trouble breathing. *Her parents were in politics. She was the mayor's secretary.* I thought back to the hand-written notation Missy had jotted on the top of that hotel brochure. The one that tipped me off to Blake's location in Albuquerque.

"Where's the blackmail letter?" I asked him. Blake wanted an explanation, but we didn't have time. "Just show me."

He went to the same mirror where he'd just been admiring himself and took it off the wall to reveal an antique wall safe. The large silver-toned dial shone. An ornate, hand-painted image of an eagle with outstretched wings decorated the front. Blake spun the dial first one way and then the other, stopping at various points. It opened on his first try.

"Just in case you're wondering, I had this re-keyed when I took office," he mentioned.

If my suspicions about his secretary proved correct, he'd made a wise decision.

Blake reached underneath a stack of files and binders to find a manilla envelope. He turned and handed it to me. I knew I better take a seat. My anxiety level was reaching a peak, and if I found what I expected to, I just might faint dead away.

With shaky fingers, I fumbled with the metal clip at the top of the envelope and withdrew the letter. I scanned the page quickly, knowing at once who had written it. I didn't fault Blake for not immediately recognizing Missy's hand-writing. There was a youthful feel to it; rounded letters and circles to dot the i's. Missy had matured and so had her cursive. But there was no denying it was her writing.

"It's Missy..." I whispered.

"What about her?" asked Blake.

I answered by handing him the letter. At first, he simply frowned. Then his eyes widened. Blake took a step backward, his mental gears grinding just like mine.

I said, "Missy's what, ten years older than us? But she must have known Brian somehow. Why else try to keep him out of trouble with the law?"

The phone on Blake's desk buzzed and, speak of the devil, Missy's voice filled the room. "Mayor White, you're needed in the assessor's office right away."

Blake rolled his eyes. "Great timing," he sighed. "Wait here. I'll be back as soon as I can."

With that, he closed the door behind him, and I was left to my own devices. I laid the blackmail letter on the large desk. I sat in Blake's cushy leather chair and concentrated. Somewhere along the way, I'd missed something. Just one little thing. That's all I needed to figure out Missy's secret connection to all this. I tried retracing some steps; Mayor Luna was Missy's boss, and Mayor Luna was known for hiring high school kids for summer jobs. Could Brian Simmons have been one of the lucky kids to ace Blake out of a position?

I thought again about the necklace that Barbara Duvall mentioned taking home with her. It had somehow let her know that 'b.s.' meant Brian Simmons. And it surely must have been the shiny object I'd seen in the pool. Strangely, the necklace was lost before it made it into official evidence. Could that have been Missy's handiwork, too? She had ample access to the place—buying coffee for the police officers as an excuse to poke around on their desks was child's play compared with blackmailing the mayor.

I really wish Blake would hurry up.

In my reverie, I turned to the window. I drew back the long drapes to look outside. It had started to rain again. If I didn't know any better, I'd say it was a run-of-the-mill spring day in Jericho Falls. But I knew that underneath this quaint, picturesque facade, we had ominous revelations about to surface. To my right, something caught my eye. Someone was going down the steps of the building. I watched a young man dressed in jeans and wearing a baseball cap hurry away from the building. Just before making it out of sight, he took the red hat off and shook out a mane of lovely, dark hair.

It wasn't a guy at all! It was Missy Bray.

38

Someone to Blame

I BOOKED IT OUT OF Blake's office, skidded through the foyer and dashed down the steep steps of city hall, to run in the direction Missy had gone. But once on Main Street, I found no sign of her. She could have ducked into any of the businesses. I hurried down the boardwalk, frantically checking each storefront window for Missy, AKA the Jericho House burglar, AKA the blackmailer. I finally spotted her up ahead, entering Nick's Knacks. I broke into a full run to catch up, rain pelting my face.

I slipped inside the shop quietly and heard Nick's deep, velvety voice say, "I'm not a pawnshop, ma'am. I don't buy used jewelry."

Edging my way behind a large display of yarn, I peeked around to watch them. Missy dangled a gold locket in front of Nick. "Are you sure? You could get a good price for this and I'm not asking for much. Just enough for a trip out of the country."

"I'll buy it," I announced, stepping out to reveal myself.

Missy spun around. Her surprise at seeing me was obvious. She lowered her arm briskly, the locket now swinging at her side.

"What do you have there, Missy?" I asked, going closer.

She moved, looking like she wanted to hide the necklace in her pocket, but I lunged at her and got a hold of the chain. I yanked hard and stripped it from Missy's hand, then fell into a heap on the hardwood floor. Unfortunately, all I came away with was the gold chain. The locket pendant flung away and skittered under some merchandise in the corner. There I sat on the floor of Nick's shop, wet, filthy, and probably looking a little deranged.

"She's a maniac!" Missy screamed at Nick. "Do something."

I looked at Nick, shocked to see that his eyes revealed fear. "You stay back now, Chloe." He motioned to Missy. "Come on, ma'am. Follow me."

Missy glanced first at me and then back at Nick. She didn't know what to do. "*Hurry*, ma'am. I'll get us help," Nick told her, his usual suave voice edged in worry.

I couldn't believe my ears. Was Nick actually afraid of me and siding with malicious Missy? He put an arm around her shoulders and they disappeared into the back of the shop.

I had no time to lose. I rushed to the spot where I guessed the locket ended up and began sorting through the odds and ends Nick stocked. I moved a broom, a basket of silk flowers, a footstool, and several books before finding it. Just then, Nick reappeared behind me. "What's this all about, Chloe?" he boomed.

I turned to face him, still on my knees, with the locket pendant cupped in my outstretched hands. I expected to find him angry, maybe even wielding a hoe or flyswatter in self-defense against me. Instead, I noticed a set of old keys dangling from his hand. Finding me staring at them, he looked too. "Oh. I locked that pushy woman in the storeroom," he explained.

"Then you're not calling the cops on me? You seemed so scared."

Nick waggled his head with a satisfied grin. "I've done my share of community theater. Now explain to me what's going on."

"Missy Bray is the mayor's secretary, and I think she stole this necklace from the police department. It was at the scene when Barbara Duvall died. But according to Chief Garner, it got lost along the way and never made it into evidence." I told Nick this as I scrutinized the oblong locket. It was smooth, gold-toned, and etched with a single long-stemmed rose.

"I'm going to open it," I said to Nick. I'm not sure why I announced this out loud. Maybe because I didn't want him accusing me of tampering with evidence, or maybe because I could feel his eyes watching my every move. But I also felt compelled to say it, in order to coax myself to do it. So much hinged on these tiny hinges, after all.

I slid my thumbnail into the edge and pried the pendant open. There weren't any photographs inside, as I'd seen in many antique lockets. They may have been removed or ruined in the pool. No matter though. Clearly engraved in the back of the locket was the image of a heart containing the message, *BS+MB4ever.*

That spinny feeling I'd been experiencing lately returned, so I was glad to still be sitting on my knees. Nick kneeled down beside me to see what had me confused. "What is it?"

I looked up into his eyes. "I think we have a small-town teenage Casanova on our hands."

This, of course, meant absolutely nothing to Nick. His eyebrows knit together firmly as he turned up his palms, urging me for more explanation.

"I may have just figured out who killed Barbara Duvall," I said. Nick helped me to my feet while I continued. "Take me to Missy. She's got some explaining to do."

Nick led the way to the back of his shop and went to a panel door on one side. He pushed a large skeleton key into its lock and opened it. This storage space was larger than I expected and well lit. Inside, Missy sat on a wooden chair. She looked madder than a wet cat.

"Close the door, Nick," I told him. "I want a word with Missy. Alone."

"I'll be right here," he said with a frown, "if you need anything."

I nodded to let him know I was all right.

The door clicked behind me.

"What do you think you're doing, Chloe? Besides earning a kidnapping charge, of course," Missy sneered.

"Nah, I don't think I'm the person who'll be charged with a crime today. Not Lottie Sloan either. It's going to be you."

Missy tried an innocent face. "What are you talking about?"

"Stealing this evidence, for one." I held up the locket for her to see and then stuffed it into my back pocket for safekeeping. "You couldn't let Barbara or the police know you were involved with Brian Simmons way back when, could you?"

"Why would I care? He was just a dumb kid with a crush on an older girl at work." She shrugged to prove her nonchalance.

I chuckled. "You do care, because your blackmail letter to Mayor Luna surfaced again and, as Blake's secretary, you knew that. You found out that Blake was poking around in the old case with Barbara Duvall, so you started listening in on their phone calls, right?"

Missy's cheeks reddened. I was onto her.

"It's my job to receive and transfer calls...sometimes I hear things."

"Well, what you heard Friday was that Barbara found something that let her know what 'b.s.' really meant. And that put Brian Simmons, and possibly you, in the hot seat." I shook my head, then frowned. "I'm confused about why the locket was ever part of the evidence in Christy's case in the first place."

Now, I was simply thinking aloud, playing out a possible scenario. "Unless—Brian had the necklace on him that fateful day and intended to give it to you after he broke up with his *other* two girlfriends. Oh Missy, now that's romantic."

Missy shivered. Whether it was from vicious anger or fear, I wasn't sure. I was glad to know that Nick was right outside the door, because this was the perfect time for me to push her a little more.

"Here's what I think happened," I began. "With flowers in hand, you went to Barbara Duvall's office and suggested a drink at her place after work. Maybe you told her you were sorry about her forced retirement, you know, just to soften her up. You rode out of town with her so you wouldn't have a car at Pioneer RV Park. It's a pretty good jaunt back to town, but I suppose that was a small price to pay to stay out of jail.

The wildflowers you brought along were Cut-throat Nightshade. They can be extremely poisonous if overdone, but will only cause drowsiness at a low dose. You put some petals in Barbara's wine glass, thinking that if she got sleepy, you could rummage around and find the locket.

But you miscalculated, Missy. Mixed with alcohol and the prescription medication Barbara was taking, the effect on her was extreme. At some point, you must have told Barbara you were there for the locket and she put it all together. She realized you are the 'MB' in the locket's engraving and you were the blackmailer."

I paused, waiting for Missy's reply. When she stayed stoically silent, I went on.

"Barbara was probably experiencing some terrible effects from the poison by then. In fear for her life, and to keep the locket from you, she went out her back door to the pool area. But you couldn't let her leave with the locket. To stop her, you took the pool skimmer and swatted her with it, knocking her into the pool. If it hadn't been for the Nightshade poisoning, she probably could have saved herself. Instead, Barbara Duvall drowned."

Missy's breath came faster now. "If she would have handed the necklace over to me, I would have been on my way. I never planned to hurt her."

"You know, you were extremely lucky that neither Lottie nor Jim spotted you."

Missy opened her mouth, then closed it.

"You see, Lottie Sloan likely went in the front door about the same time you and Barbara went out back. At least that's the timeline I'm guessing, since she ended up in the photos I took. She must have forgotten something—or maybe she was going to enjoy a glass of vino with Barbara. Anyway, when Lottie arrived inside the house, all the commotion began outside. From you and Barbara, and eventually from Jim Holt. Unsure what was going on, Lottie must have stayed put until things quieted down."

Defeat was in Missy's eyes. I probably didn't have everything right, but enough of this rang true that Missy knew she was just as sunk as that gold locket in the swimming pool.

"I hid too," she explained. "When that guy started yelling and calling out for Barbara, I climbed over the pool fence and went into the adjoining field. I huddled behind a sagebrush until the cops left that night."

"But without the locket." I gave her a satisfied smile.

Missy glared. "Barbara had the necklace in her hand when she went into the water. I didn't have time to fish it out. But that was okay. I got ahold of it, eventually. In fact, your fake emergency helped me, Chloe. It gave me the excuse I needed to go to the police department. While I was there, I had a look around. There was the locket in a little baggie on Officer Meyers' desk."

A deep satisfaction swelled in my chest. In getting Missy's confession, I'd successfully solved another case. But the sweet sensation quickly faded. This explained one death, but not the other. Somehow, Missy was involved in what happened to Christy, too. And I wanted to know how.

"Tell me about Brian Simmons."

"What's there to tell? Like I said, he was a teenage kid with a crush on an older girl he worked with. End of story."

I shook my head. "There's no way you would have written a blackmail letter to the Mayor of Jericho Falls to keep him out of trouble if that was the case."

We stared at one another. A long moment passed. Too long for my liking. Was she clamming up? But in the silence, Missy's eyes filled with tears. She put her face into her hands. I stood there, unmoved, watching her shoulders shake as she sobbed.

Eventually, her crying quieted, and she looked up. "I loved him. It was stupid. But I did. When I found out I was pregnant, I told him he had to marry me or I would be ruined. He agreed and promised to break up with Jeannie. I didn't even know about Christy then."

"So it was you who was expecting Brian's baby, not Jeannie. And Brian was planning to break up with both of them," I said. Maybe Jeannie had been telling me the truth all along. "But, wait. Brian was still with Jeannie," I said to Missy. "They were spending time together the day Christy died."

Missy explained, "That was the day Brian went to Jeannie's house to break up with her. He didn't get the job done though, before you all showed up to invite them to the falls. Brian had real trouble on his hands then with two girls he was seeing in one place. He knew Christy was angry at him for being at Jeannie's. So, he followed her to the top of the mountain to explain the whole truth—about me and the baby, about everything."

A prickly tingle started at the scar on my knee and traveled throughout my body. I hadn't been imagining things after all. There really had been someone else at the top of the falls when we were searching for Christy—I thought I'd seen them dash through the woods. It was Brian.

Now I felt like *I* might cry, but I couldn't let myself show Missy any emotion. I swallowed hard to press down my tears before asking the question I desperately wanted the answer to, but also hated the thought of. "Did Brian push Christy? Is that why his interview had to be kept secret?"

Missy gazed at her lap and shook her head.

"Then how?" I yelled. "How did Christy die?"

Missy looked up. She appeared to be weighing whether to satisfy my fourteen-year curiosity. "It happened the way everyone thought. Except, it wasn't you and Christy fighting near the waterfall. It was Christy and Brian."

In my mind, I imagined them having such an emotional conversation at the edge of the waterfall. It would have been loud with the roar of the water.

"He broke her heart," I whispered. "She was probably crying and upset."

Missy looked sad now, and plain worn out. "Brian told me he reached for her, to comfort her. But she yanked away from him. She was right at the edge..." Missy's voice faltered.

My heart ached thinking of my friend losing her balance, slipping into the rushing water. There was no way Brian could have saved her.

"But, Missy, if it was truly an accident, why go to such lengths to get Brian's testimony thrown out?" I asked.

"He still might have been convicted if it went to trial. The town wanted someone to blame."

I, better than anyone, knew that.

A rush of adrenaline mixed with sadness and, strangely, a little relief made my whole body feel funny. I thought my legs might give out.

At this moment, Missy stood abruptly and lunged past me. She was making a break for it! But as her hand grasped the doorknob, I took her by the shoulders and pulled hard. She spun around and slapped me, her eyes wild. "I won't go down for this," she cried.

With my cheek searing, I gripped her arms and pushed her against the wall. I knew I couldn't hold her for long, so I yelled, and yelled for Nick.

The door burst open to reveal not only Nick but also Officer Ellie Porter and Chief Garner. "We've been looking all over town for you," Officer Porter remarked as the chief put handcuffs on Missy.

Ellie went on, "After Missy sent Blake on a bogus errand to the assessor's office, she wasn't at her desk and you were gone, too. He came to us with the blackmail letter."

I flashed a glance at Garner, who was now guiding Missy past me with her hands cuffed behind her back. "The blackmail letter we should have seen *days* ago," he muttered. I offered him a cringey smile in reply.

Officer Ellie put a hand on my back. "You gonna be okay, Chloe?" she asked firmly.

"Yeah." I reached into the pocket of my jeans, withdrew the locket, and handed it to her. Our eyes met. "I think we all are."

39

One Boy and One Girl

"GRANDMA, I HOPE YOU'VE learned your lesson and will stop the matchmaking," I said, buttering a piece of sourdough toast for each of us.

"And I hope you'll stop all this detective work." She looked over the top of her tortoise-shell glasses at me. "But I don't hear either of us making any promises."

I laughed. "What is it you always say? Tigers don't change their stripes?"

Grandma nodded and took a sip of her favorite sweet and spicy tea. The scent of cinnamon, citrus, and cloves filled the kitchen, making me feel even more cozy. It was nice to be comfy again instead of worried and confused. Missy Bray was behind bars for the murder of Barbara Duvall and we could all rest easy once again.

"To be clear," Grandma said, "Missy didn't set out to kill Barbara, did she?"

"No. Missy was only continuing to protect Brian Simmons—and herself, for that matter."

"Like I told you, secrets always take a toll, even if they're kept for good reason," Grandma said.

"That's for sure."

"What happened to Missy and Brian's baby? And where'd he end up, anyway?"

"Apparently, Missy lost the baby later that summer. Sad, but not too hard to imagine, considering all the stress she was under. After that, Brian left town. Chief Garner tried to track him down to corroborate Missy's version of how Christy died. It turns out, though, Brian's womanizing ways were his eventual undoing."

"How so?" Grandma set her teacup down and leaned in for the details.

"Seems he got involved with a married woman. When the husband found out..." I drew my thumb across my throat.

"Nooo," Grandma Lily's amber eyes widened. "Talk about karma."

"And you'll never believe how the man learned about the affair." Grandma just shrugged.

"He intercepted a package intended for his wife. When he opened it, he found a bracelet inside with a heart-shaped charm engraved with *B+L4ever.*"

"Talk about a tiger and his stripes," she shook her head in disgust. "Which reminds me, have you seen today's newspaper?"

I hadn't. Grandma Lily fetched the latest copy of the Jericho Chronicle from the parlour. The front-page headline stated, *Mayor White, Our Hometown Hero,* followed by an in-depth article detailing how Blake single-handedly solved a decade's old cold case *and* Barbara Duvall's murder in one fell swoop. "Oh, brother," I said, rolling my eyes. "Well, I told him he could take the credit. He certainly didn't waste any time calling the press, did he?"

Grandma scooped up Elliot, rubbing his neck. She came up beside me. "Listen dear, I know this has been a hard week for you. You uncovered a lot of secrets...Chief Garner's and Christy's too. But at least you have the answers you've been searching for all these years."

"Most of them," I whispered.

"What's that supposed to mean?"

I narrowed my eyes and bit the inside of my cheek. "I'm still curious to know what Missy Bray knew about Mayor Luna, in order to blackmail him. And who are those people in the photo with the mayor and Governor Finney? Were they involved, too?"

Grandma sighed. She sat Elliot down and moved a sky-blue hair scrunchy from her wrist to her high ponytail. It looked good on her; such a hopeful spring color. "I'm going to pretend I didn't hear you say any of that and set out for my walk. Come on, Jed. Oh, and don't forget, we're video chatting with your parents tonight. Hopefully, their wi-fi signal will hold out long enough to hear this long, crazy story."

I smiled.

With Grandma and Jed out and about, I decided it was finally time to move back into my cozy apartment. I took the cherry wood stairs two at a time, with Elliot on my heels. I filled my duffle bag once again and did a quick tidy. Then I cheerfully trotted back downstairs and out the back door.

This time when I rounded the garage building, there was no unruly mess, no unsightly garbage strewn about. But there was a big surprise waiting for me.

My grandfather's red stool stood in the perfect spot next to my new sturdy door. The white petunias and lavender pansies I'd neglected for days were freshly potted and sitting on top of the stool looking charming. And beside this display stood a set of brightly painted garden gnomes, one boy and one girl.

An envelope was taped to my door. Inside I found two tickets to the Jericho Falls Opera House opening weekend presentation of *Barefoot In The Park,* starring none other than Nick Newsom. An enclosed note read,

Dear Chloe,

While I don't approve of your secret keeping this past week, I doubt I have much room to talk. Despite the mayor's boasting, everyone knows who the real sleuth in town is.

I hope you like the gnomes. Now we have matching sets.

Garner

EPILOGUE

BY THE END OF APRIL, business at Pioneer RV Park was booming once again. The Browns purchased the RV Park from Daniel Duvall with a portion of their lottery winnings. This delighted RVers (and Mr. Cooper, the grocer).

After learning that Lottie Sloan only returned to the RV office the day Barbara died because she forgot her cell phone charger and needed it for video chatting, the Browns asked her to become the full-time park manager. They even allowed her to move into the Duvall home. The Browns would be in sunny Arizona each winter, but Lottie had everything under control—especially with Jim Holt as the new park maintenance manager. Under his watchful eye, campers would no longer have to worry about empty change machines or broken washers and dryers.

As I sat at Jim's tiny dinette, enjoying another cup of his delicious percolated coffee, he beamed when discussing his new position. "I think I'll ask Lottie about plantin' some flowers around the place—you know, spruce it up some."

"That'd be nice and Barbara would have loved it."

He nodded reverently.

"Anyway," I said, "I dropped by because I have a favor to ask."

Jim took a gulp of coffee. "What's that?"

I motioned towards his little fish aquarium, softly gurgling nearby. "Could I talk you out of a goldfish? It's for a friend."

Acknowledgements

SPECIAL THANKS TO MY wonderful husband and daughter for their love and support, to Annette Moser and Melaney Taylor Auxier for helping me polish my stories week by week, and to my mom for being my very first reader. I couldn't do it without any of you.

Hear More From Brook Peterson

THANK YOU FOR READING. I hope you enjoyed this Jericho Falls Mystery. Please consider leaving a review where you purchased this book.

Want to join my Cozy Community? You'll get instant access to The Cozy Library, including behind-the-scenes photos and details on the inspiration behind Jericho Falls. I share monthly updates with sneak peeks and freebies such as recipes for the dishes in my stories.

Sign up: https://www.subscribepage.com/brookpetersonauthor

I promise to never share your email and you may unsubscribe at any time.

Let's connect:

Facebook: @brooktheauthor

Instagram: brookpetersonauthor

Email: brook@brookpetersonauthor.com

Snail mail: P.O. Box 675, Payette Idaho 83661

Did you love *A Collection of Secrets*? Then you should read *A History of Murder*[1] by Brook Peterson!

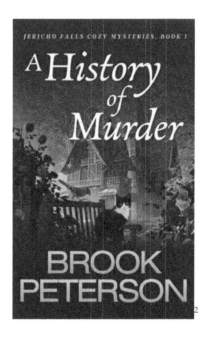

[2]

Once a booming gold town, now a quiet tourist spot with a history of murder...

When Chloe Martin makes the long overdue trip to Jericho Falls, Nevada, to check on her grandma, she doesn't plan to stay long. In fact, she has every intention of hightailing it right back to Idaho and leaving the historic mining town she loves to hate, for good.

But when a man turns up dead in their flowerbed, Grandma Lily becomes the prime suspect. Chloe is forced to stay in town long enough to prove her innocence. To complicate matters, Chloe finds herself in a love triangle almost as tricky as the mystery she has to

1. https://books2read.com/u/4A7a7A

2. https://books2read.com/u/4A7a7A

solve. Will Chloe be able to solve the murder and keep Grandma out of jail? Just as important---will she finally find peace in Jericho Falls?

If you love mysteries set in small towns, with cute sidekick pets and a bit of romance, the Jericho Falls Cozy Mysteries are for you.

―――

"When Chloe returns once again to her hometown, she must face old memories and new dangers. Does she have the courage to confront the pain of the past, unravel the mysteries of the present, and achieve her hopes for the future, or will she once again run from her problems--or be overwhelmed by them? This intense tale of secrets, vengeance, and love is sure to please!"

- Irene S., Proofreader, Red Adept Editing

Read more at https://www.brookpetersonauthor.com/.

Also by Brook Peterson

Jericho Falls Cozy Mysteries
A History of Murder
A Collection of Secrets
The Present Predicament, A Jericho Falls Holiday Novella

Watch for more at https://www.brookpetersonauthor.com/.

Brook Peterson
Mystery Author

About the Author

As long as she can remember Brook Peterson has been reading mysteries. By the time she was ten, she was writing her own and turning them into little stapled paperbacks to share with her family.

Her cozy mysteries are sure to include long held secrets, an antique or two, and a little bit of romance.

Read more at https://www.brookpetersonauthor.com/.

Made in the USA
Coppell, TX
10 February 2022

73275524R00156